# A Risk
# Worth Taking

# A Risk Worth Taking

## LAURA LANDON

Montlake
Romance

Text copyright © 2013 Laura Landon
All rights reserved.
Printed in the United States of America.
No part of this book may be reproduced, or stored in a retrieval system, or transmitted in any form or by any means, electronic, mechanical, photocopying, recording, or otherwise, without express written permission of the publisher.

Published by Montlake Romance
PO Box 400818
Las Vegas, NV 89140

ISBN-13: 9781477807408
ISBN-10: 1477807403

Library of Congress Control Number: 2013933192

*To all my readers…you are the best!*
*Thank you!*

# Chapter 1

❧

November 20, 1857

*G*riffin Blackmoor glanced up from where he sat in a secluded corner of the Rooster's Inn and watched with cautionary curiosity when the door opened. Out of habit long perfected, his nerves snapped to attention at the commotion at the front of the room. He relaxed when his longtime friend, Freddie Carmichael, Marquess of Brentwood, entered.

Griff leaned back in his chair and waited while Brentwood's gaze searched through the hazy smoke. A smile lit his friend's face the second he found Griff. With determined steps, Brentwood made his way across the crowded room.

"Another chance meeting, Freddie?" Griff said, unable to keep the grin from his face. "This is your third visit in the last two weeks. My company must be more enjoyable than I realized."

Freddie sat down in the chair adjacent to Griff and, with a hearty gulp, finished the last of the whiskey in Griff's glass. Griff laughed, then motioned for the barmaid to bring another glass.

"Don't flatter yourself, Griff. I didn't come here for your pleasant companionship." Freddie reached for the glass the barmaid set before him and took a swallow. He swiped the back of his hand across his mouth, then set the glass down on the table with a dull thud. "I came here because of the fine ale they serve."

Griff halted the glass halfway to his mouth and gave a snort that nearly resembled a chuckle.

"Bloody hell," Freddie said. "Was that a smile I saw cross your face? Drinks for the house," he added, almost loud enough to be taken seriously. "We are indeed in peril of seeing the world's last days."

"Save your money, Brentwood."

Griff finished his drink and gave Freddie's expensively cut black tails a cursory glance. "So, what brings you here? From your attire, I'd say you didn't exactly dress for an evening at the Rooster's Inn."

Freddie rolled his eyes. "Lady Ashworth's ball. Quite a bore."

"My sympathies. You must have left quite early to make it here before dawn."

"Actually"—Freddie motioned for the barmaid to refill their glasses—"I was glad to get away. The atmosphere was extremely stuffy and the company overly confining."

"So you traveled to the country in hopes I'd provide better entertainment?"

"Actually, yes. And…"

Griff raised his brows and waited.

"I ran into your brother at the ball."

Griff ran his fingers over the mars and cuts in the wooden tabletop. He tried to think of another topic to

introduce but couldn't. He finally gave in. "And how is the earl?"

"He's fine. He's anxious to see you."

"I made an appearance at Christmas."

Freddie laughed. "That was nearly a year ago."

"I thought my visit was memorable enough to last the year."

"Obviously it wasn't. I think he's of the opinion that you've been the recluse long enough and it's time you returned to civilization."

"I hardly call living at Covington Manor an existence in the wilds. It may not be London at the height of the Season, but we're quite civilized in the country."

"And lonely."

"Don't, Freddie." Griff lifted his palm to stop his friend from continuing.

"Adam is concerned for you, Griff. He only wants—"

"I know what he wants, but I'm perfectly content with life as it is."

Griff sucked in a harsh breath, then released it in a rush. "You surely didn't come all this way just to give me Adam's message? What other reason brought you here?"

Freddie leaned back in his chair and groaned. "You're right, of course. There is another reason." He paused. When he spoke, his voice was filled with frustration. "I have decided to marry."

Griff tried to hide his surprise but failed. "And who is the lucky lady you wish to make your marchioness?"

"I don't know. I haven't picked her out yet."

Griff did laugh this time. "I don't believe it. What brought this about?"

"I turned twenty-six last week."

"And…"

"I am in need of an heir."

"I see."

"Everything I have is entailed. My London town house. The country estate. Everything. If something were to happen to me, Annie and Rebecca would have nowhere to go. They would be without even a roof over their heads."

"It took you all this time to realize this?"

Freddie raked his fingers through his dark, curly hair. "Perhaps I'm finally growing up." He gave a short laugh. "That's a surprise, isn't it? Father would be shocked if he were still alive to hear me say that. Or perhaps I have finally accepted my own mortality. None of us knows what tomorrow will hold. You more than anyone can attest to that."

Griff's blood turned to ice. "Yes. The future is uncertain for all of us."

"I don't see why Father couldn't have supplied the Brentwood line with at least one more male instead of just Annie and Rebecca, but he didn't." He took another swallow of ale and set the glass back on the table with a great deal of concentration. "Although considering his failure at being a husband and father, I suppose I should be thankful I'm not an only child."

Griff thought of his own childhood. It had been so different from Freddie's, his parents so loving. "Not all marriages are like your parents'."

"So I've heard. And it wasn't so bad, really. At least I was sent away to school and could escape the upheaval for part of the year." Freddie slowly turned his glass in tiny circles on the table. "It was worse for Annie. She had nowhere to go."

Freddie lifted his glass and took another swallow. "It's no wonder neither of us have jumped at the chance to marry."

Griff absorbed Freddie's words, then softly asked, "So, have you begun the search for your perfect candidate?"

"I began tonight but tired of it after dancing with the fifth or sixth blonde-haired, blue-eyed twit. Bloody hell, Griff. They all seem so…young."

"They are. You should have chosen your bride years ago, when the eligible young ladies were your age."

"What a depressing thought."

Griff smiled. "So you're seeking out my company on the rebound? I am indeed flattered."

"You should be. At least I have no intention of letting you step on my toes, then whispering my apologies as if *your* clumsiness was *my* fault."

"It must indeed have been a trial for you."

"It was."

Griff smiled. "Drink up. You can spend the night at Covington Manor. Things will look better in the morning, after a good night's sleep and a hearty breakfast."

The two friends finished their drinks, then walked together into the cool evening air.

Thousands of bright stars twinkled above them, and a gentle breeze washed over them as they made their way across the rutted yard to the stables beyond.

Perhaps it was due to Griff's years in the army as a spy, but the hairs at the back of his neck pricked in warning. Griff took in his surroundings to evaluate the danger he felt.

He noticed a movement to his left. Then Freddie noticed it, too. They both paused. Their footsteps halted as they turned to the side.

A glint of metal shone in the moonlight. The realization of what was happening sent a wave of panic racing through Griff's body.

"Get down, Freddie!"

Griff reached for the pistol he always kept in the pocket of his jacket—but not in time. A loud explosion shattered the peaceful country air as Freddie spun against him, taking them both to the ground. A second shot followed the first.

The force of Freddie's body was too much, and Griff fell backward, his arms splayed out on either side of him. His chest heaved as much from careening against the hard earth beneath him as from the jolt of Freddie's weight.

Bloody hell! He thought he'd left all this behind him. He was sure they'd executed all the traitors. Just as he was sure the sniper who'd tried to kill him after the war hadn't followed him to England. He must have been wrong. Whoever it was evidently had no intention of stopping until he was dead.

Griff's blood ran cold; dread and disbelief ran rampant through his brain. He put his hands on Freddie's arms and gripped hard as he tried to move him.

"Freddie." Griff rolled Freddie to the side. "Are you all right?"

Griff heard a soft, muffled groan and passed his hands over Freddie's face and arms to see where he'd been hurt. Then he felt the warm, sticky liquid at Freddie's chest.

The pain of a dozen cannonballs slammed into Griff's gut. He looked down and, instead of seeing Freddie's face, relived the death of another friend. A spy's bullet had also killed Gerald Fespoint, a fellow officer—a bullet Griff knew had been intended for him.

Cold fingers of fear clenched his heart. "Dear God! No!"

"Griff," Freddie whispered.

"You're going to be all right, Freddie. Just lie still."

Griff was frantic. This couldn't be happening. Not again. Not to Freddie.

"Griff?" he whispered again, his voice weaker.

"Shh, Freddie. Don't try to talk. I've got to get you inside. Don't worry. I'll take care of you."

"No, Griff. It's too…late."

"No! You're going to be fine. I'm not going to let you die. Not you, too." He turned and yelled to the growing crowd gathering around them. "Someone! Get a blanket and help me carry him inside."

Griff stared into Freddie's eyes and saw the same look he'd seen a hundred times during the war. The look of death. "Don't talk, Freddie. Save your strength."

"Take care of…Annie. Promise me."

"Damn you, Freddie. Don't you dare die. Don't you dare!"

Griff's mind reeled in alarm. His heart thundered in his chest. His head wanted to explode from the terror that raged through his body. He knew what was happening, yet his mind refused to believe it.

"You're going to be fine. Just hang on." Griff reached for the blanket someone handed him and threw it over Freddie.

Freddie lifted his arm and clutched Griff's shirt. "Annie. Promise me you'll…take care of…Annie."

He whispered his final words, then went limp in Griff's arms.

"No! Dear God, no!"

Griff stared at Freddie in numb disbelief. He was dead.

There was nothing left to do but hold his friend's lifeless body in his arms as he gently rocked him back and forth. With eyes shut tight, Griff lifted his face toward heaven and let a river of hot, wet tears stream down his cheeks. Tears that burned a hole deep into his heart.

A heart he'd thought was incapable of feeling more pain.

\* \* \*

Griff pulled on the reins and stopped his horse at the entrance to the drive of the late Marquess of Brentwood's country estate. He wasn't sure he had the courage to go the rest of the distance. He wasn't sure he could stand at Freddie's graveside and watch while they lowered his friend's body into the ground and covered his coffin with shovel after shovel of cold, black dirt. He wasn't sure he was strong enough to face Freddie's family, knowing that Freddie was dead and he was not.

He reached for the flask inside his topcoat pocket and took another long swallow. Liquor afforded him a level of comfort he desperately needed. It was the panacea to dull the pain and ease the guilt that consumed him, that threatened to tear his heart from deep inside his chest.

He took one more swallow, knowing he'd need it to make it through this day.

Griff nudged his horse with his heels and let the animal make his way up the long lane to Freddie's home.

A groom rushed to take his horse when he dismounted. Griff hesitated until the ground felt solid beneath him, then forced himself to take the first step toward the door, then a second. Before he lifted the muffled knocker, a tall, somber-looking butler opened the door. The man gave Griff a respectful nod, then stepped aside to let him enter.

"I've come for the marquess's funeral," Griff said, praying he hadn't slurred his words.

The butler took his hat and coat. "I'm afraid the services are over, sir. But the guests are gathered in the morning room with Lady Anne and Lady Rebecca. If you'll follow me."

The butler turned to lead the way to the morning room. Out of habit, Griff reached for the flask in his pocket. He stopped himself, a small voice warning him he'd had enough—for at least an hour or two.

With slow, hesitant steps, the butler led Griff down a narrow hallway, stopping just outside an open doorway. Inside, he heard the low, murmuring sounds of muffled voices. Griff took a step toward the doorway and stopped. Dear God, he couldn't do this. Yet what choice did he have?

With a heavy sigh, he sucked in a painful breath and walked through the portal.

The room was crowded. Each guest was dressed in a more depressing shade of black than the last. Droll bits of their whispered conversations blanketed the room in suffocating closeness.

Griff fought the urge to flee. He fought the greater urge to reach for the flask in his jacket pocket and drain it. Instead, he stepped forward and let his gaze move around the room. He focused on the first familiar face he recognized—the last face he wanted to see today of all days. His brother Adam, Earl of Covington.

He watched the frown on Adam's face darken, the concern that etched his features. It was an expression Griff knew only too well. He stepped closer and braced himself for the confrontation he knew would come.

"Hello, Adam. What a surprise."

"It shouldn't be, Griff. Brentwood was, after all, a peer as well as a neighbor and friend."

Adam leveled Griff a discerning gaze, his serious expression every inch the earl. Adam clasped his hands behind his back, the tense pull of his expensively tailored jacket an indication of the fragile rein on his emotions. His every movement was an unmistakable example of propriety.

"I've tried to find you for the last three days, Griff. Where have you been?"

Griff remained focused on a black-clad footman carrying a tray of sandwiches he offered to the guests. He could hardly tell Adam where he'd spent his time over the last few days when he had no idea himself.

"Damnation, Griff," Adam said, his harsh whisper pulling Griff's attention back to the scowl on his brother's face. "Don't you know how worried I've been?"

Griff tried to smile. "There's no need, Adam. I'm perfectly fine."

"No, you're not. Anyone can see by looking at you that Freddie's death has taken a toll on you."

"Of course it has taken a toll. Freddie was my friend. Now, if you'll excuse me."

Griff tried to escape his brother's scrutiny but staggered when he took his first step. Adam's fingers clasped around his arm.

"Have you been drinking, Griff?"

"Not nearly enough to matter." Griff ignored Adam's shocked expression and looked away.

"I want you to come with me to London, Griff," Adam said before Griff could turn away. "You need to be with family."

Griff smiled as he fingered the flask in his pocket. Family was the last thing he needed right now. Being the cause of one more person's death would be the final blow that would drive him over the edge. He was suddenly very anxious to make his escape. "I need to pay my respects to Freddie's sisters. Which ones are they?"

"Perhaps it would be best if you talked to them later. When you haven't been drinking."

Griff shrugged out of Adam's grasp. "Never mind, Adam. I'll find them myself."

He had only taken one step forward before Adam stepped in front of him.

Griff glared at his brother with every bit of his anger. "I wouldn't if I were you, Adam. Not unless you want to cause a scene that will have the whole of London talking for weeks."

"All right," Adam said through clenched teeth. "But take care. They are both terribly upset. Brentwood's death was a horrible shock."

Griff wanted to laugh. He knew better than anyone the horrible shock of Freddie's death. Freddie had died in his arms. Freddie had died in his place. All because he hadn't made sure the last sniper couldn't harm anyone else. He sucked in a shuddering breath, anxious to pay his respects and get out of here. "Where are they?"

Adam hesitated a second more, then breathed a sigh of resignation. "The younger sister, Lady Rebecca, is sitting on the sofa." He nodded toward the other side of the room. "Please leave her be. She's barely fifteen."

Griff ignored Adam's warning and focused his gaze on Freddie's youngest sister.

She wasn't alone. Several guests were gathered around her to comfort her. A plump lady held her hand. Another older woman sat at her other side, and a kindly looking gentleman, perhaps one of the women's husbands, stood to the side, resting his hand on the back of the sofa.

The minute Griff saw her he knew he couldn't face her. He swiped his hand across his damp face. "Where's the oldest?"

"Don't cause a scene, Griff. She's been through quite enough—"

Griff ignored the sharp tone of Adam's voice and looked around the room. "Which one is she?"

With a second harsh look of warning, Adam turned his gaze to the far corner of the room, to a spot where the light from the windows and from the glowing candles placed throughout the room did not seem to reach—a place of isolation no one in the vast crowd seemed able to breach.

She stood alone with her back to him, with her deep mahogany hair pulled back in a loose chignon, her narrow shoulders braced in stoic bravery. He couldn't tear his gaze from her.

*Take care of Annie. Promise me you'll take care of Annie.*

Griff ordered his feet to move. Ordered his body to go to where she stood and tell her how sorry he was that Freddie was dead. But his feet seemed rooted to the floor. He couldn't face her. Not when she'd look at him, a stranger she hadn't seen since she was a young girl, and wonder why he'd allowed Freddie to die.

He tried to step forward again but failed. Guilt ate away at him until he found it hard to breathe. He shouldn't have come.

He shouldn't even be alive. Freddie should be the one visiting Griff's family, sharing in their grief. Griff should be the one buried in the ground.

He kept his gaze focused on the slight figure standing in the shadows and knew his paltry words of regret were inadequate.

He had to leave. Leave before she turned around and saw him. Leave before she looked into his eyes and saw the guilt.

As if she realized he was there, her hands dropped to her sides and she slowly turned.

Her eyes were as black as midnight—big, beautiful, sad. Her gaze went directly to him, focusing on him. A jolt belted him in the gut with the force of a heavy fist.

She knew.

She knew the bullet that had killed Freddie had been intended for him. She knew Freddie had given his life to save him.

She knew he wasn't worth the sacrifice.

Griff felt sick. His stomach churned; his shallow breaths came in harsh, ragged gasps. He needed to leave. He needed a drink. He needed to forget.

*Take care of Annie, Griff.*

He couldn't. He wanted to scream that no one was safe unless they stayed far, far away from him.

He held her burning gaze as long as he could, then spun on his heels and stormed from the room.

By the time he reached the nearest inn, he was desperate for a drink. Then another. And another. As many as it took until he could forget. Forget the lives he'd destroyed.

There'd been so many.

How the hell did Freddie think he could take care of his sister? Why the bloody hell had he asked? Griff could no more protect her than he'd protected his wife, or his son, or Gerald Fespoint, or Freddie himself.

A painful stabbing carved a ridge deep in his chest. He would drink until he succeeded in drowning the painful memories he couldn't live with.

Just like he'd succeeded in drowning his family.

# Chapter 2

✤

"What is going to happen to us?" Becca asked. Worry clouded her pretty features.

Anne Carmichael dropped her gaze back to the papers in front of her, trying desperately to appear calm. How could Freddie have left them in such a precarious position? "I'm not sure, Becca, but we'll know soon enough."

"Reverend Talbert said we would have to—"

"Don't worry," Anne interrupted, looking up from the papers she'd been studying. "We'll be all right."

Anne rubbed a hand over her eyes and noticed the confused expression on Becca's cherub face. Thank heaven she was too young to completely understand their dire straits.

Anne gave her younger sister a pensive smile. In looks, Rebecca was much like their mother, with her honey-blonde hair, sky-blue eyes, and face of an angel. At fifteen, she already had a hint of beauty that promised to make her one of the most sought after debutantes when she had her coming out. She was not like Anne, who was dark like her father and like Freddie had been.

Although Anne was not plain, she did have a serious countenance many found unapproachable. It was an attribute for which she was very thankful.

Anne sighed, then went back to the numbers in Freddie's ledger and added them again. And again. Nothing changed. No matter how often she calculated the columns of figures, the end result was the same. They were destitute.

"I overheard Cook tell Mr. Flounders that the new Marquess of Brentwood will come here to live." Rebecca had resumed the nervous habit of chewing her nails. "Is it true he will get our home?"

"Yes, it's true."

"Then we will have to find someplace else to live," Becca said matter-of-factly. "Do you have any idea where we will go?"

Anne felt the air being sucked from her lungs. "I'm not sure. I will know more after I meet with the new marquess and Freddie's solicitor. They will be here any moment."

"Do you think the marquess will be kind? Perhaps he will let us live in one of the cottages on the estate." Rebecca voiced some of the same questions that had gone through Anne's mind during the past month—ever since she had realized their desperate situation, and what Freddie's death meant for them.

"Perhaps the one the caretaker used to live in before he left," Becca added.

"Perhaps." Anne tried to hide how concerned she really was. How could she give her sister an answer when she didn't have one herself? How could she reassure Becca that everything would be all right when she didn't think anything would ever be right again? Anne started to add the figures again, praying she'd made a mistake and the numbers would come out differently this time.

"Will I be able to go back to school?"

Anne glanced up. The wide-eyed anticipation in Becca's eyes caused her heart to twist in her chest. At least Freddie had taken care of that expense for the next term, and Becca would not have to leave school. Her enrollment in Lady Agnes's School for Young Ladies was paid for the entire year.

Anne walked from behind the desk and took Rebecca's hands in hers. "Of course you'll be able to finish school. But if you don't stop biting your nails, Lady Agnes won't allow you to return, regardless of whether your fees have been paid or not. Lady Agnes said it took her all of two full terms to break you of that awful habit when you first came. She will never forgive me if I send you back with your nails chewed to the quick."

Rebecca tucked her hands in the folds of her skirt. "I have time to grow them out before I go back. I won't have to leave you yet. Will I?"

Anne gave her sister a quick hug. "Of course not. You will stay with me for at least a few more weeks."

The leaden weight in the pit of Anne's stomach seemed even heavier. With a sense of desperation, she returned to her place behind the desk and closed the cover on the ledger that proved how destitute they were. What on earth was she going to do if things turned out as she feared? What if they were left with nowhere to live and no income to purchase even food?

A knock at the door stopped her thoughts. Freddie's solicitor and the new marquess were here. It would not be long before she would know just how bad things really were.

"The Marquess of Brentwood and Mr. Harold Woolsey to see you, my lady," their butler, Ruskins, announced from the doorway.

"Thank you, Ruskins," Anne answered, trying desperately to keep her voice steady. "Will you see that tea is served?"

"Yes, my lady."

Anne shifted her gaze to the two men who'd entered the room.

She'd met Harold Woolsey once before when he'd come to Brentwood Manor on business. He hadn't changed since she'd first seen him. He was still…average. Average in height, as well as in looks and in physical build. Average in coloring and dress, and almost nondescript in the way he blended into his surroundings. The total antithesis of the man standing next to him.

The new Marquess of Brentwood was tall and broad shouldered, almost as large as Freddie had been. And he was as dark. His shadowed features, so prevalent in the Carmichael ancestry, left no doubt as to his parentage.

She looked into his face, a face she found unusually handsome—handsome in the same way Freddie had been, yet different. Those same distinguishing features that had endeared Freddie to Anne hardened the new marquess's looks. The sight of him caused her a hint of trepidation.

"Lady Anne," Harold Woolsey said, making his way into the room. "I would first like to express my sympathy to you and your sister."

"Thank you, Mr. Woolsey."

"I would like to present the Marquess of Brentwood."

The marquess closed the space between them. With flawless elegance, he bowed formally, then lifted Anne's hand to his lips and kissed the tips of her fingers.

"My lord," she said, resisting the urge to pull her hand from his grasp.

"Lady Anne, I cannot tell you how distressed I was to learn of your brother's death. You have my heartfelt sympathy."

"Thank you, my lord." Anne stepped back from him. She experienced an innate desire to put an adequate amount of distance between them.

The new marquess straightened his shoulders and clasped his hands behind his back, which made him appear even taller, even larger. "I am deeply honored to bear the title bestowed upon me, but I would gladly give it up if I could change the circumstances that brought about my good fortune. Please believe me when I say I regret your brother's untimely death more than I can say."

Anne heard the sincerity in his voice and reprimanded herself for the unkind thoughts she'd had earlier.

"Thank you, my lord." Anne held his gaze for a moment, then turned away from him to where Becca stood before the sofa. "May I present my sister, Lady Rebecca Carmichael."

Brentwood executed a perfect bow when he greeted Rebecca, then took her hand and lightly kissed her fingers. When he lifted his gaze to her face, he flashed her a most startling smile.

The manner in which Rebecca received Brentwood's greeting would have made Lady Agnes proud. Anne was terrified. She wasn't sure when Rebecca had grown up on her. She suddenly realized what a threat Brentwood posed and didn't know how she could protect Rebecca from being taken in by a man's handsome face and easy charm.

Anne struggled to regain her composure. "Won't you please sit down," she said to both Mr. Woolsey and Lord Brentwood, indicating two chairs opposite the sofa.

Anne took a seat on the sofa and Rebecca sat beside her. Anne poured tea when it arrived and served it with the small cakes Cook provided. When she finished, she took a sip of her tea, then set the cup and saucer back on the table.

"If it would not be too unseemly, I would appreciate it if we might dispense with any pleasantries and proceed directly to the reading of Freddie's will. As I'm sure you can understand, none of us want to prolong this any longer than necessary."

"Of course, Lady Anne," Mr. Woolsey said, setting down his cup of tea and picking up the leather binder that would reveal their futures. "I have the late marquess's papers right here."

Anne tried to conceal her nervousness while Mr. Woolsey removed the papers and held them in his hands. "Are you certain there isn't someone you would like to have with you while we go through your brother's will?" he asked before he began. "A friend, a guardian, a—"

"Someone of the male populace, you mean," Anne interrupted. "No, Mr. Woolsey. My sister and I will be fine. Although being mere women, we will probably need your guidance on matters."

"Of course. Of course," Mr. Woolsey murmured, oblivious to the cut he had just received. It was not, however, lost on the marquess. The superior expression on his face said as much.

"Perhaps we should begin," Brentwood said, "and Lady Anne can stop us if she has any questions."

"Very well," Woolsey agreed, bobbing his head up and down.

Thus began the reading of the will.

Anne searched for one thread of hope as Woolsey read through the volume of papers, but each page verified every dreaded fear that had plagued her since Freddie's death. Each detail negated every fervent prayer she'd made that she would find a way to take care of Rebecca. Her scrutiny was useless. There was no hope.

The title and Brentwood Manor went to the new marquess, as well as the London town house, the mining and lumber interests, and three other estates, one of which Anne had not even known existed.

Minutes stretched into what seemed hours as the solicitor read the legal descriptions of each and every property that now belonged to the new Marquess of Brentwood.

She clenched her hands in her lap, fearful that she would not be able to keep up her brave facade until he finished. Finally, the legal description of each landholding was finished, and Mr. Woolsey began with the actual cash bequeaths. Anticipation mounted. Her heart pounded against her ribs and the tempo of the constant thudding inside her chest raced faster and faster.

She was relieved when Mr. Woolsey read that each loyal employee would receive an adequate allowance, as well as an amount allotted for a generous donation to the church. When these bequeaths were made, the solicitor revealed the remaining sum of money Freddie had amassed from his personal investments. The amount left wasn't a staggering sum, but it did give her some room for hope.

There were, of course, a number of outstanding debts that had to be paid first. Mr. Woolsey began with the tailor, then a bill for a carriage. There was the bill to Tattersall's for a pair of matching grays and a gambling debt of two hundred pounds, another of four hundred. There was a payment for the last shipment of wine and brandy, and… The list seemed endless, leaving a sum total of…

Anne's heart fell to the pit of her stomach. She knew there would not be much, but…*Freddie*, an angry voice screamed from inside her, *didn't you think to leave us at least enough to get by?*

How did he think she and Becca could survive on so little?

"I am terribly sorry, Lady Anne," Mr. Woolsey said softly. "I don't know what to say."

Anne squared her shoulders and gathered all the courage she could find to accept what she'd known would happen all along. "It is what I expected. If you would, Mr. Woolsey, please itemize what we do possess."

"Of course, Lady Anne."

A whirlpool of fear and unease churned deep in her stomach as Anne watched Mr. Woolsey sift through the documents, stopping when he reached a single sheet of paper at the back of the large stack. Unsightly red splotches covered his neck, either a sign of nervousness or an indication of his pity for her plight. The sympathy she read in his expression instilled within her a renewed determination.

A stronger sense of resolve bolstered her, strengthening her with a blanket of fierce determination. She could not stand it if what he felt was pity. Anything but that.

"As I'm sure you realize, Lady Anne, your brother did not anticipate something happening to him at so young an age. If he had, I have no doubt he would have made greater provisions for you and Lady Rebecca."

"No doubt," Anne agreed. "But that was not the case, was it?"

"No, it was not." Mr. Woolsey shifted uncomfortably in his seat, then adjusted his spectacles before continuing. "This is a list of what you and your sister are entitled to. A list of everything that is not entailed."

The solicitor cleared his throat, then began. "Your mother, the late Marchioness of Brentwood, brought with her to her marriage the following items of value: one ruby pendant necklace; a diamond-and-emerald necklace with a matching emerald ring; two pearl rings, one black, one pink; a pearl necklace; and a diamond-and-sapphire necklace with earbobs to match. In addition, there are a few items of furniture and mementos not entailed to which you and your sister have ownership, and finally, the sum of one thousand pounds you will each receive upon your marriage."

"Upon our marriage?"

"Yes. It was a provision required by your maternal great-grandmother. She thought it gave a woman a sense of independence to have money of her own."

A knot clenched in her stomach. Money of her own did not just give a woman a sense of independence; it was necessary for survival. "Is there a stipulation in the will that prohibits us from receiving the money now?"

Mr. Woolsey nodded. "I'm afraid there is. You can only receive your inheritance upon your marriage."

Anne wanted to laugh. That day would never come for her. A paltry thousand pounds was not worth sacrificing her freedom to endure the hell that constituted a marriage. Even a hundred times that amount would not be worth it. A thousand pounds, however, did mean the difference between survival and starvation.

"Is there anything else?" Anne asked, feeling the need to escape before it was impossible to keep up the pretense of calm.

"One more item, Lady Anne. Less than a year ago, your brother added a piece of property to his holdings."

"What property?"

"I'm afraid it is nothing of any real value. It is a stretch of land that used to be a part of Brentwood Estate on the north, reaching as far east as the ocean. I took the liberty of looking at it when I heard of the late marquess's death." He shook his head. "I'm afraid I cannot imagine why your brother purchased it. It's nothing but craggy rocks filled with dangerous caves."

Anne smiled. "Freddie often saw beauty where others did not. It does not surprise me that he purchased something for the sheer pleasure of looking at it."

"Where is this land located?" the marquess asked, speaking for the first time since Mr. Woolsey had begun.

"It borders Brentwood Estate at its northeastern corner, next to Covington Estate."

"But that land is entailed," Brentwood said.

Woolsey turned to face the marquess. "Yes, it was. Until the late marquess petitioned the courts to have it separated. Although I can't see why. It's quite desolate and traveled very little. I doubt anyone has set foot there for years, except, of course, the late marquess. That's perhaps why he wanted it."

"I'm sure it was." Anne had already dismissed the piece of land that had no value. A small patch of worthless property would not save Becca and her from starvation. What she needed was enough money to support them until she figured out what to do.

"He also left this letter, with instructions that it be given to you in the event of his death."

"Thank you." Anne reached out to take the letter. The writing was in Freddie's hand and she choked back the lump that wanted to form in her throat.

"I'm terribly sorry I do not have better news for you, Lady Anne."

Anne smiled. *Dear God,* she prayed. *Just let me survive this until they're gone. Please.* "It was expected, Mr. Woolsey."

"Lady Anne?" the marquess asked as he sat forward in his chair. "What are your plans now?"

"Don't worry, my lord," Anne said, forcing her voice to sound strong and confident. "You are not responsible for us. Becca and I would be extremely embarrassed if you considered yourself thus."

"Do you have somewhere to go?"

"I'm sure it won't be too difficult to find an empty house somewhere. Perhaps in London. We do have a little income, as you recall Mr. Woolsey mentioning."

"But not enough to live as you are accustomed." His words brought the desperation of their situation into full focus. "And for how long?"

She sat even straighter. "Long enough, my lord. You are not responsible for us. Please understand that neither I nor my sister will accept charity from you or anyone else."

"Wanting to help you is not charity," he said in a gruff tone. "Although distant, you are, after all, my only relation. I wouldn't be able to live with myself knowing you were in dire straits. I won't insult you by inviting you to remain here at Brentwood Manor. It would be most improper once I take up residence, and I know staying here for any length of time would be too difficult an adjustment. I will, however, offer one of the other cottages on the estate. The caretaker's cottage, which I understand is unoccupied. Or the hunter's lodge, which I have been told is open and quite roomy."

Anne felt as if her prayers had been answered. They had no place to go. Nowhere to live. The caretaker's cottage would give them at least a roof over their heads until she could figure out what options were open to them.

She turned to face Becca, and it was almost her undoing. The look on her sister's face was filled with trusting confidence.

In a gesture too small to be noticed by anyone but her, Becca reached out and squeezed Anne's fingers. The message pure and simple. She trusted that Anne would take care of her, not realizing that they were now left with little to call their own.

Anne braced her shoulders in resolve. "I would greatly appreciate your offer of the caretaker's cottage, my lord. Your generosity is overwhelming."

"Not at all, my lady," the marquess said.

His glance lingered far longer than was seemly—or necessary. She didn't like the manner in which he looked at her. It hinted at things she would never consider.

"I couldn't bear it if some hardship were to befall someone so lovely," he said, still holding her gaze. "You and your sister are welcome to stay as long as you need."

"Thank you. You will be free to take up residence in the manor house by the end of the week."

"There is no need to hurry."

"Yes, there is. Brentwood Manor is now yours. I'm sure you are anxious to take possession of it."

The serious look he gave her hinted at a newfound sense of self-importance.

"As you wish."

Anne stood, praying that their guests would take the hint that their discussion was at an end. Thankfully, they did.

"If you have any further need of my services," Mr. Woolsey said, clutching his folder to his chest, "please, do not hesitate to call on me."

"Thank you, Mr. Woolsey."

"The same applies to me, Lady Anne," the marquess said. "And consider my servants at your disposal. They will see to anything you need."

"Thank you, my lord."

Wordlessly, Ruskins appeared to usher the two men from the room. Only when she heard the soft closing of the front door was Anne able to move. She walked to the window and stared out onto the beautifully cared-for garden.

She would miss Brentwood Manor more than she let herself admit. She loved it here and thought of it as the home where she would grow old and die. She'd never dreamt of living anywhere else, of having a home other than this one. A home of her own would come with a husband, and that was a part of life she did not want. Would not have.

She took a swallow that burned her throat. She was suddenly very tired. She wanted to lie down and close her eyes and pretend that when she awoke, Freddie would be alive and the past few weeks would have been a terrible nightmare. But that wouldn't happen.

"I think I have the answer to our problem," Becca said from behind her.

Anne had almost forgotten her sister was still there. She turned. "What answer? What answer do you see that I have missed?"

"You, Annie. Oh, it will be so wonderful." Becca clasped her hands in jubilation. "The London Season is about to begin. You can put yourself on the marriage mart and find a husband. It will be perfect." Rebecca nearly skipped across the room in her excitement. "There are ever so many eligible men out there, each one more handsome than the last. Perhaps even the new marquess will be one of your suitors. You are not that closely related, you know."

Anne shook her head from side to side. "No, Becca. I will not have you even suggest it. Marriage has never been the answer to any problem. A marriage of convenience is decidedly worse."

"But marrying some wonderful man who will take care of us would be the perfect solution."

"No. Marrying a man you do not love is like walking into a trap you have no hope of ever escaping. And loving a man who will never love you in return is even worse."

The happy look on Rebecca's face fell. "Was it really so terrible between Mother and Father?"

Anne lowered her gaze to the floor. How could she tell her sister, who was too young to remember their mother's tears and the endless quarrels? How could she shatter the illusion of matrimonial bliss with tales of her parents' unhappy union? She could not. She could do nothing but lie.

"No, Becca. It was not so terrible. Mother just loved Father too much, and Father…"

"And Father loved his liquor more than Mother or his children," Rebecca finished for her.

Anne nodded. "Yes. He loved his liquor more."

"But not every man is like that." There was a glimmer of hope in Rebecca's eyes that yearned for Anne to deny her fears. "Freddie was never like that."

"No, he wasn't. Perhaps he saw the heartache being a drunkard caused and knew how drinking destroyed everyone who cared for you."

"I don't want to believe it's impossible to fall in love with a man who loves you just as desperately as you love him, Annie."

Anne wanted to tell Rebecca that her dream was impossible. That she was not sure any man could ever love that much. That her mother had found that out and died when she had to face her failure.

But Anne couldn't disillusion Becca. She was so young. "You're right, Becca. It is possible to find your prince charming and live happily ever after. And some day you will do exactly that."

"Just as you, too, will find your prince charming, Annie."

"We'll worry about that later." Anne put her arm around her sister's shoulder and held her tight. "Right now, it would be most improper to even consider marriage while we are in mourning."

"But some day—"

"Let's get over this hurdle first, Becca. In a few years I will give you a Season in London. You can search for the man of your dreams."

"Oh, Annie," Rebecca said, turning into Anne's arms and hugging her in return. "I don't want to get married right this moment, but marrying the perfect man is such a wonderful dream."

Anne breathed a deep sigh and touched the flawless skin of her sister's rosy cheeks. "Of course it is," she answered her sister, although deep in her heart she was terrified of marrying a man who might turn out just like her father. Terrified of being stuck in a loveless marriage with no hope of escape. And terrified of loving someone so much you didn't want to go on living when you realized he could never love you in return.

The risk was just not worth taking.

Anne pushed such thoughts away and gave her sister an open smile. She hugged her even tighter. "Why don't you make a list of what we will take with us when we leave? I would like to go to my room for a while. I'll be down in time for dinner."

"You rest, Annie. I know what little sleep you've gotten since…since they brought Freddie home."

Anne made her way to the door with Freddie's letter clutched in her hand.

"We'll be just fine, Annie," Becca said from behind her.

Anne turned and forced herself to smile. She was thankful that Becca didn't realize they would never be fine again.

Anne took Freddie's letter with her to her room and sank down on the edge of the bed as if the weight of the world rested on her shoulders. With trembling fingers she opened the envelope and unfolded the papers. A river of hot tears filled her eyes and blurred the words she read.

*Annie,*

*If you have cause to read this, then I regret that I have left you to face the future alone and without the financial security you deserve. As you probably know by now, everything you and Rebecca have always considered your own is entailed and belongs to someone else. Everything except the deed to the property you received along with this letter. I regret that I have not yet acquired enough wealth to adequately support you, Annie, but at the moment this parcel of land is all I have to leave you to preserve the Brentwood name. Know that there is no one else I would have possess it but you, and promise that you will never sell it.*

*Tell Rebecca that I loved her dearly, even though you have always possessed the greatest part of my heart. Perhaps it was because of the unhappiness we endured growing up. That bound us to each other like nothing else could.*

*If it is possible, I will watch out for you from above.*

*Your loving brother,*
*Freddie*

*P.S. When all is said and done, all any of us have left are our honor and our good name. These are riches beyond what is seen by the human eye.*

When Anne finished, she folded the letter, then held it to her breast. She tried desperately not to feel any anger toward the brother who'd left them so desolate and alone, but pangs of vexation plagued her.

She also tried not to think of the man who had been with Freddie when he died. The man she blamed for Freddie's death.

The man she wished had died instead of her brother.

# Chapter 3

✣

Griff stopped to take a swallow from the flask he kept in his pocket, then continued his way down the deserted wharf.

It had been over a month since Freddie's death, and Griff hadn't uncovered one clue that pointed him to whoever was responsible. He'd turned over every rock he thought might reveal something, but any information he found turned out to be nothing. He was here because there was one man who might have some answers, Colonel Rupert Fitzhugh, the man who'd issued the orders for every mission Griff had been a part of. The same man who might have been able to prevent Freddie's death and hadn't.

Griff had chosen the docks of London to meet Colonel Fitzhugh for a reason. After dark, the docks were the closest place to hell he knew.

Transformed under a cloak of darkness, London's waterfront turned into a vile cesspit at night, overrun with thieves, hooligans, and deadly dangers hiding around every corner. Griff walked through the maze of hazards as if he owned the night. Safety was his last concern.

Farther down the long stretch of docks, bawdy laughter and raucous music floated out from smoke-filled taverns, rising above the yelling and cursing associated with an occasional drunken brawl. Griff was well acquainted with every filthy hovel along the wharf.

But it was quiet here. The only sound that intruded on the haunting silence was the steady lapping of the water against the moored ships.

The hollow clomping of his boots echoed through the heavy fog. The danger that awaited him down every darkened alleyway and hidden recess was as familiar as if he'd been born here. Sometimes he felt as if he had. He'd lived in this environ since Freddie had been killed. He'd spent as many hours here as he had in even less respectable parts of London, searching for the sniper who had shot Freddie. This was the most likely place to hide for someone who didn't want to be found. The easiest place from which to make an escape.

Griff walked a few feet farther down the boardwalk and stopped to lean against a wooden railing between the moored *Angela Bay* and *Caribbean Lady*. By design, he was not early. Fitzhugh was probably here, undoubtedly waiting for him in the shadows. He enjoyed knowing that the colonel's wait hadn't been comfortable.

"I'm glad you finally showed up," Fitzhugh said, appearing from nowhere. He stopped when he reached Griff and leaned against the wooden railing. "This isn't my favorite place to stroll after dark."

Griff didn't turn to face the man who had been his commanding officer during the war, but kept his gaze focused out into the dense fog that seemed to grow heavier by the second. "I didn't think you would feel too out of place mixing with the rats and vermin that only come out when no one can see them."

"Is there a point to your comment, Captain Blackmoor?"

Griff spun to face his former commanding officer. The threat he presented forced Fitzhugh to step back.

"Why the bloody hell didn't you tell me there were still loose ends from our last mission during the war?"

Fitzhugh stiffened. "We thought we'd taken care of them."

"Damn you, Fitzhugh! You're the head of British Intelligence! You're the one who sees the reports first. Why the hell didn't you warn me that we hadn't eliminated all of them?"

"We thought we had. The last *loose end*, as you call it, was eliminated after Fespoint was killed."

"Who took care of it?"

"Hawkins."

"Then there must have been someone else."

"There couldn't have been."

Griff took a step closer to Fitzhugh. "If you don't think there is a possibility of another agent out there, then why the hell are Hawkins and Johnston and Turner still following surveillance procedures? I've tailed them for nearly a month. They're hunting for someone."

"They're following my orders. I'm simply making sure we didn't overlook anything."

Griff slammed his fist on the wooden railing and glared at Fitzhugh. "Now is a hell of a time to think you may have overlooked a stray killer."

Several long, uncomfortable seconds of silence hung between them. Fitzhugh was the first to speak. "I'm going to credit your rudeness to the fact that you lost a dear friend, Blackmoor. And your accusations to the liquor you've consumed. But don't push me too far. I'm warning you. We've done everything possible and can't find any evidence that anyone followed you to England."

"Tell that to the late Marquess of Brentwood's family. I'm sure it will be a great comfort to them."

Fitzhugh reached into his pocket to pull out some papers. "These are Hawkins's reports. Everything is included in them."

Griff snatched the papers out of his former commander's hand. It was too dark to read them here. But he didn't want to wait to find out what they contained. "Humor me. What do they say?"

"Only what you already know. We discovered one more member of the spy ring. He was the one who killed Fespoint. We thought he was the last. We assumed that when Hawkins eliminated him, any threat to you was over."

"Well, it wasn't. Or the Marquess of Brentwood wouldn't be dead."

"You can't be sure his death is related to what happened over there, Captain. There's no proof."

"What other reason can there be?"

"Maybe Brentwood had enemies and it was just your bad luck to be with him when he died."

"You can't be serious. Brentwood had no enemies." Griff fisted his hands at his side. He'd lost the battle to hold his temper at bay.

Fitzhugh turned away from Griff and stared out into the fog. The message was clear. Their conversation was at an end.

Griff put the papers in his pocket and took a step back. "If you find out anything," he said through clenched teeth, "I want to know."

"You're no longer under my command, Blackmoor. You resigned your commission."

"I don't give a good bloody damn. You'll tell me what you know or I'll find out on my own, Colonel. And you won't like my methods. I can promise you."

Griff walked away from the man who had been a friend to him since he'd been assigned to intelligence.

When he was far enough away to regain his temper, he reached into his pocket and drained the flask in one long swallow.

Then he headed for the nearest tavern.

# Chapter 4

✿

Over the last three months, Griff had used every skill he'd perfected during the war to find the gunman responsible for Freddie's death—and come up with nothing to show for his efforts. He was perilously close to running out of options, perilously close to running out of leads. But not once did he consider giving up. Vengeance was strong motivation.

He put his half-empty flask back in his pocket and made his way down the walk, keeping close to the rows of storefront buildings already locked up for the night.

He'd turned over every rock, followed up on every lead, talked to every person who might have seen anything that night. But as each lead ended in futility, his frustration consumed more of him. His fear that the killer had gotten away with another murder, and that he, Griffin Blackmoor, was the cause of another innocent person's death, ate away at him like a deadly cancer.

At first he thought he'd lose his mind trying to battle the unrelenting guilt that refused to go away. But he'd figured out the amount of liquor he needed to consume every day to numb his emotions without affecting his ability to think. It was important that he always remain alert enough to function—at least until the nightmares came. Nightmares that drove him to the brink of insanity.

Griff pulled the flask from his pocket and took another long swallow. Now he simply subsisted in a haze of blessed numbness, not sober enough to recall the faces of the people he'd condemned because of their association to him, yet not drunk enough to completely forget.

Griff kept his feet moving until he reached Waterman's, the club to which every member of his family had belonged for generations. He stopped and stared at the doorway, not sure when he'd been here last. Not sure when he'd been anywhere last.

He swiped a hand over his brow and entered through the door the ever-present Harry held open for him.

"Good evening, Mr. Blackmoor."

"Good evening, Harry. How are you this evening?"

"Fine, sir. And you?"

"Fine. Just fine. Send over a bottle, would you?"

"Right away, sir," Harry said, but he didn't rush off as he usually did. "Sir?"

Griff turned. "Is something wrong?"

"Not exactly wrong, sir. But you might want to consider that Lord Bington is here and avoid him tonight."

Griff tried to recall the last time he'd seen Bingy. He couldn't. "I take it I offended Lord Bington recently," Griff said, handing over his coat and hat.

"Yes, I believe you did. It seems Lord Bington took offense at a disparaging remark you made regarding the lack of participation by any of his offspring in our war in the Crimea."

The air caught in Griff's chest. "A disparaging remark?" he asked, trying to remember the incident.

"Well, actually it wasn't a remark, sir, but more an accusation because not one of Lord Bington's six sons considered it their duty to serve their country. If I recall correctly, you compared several of Lord Bington's sons to those brave soldiers who had given their lives for their country and found Lord Bington's heirs, um…lacking."

Griff ignored the stabbings of guilt that tore at him. Even if what he said was true, he'd had no right to make such comments in public. "I'll try my best to avoid Lord Bington, Harry. Thanks for the warning."

"My pleasure." Harry cleared his throat and looked a little sheepish. "It's only that I overheard Mr. Waterman himself remark that he wouldn't tolerate any more disturbances where you are involved, Mr. Blackmoor."

Griff nodded his understanding, then walked into the room. He found a table in the corner where he could be by himself, and waited impatiently for the bottle he'd ordered. The minute a footman brought it, he poured a liberal amount in a glass and drank it. He reached to fill the glass again but stopped when Viscount Sheridan, who was seated at a nearby table, greeted a stranger approaching him.

Griff intended to ignore Sheridan. They had never been close acquaintances, and from what Griff had heard of him, he had no intention of making any change in their relationship. But his intentions evaporated when Sheridan used Freddie's title to greet the stranger.

"Brentwood," Sheridan said, pulling out a chair for his guest. "Sit down and join me. I haven't seen you since you came into all that Brentwood wealth. I thought perhaps you considered friends from your old life too insignificant to bother with now that you possessed such a lofty title."

"Don't be ridiculous, Sherry. You and I spent too much time in each other's homes as youths. You know me better than that."

"I do, friend. So, what has kept you from coming to London before now? It's been more than three months since you've inherited. Is it true you've been so busy entertaining the late marquess's sisters that you couldn't tear yourself from their pleasant company to visit us?"

"Hardly. Lady Anne and her sister moved out of Brentwood Manor the day after the solicitor read the will. I've seen very little of them since. As the oldest, she watches out for her sibling as if I were the bad wolf in that appalling fairy tale."

"Well, aren't you?" Sheridan laughed a lot more raucously than Griff wanted to hear. "I thought maybe you'd be sharing your bed with at least one of them by now."

"You wound me, Sherry. As their only remaining relative, I've taken them both under my wing for safekeeping."

Viscount Sheridan slapped his hand on the table and laughed. "I thought you were going to tell me you'd taken them both into your bed."

"Not yet, friend. Not yet. My first step was to offer them the old caretaker's cottage to live in until they find another residence."

"And when will that be?"

"Never." Brentwood's tone dripped with condescension. "Rumor has it they've already had to pawn some of their mother's jewelry in order to put food on the table and buy a few necessities. If they're that lacking in funds, they can hardly afford to pay rent on a place to live as well. It won't be long before they'll have to accept my generosity."

"You haven't opened your pantry to them?"

"Such a magnanimous offer would only hinder my goal."

"Which is?"

"To wait until they are desperate."

"And then?"

"I'll make my offer."

"What offer?"

"Marriage, of course."

"You intend to marry the late marquess's sister? Lady Anne?"

"Of course. Why wouldn't I?"

"Because she's hardly your type, Brentwood. She must be all of twenty-five. It's a well-known fact that when she had her coming out a few years back, she all but chased every eligible suitor away. Society still talks about it."

Brentwood laughed. "I don't doubt it. She hasn't changed since then."

Sheridan continued. "By all accounts, she's turned into something of a recluse. Some even call her odd."

"The only thing odd about her is she's as cold as a block of ice. Being in the same room with her is like sitting next to a frozen statue."

"Then why would you choose her for your bride?"

Brentwood laughed again and set his glass down with a loud thud. "I have my reasons. Besides, can you imagine anything more exciting than the submission of an unwilling wife?"

Griff fisted his hands around the glass in front of him and took a deep breath. Freddie had mentioned the distant cousin who would inherit his title and land if anything happened to him. Griff also remembered he hadn't said anything good about him. The new marquess had a violent reputation with women that his overprotective family had kept secret. That did not speak well for the man who'd given Freddie's sisters shelter—the man who intended to wed the sister Freddie called Annie.

*Take care of Annie. Promise me.*

Griff ignored the rest of the conversation between the two men and concentrated on refilling his glass, then emptying it. He refused to let Brentwood's bragging over his good fortune due to Freddie's death affect him. He refused to consider helping Freddie's sister as Freddie had begged him to. The only way he could protect her was to stay as far away from her as possible.

Eventually, the two men rose to visit a brothel that specialized in satisfying the darker side of a man's sexual appetites. Griff watched them go, then finished another glass of liquor. He tried to forget what he'd overheard but couldn't. He tried to forget about Freddie's sisters—but couldn't. Especially the one he remembered standing alone at the window. The one called Annie, who seemed able to see through him to his very soul.

She was alone now. What if she found herself forced to marry such a man to support herself and her sister? What if she had no choice but to submit to such a man night after night?

Griff released the glass before it broke.

*Take care of Annie. Promise me.*

He pushed his chair back and stumbled to his feet. He needed to get out of here. Needed to go where he could be alone.

He threw the remaining liquor to the back of his throat and took one step forward. Fingers of iron clamped tight around his arm and stopped him.

"Griff. Sit down."

Griff turned around too fast and took an unsteady step backward. When he was able to focus, he found himself looking into his brother's angry features.

"Adam. What an unpleasant surprise." Griff pulled his arm free with a jerk. "If you'll excuse me, I was about to leave."

Adam pointed to the chair Griff had just vacated. "I'd like to talk to you if you don't mind."

"Well, I do mind."

"It's important, Griff."

Griff stared at his brother. A knot of unease welled inside him. "Leave me alone, Adam. It's late. I want to go home."

Griff staggered toward the door. He had to get out of here. Had to go someplace where he could be alone. Someplace where he could forget the deaths he'd been responsible for. Someplace where the memories wouldn't haunt him.

He moved toward the door, thankful when he was outside in the cool evening air.

He forced one foot in front of the other, weaving from the left to the right. He could still hear the new Marquess of Brentwood's voice, still hear the man who'd inherited Freddie's title say what he intended to do to Freddie's sister.

*Take care of Annie. Please.*

He reached inside his pocket and tipped the flask to his lips. He took a long drink.

Bloody hell. She was already pawning her mother's jewelry to put food on the table.

*Take care of Annie. Please.*

He brushed Freddie's words aside. He couldn't take care of her. She wouldn't be safe anywhere near him.

He picked up his pace, staggering even more in his desperation to escape Freddie's words. Freddie was dead because of him and his sisters were alone to fend for themselves.

*Take care of Annie. Please.*

Griff stepped off the walk and into the gutter. He needed to make his way across the narrow cobblestoned street. Needed to get as far away as he could from Waterman's and the conversation he'd heard between Lord Sheridan and the new Marquess of Brentwood.

"Stop, Griff!" Adam called from behind him.

Griff spun around. He lost his balance and slammed into a pair of horses pulling a carriage down the street.

The piercing screams from the panicked horses shattered the silence around him as he flew through the air. He landed on the ground with the air knocked out of his body. A sharp pain grabbed at his ribs and another shot through his head.

The last thing he saw before the world around him went black was the concerned expression on Adam's face.

As darkness consumed him he recognized the only emotion that was strong enough to overshadow the pain— that of regret.

Regret because he hadn't been hurt severely enough to die.

# Chapter 5

❋

*G*riff opened one eye at a time, then slowly closed each one. Last night must have been worse than usual. He hurt like hell this morning. Or afternoon. He wasn't quite sure which. Thankfully, the drapes were still shut and he didn't have to face the blinding sun.

He opened his eyes a slit and tried to move his head. The pain was too intense and he quickly closed them.

He needed a drink. With his eyes closed, he reached out his hand to the table beside the bed. His hand came back empty. Where the hell was the bottle he always kept there?

He attempted to open his eyes again, then slowly turned his head. A sharp pain pounded at his temples, causing him to groan. He squeezed his eyes shut and swore a vicious oath, then lay in the comfort of the soft bed without moving. He felt like hell. Like someone had hit him over the head with a club.

He needed that drink.

He forced himself to lift his eyelids and look around the room. Where the hell was he? He certainly wasn't in his own home. Then he remembered the running horses and Adam leaning over him.

Using more strength than he thought he had in him, he threw off the bedcovers and swung one leg over the edge of the bed. He needed to find a bottle. He needed a drink before his head split wide open.

He sat upright and clutched his fists into the covers to keep from toppling over. He wore a nightshirt. He hadn't slept in a bloody nightshirt for years. He let his eyes scan the entire room. There wasn't a bottle anywhere. His stomach lurched and he thought he was going to be ill.

Damn it to hell! He needed a drink!

By the time he had the nightshirt off and his shirt and breeches on, his hands were trembling so violently he could barely button his breeches. He left his shirt gaping at the neck. He knew he wouldn't find anything to drink up here. He had to get downstairs.

He staggered across the room and out the door. A heavy film of perspiration covered his forehead before he reached the stairs. By the time he made it to the first floor, his knees felt like pudding beneath him.

"Good morning, Mr. Blackmoor," Adam's butler, Fenwick, said from behind him.

Griff clung to the thick, oak column at the bottom of the banister to hold himself steady. "Where's the earl, Fenwick?"

"In his study, sir. Should I announce you?"

"No." Griff forced himself to walk across the marble vestibule floor. "I'll announce myself."

Griff grabbed the handle on Adam's study door and flung it open. Adam Blackmoor, Earl of Covington, raised his head and stared at him with a look that was part concern and part disgust. Griff didn't care. His only thought at the moment was making it to Adam's well-stocked supply of fine liquors and pouring himself a tall glass of anything that would numb the pain in his head and stop his hands from shaking. He filled a glass and took several long swallows, then wiped his mouth with the back of his hand.

Adam rose and walked to the door. "Fenwick, bring a tray with coffee," he ordered from the doorway, then closed the door behind him, leaving the two of them alone. The two brothers stared at each other for a moment. "I didn't expect you to be up so early," Adam said.

"Just as I didn't expect to find myself in your home when I woke."

"Where did you expect to find yourself, Griff? Or do you even care anymore?"

Griff ignored the sarcasm in the accusations and refilled his glass with scotch. After another swallow, he lowered his aching body to a chair beside the fireplace and sat there while Fenwick placed a tray of hot, steaming coffee on the table nearby. Griff clutched the glass of scotch in his hand and leaned back into the chair to wait until Fenwick was gone. "I have decided to go back to the country," he said when they were alone.

"Why?"

Griff laughed. "You sound disappointed. I thought you would be glad to hear I was leaving London."

"Well, I'm not. Your problems will follow you no matter where you go. All you will accomplish by hiding in the country is that a greater number of people will be spared seeing what a drunkard you have become."

Griff felt his temper flare. "I'm hardly a drunkard, Adam."

"Aren't you? Just how normal do you think it is to have finished your second glass of scotch before nine in the morning?"

Griff slashed his hand through the air. "When I choose to have a drink is hardly your concern."

"Then whose is it?"

"Mine! Only mine!"

Griff closed his eyes and took another swallow of liquor to help ease the pain. "I simply wanted you to know I was leaving London."

"Why the concern now? You haven't thought to inform me of your whereabouts for the last three months. I've searched for you but only discover where you've been after reading the scandal sheet each morning to learn about the latest brawl in which you were involved." Adam walked to the tray and filled a cup with coffee. "I wouldn't know of your whereabouts now if I hadn't paid every doorman in every club in London to send for me the moment you showed up at their establishment."

It seemed Adam was bellowing. His voice boomed louder than Griff's head could tolerate. Griff lowered his head to his hands, but Adam didn't stop his ranting.

"You haven't cared about anyone but yourself for months. Why in bloody hell are you so concerned that I'm informed of your whereabouts now?"

Griff sat back in the chair and took another swallow. "Because I need a favor before I can leave."

"You need a favor? Don't tell me you've left debts all over London and need me to cover them?"

"No. Money isn't the problem. It never has been. You know I could never spend what I inherited from Mother's family, or what you pay me for managing Covington Estate, even if I devoted two lifetimes and more to reckless waste."

"Then what is it?"

49

"I need you to sponsor Freddie's sister into Society."

Adam's jaw dropped. "You're not serious."

"I'm afraid I am."

"Why?"

"Because she has no place else to go. Because she's destitute and has already had to pawn their mother's jewelry to put food on their table. Because that was the last demand Freddie made of me before he died. To take care of his sister."

Adam stared at him, his fixed gaze and unyielding stance exemplifying the fortitude of the respected Earl of Covington.

"It was Freddie's last wish, Adam. I owe him. He would have done it if he'd lived, but he's dead. And I'm alive."

"Is that what this is all about? Your drinking and whoring and gambling until you lose all sense of what you're doing? You feel guilty because you're alive and Freddie is dead? Because you didn't die instead of him?"

"Stop it!" Griff bellowed his demand louder than he'd intended. He clutched the side of his head to stop the pain. "I owe Freddie. I owe him my life."

Griff downed the last of his drink. "Do you honestly think Freddie was shot by some would-be robber as everyone believes? He was not. The assassin's bullet that killed Freddie was intended for me!"

"How do you know that?"

"That isn't important. I just do."

"You can't be sure," Adam argued. "It's been three months. Has there been another attempt since then?"

Griff shook his head.

"Then perhaps it *was* a robbery. If there is truly an assassin out there, why hasn't he tried to kill you again?"

Griff swept his hand over his damp brow. "I don't know. Perhaps he will. Perhaps he satisfied his revenge on me by killing my best friend. How should I know?"

Adam paced the room. "So you want me to assume your responsibility to Freddie's sister and let you go to the country and drink yourself into an early grave? You want Patience and me to fulfill Freddie's dying wish and let you go scot-free?"

"No. I only want you to provide Freddie's sister with the cover of respectability. I will cover all her expenses, her wardrobe, and anything else she needs. And you will not have to worry that she will not be snatched up. The generous dowry I intend to provide her will guarantee she'll attract every eligible male in England."

Adam shook his head. "She's a complete stranger to us."

Griff walked to the liquor decanters and poured himself another drink. Thankfully for Griff, the world had become pleasantly hazy, because his next words were damned difficult to say. "Please, Adam. Just grant this one favor and I'll never bother you again. I'll never show my face in London or be an embarrassment to you ever again."

The two brothers, as similar as night to day, stared at each other for a long moment. Finally, Adam walked across the room. With his back to Griff, he stared into the blazing flames in the fireplace.

Griff felt a sense of relief. Adam would help him. He always had. Only this would be the last favor Griff would ever ask of him. He took another swallow as he waited for Adam to answer.

"Very well, Griff. You may move Freddie's sister into my home. Patience and I will sponsor her into Society."

"Thank you, Adam," Griff acknowledged sincerely.

His brother turned to face him. "Under one condition."

"Anything."

"From the moment Freddie's sister steps foot in my house, you will not have another drink."

Griff stared at him, dumbfounded. "You can't be serious."

"That is my offer. Take it or leave it."

"No."

"Then find another way to help Freddie's sister. Sponsor her yourself."

"You know I can't! I'm not married. I can't allow a single woman to reside under my roof. Her reputation would be in shambles before the sun set on the first day. I need you and Patience to help me."

"Then agree to my condition."

"Make another condition. Anything."

"There will be no other condition, Griff. Either you stop drinking completely, or Freddie's sister can stay in the country until she starves."

"This is ridiculous! I can stop drinking anytime I want!"

"Then stop right now! Put that glass down and don't pick up another."

"No!" Griff had never felt such cold anger, such a violent explosion of his temper. He wanted to hit Adam. To double his fist and slam it into the authoritative expression on his face. Didn't Adam know Griff's guilt and grief were too devastating when he was sober? He clutched the glass tighter. "I don't want to quit."

"You will if you want the girl to come to London."

Griff slashed his hand through the air. Bloody hell. He could stop drinking anytime he chose. But he didn't want to. The pain was too great, the regret too unbearable.

"I'll get you help. I have a friend, Dr. Samuel Thornton. He'll help you."

"I don't need help."

"You do, Griff." An even harsher expression darkened Adam's face. "You aren't strong enough to do this on your own."

Griff glared at his brother. Anger raged through his body. "Damn you, Adam. Why can't you leave me alone?"

"Because you are all the family I have. I'll not allow you to kill yourself one drink at a time."

Griff raked his fingers through his hair. "You don't know. There's no way you can understand."

Adam's face softened ever so slightly. "You can't protect the world, Griff. You aren't the cause of everything that goes wrong. You didn't fire the bullet that killed Freddie, just as you didn't cause the storm that took Julia and Andrew from you. You aren't to blame, Griff. Punishing yourself will not bring them back."

"Damn you, Adam. Damn you!"

Griff held himself back from refilling his glass. Instead, he made his way to the opposite side of the room and stared out the window. He didn't have enough courage to do what Adam wanted him to do. He didn't care. Not anymore.

He fought to catch his breath. Even the liquor he'd consumed already this morning couldn't make what he had to do easier. Why hadn't God taken him instead of Freddie? Why hadn't He let him drown with his wife and son?

"How badly do you want to save Freddie's sister, Griff? You are all that stands between her and starvation, or worse. If you truly want to protect her, all you have to do is put down that glass and let me help you."

A knot tightened in Griff's gut, the panic racing through him like a raging storm at sea. He'd never been more frightened in his life. He had no choice. He knew it was only a matter of time until the liquor killed him just as dead as a bullet would. He couldn't continue like he had much longer before the black pit he'd fallen into would be too deep to climb out of. He knew Adam's offer was the only way to help Freddie's sister. The only way he could save himself.

*Take care of Annie. Please.*

Griff braced his hands against the window frame and hung his head between his outstretched arms. He had no choice. Not if he wanted to honor Freddie's last request.

"I'll bring Freddie's sister here tomorrow."

"I'll tell Patience. And I'll have a room ready for you in the east wing. You will stay here until you are well."

Griff shook his head. "I'll go to the country."

"No. You'll stay here, Griff. Thornton's already explained this won't be easy. You'll need help."

Griff clenched his fists at his side and prepared to argue. Adam's raised hand stopped him.

"Don't, Griff. Nothing you say will change my mind. I refuse to allow you to destroy yourself."

Griff wanted to argue. He wanted to scream his frustration and fear. He wasn't sure he could do this. He wasn't brave enough to face the demons that plagued him.

He opened his mouth to make a final plea, then closed it. The hard set of Adam's expression made him hold his tongue.

"Don't concern yourself, Griff. I'll be here for you."

Griff answered his brother with a sharp nod, then set his empty glass on the corner of the table. With slow, unsteady steps he left the room.

He'd buried his wife and son and somehow survived. He'd risked his life more times than he could count during the war and somehow survived. He'd watched his best friend die in his place and still survived. But this? Surely he could survive giving up drinking just until Freddie's sister was someone else's responsibility.

But a part of him wasn't sure he was brave enough to face all his nightmares sober.

# Chapter 6

❧

Anne lifted the blue chintz curtain at the window and watched as a rider made his way up the lane. It was Lord Brentwood.

She pressed her back against the cold outside wall and closed her eyes. Oh, she wished she hadn't sent Becca to Reverend Talbert's to return the books they'd borrowed. She dreaded being alone with the marquess. For some reason she did not understand, he frightened her.

The sound of his horse's hooves neared the cottage, then came to a stop outside the door. Anne smoothed down the skirt of her black bombazine gown as he knocked. She took a deep breath and opened the door.

"Good day, Lord Brentwood."

A harsh shiver raced down her spine when she looked at the man standing in her doorway.

The expression on his face was pleasant enough, and the lift to the corners of his mouth indicated an offer of friendship, yet the narrowing gleam in his eyes brimmed with predatory intent. The man who owned Freddie's title and estates was not an easy man to like.

In the various dealings she'd had with him and Mr. Woolsey since the initial reading of the will, she felt his simmering temper lying dormant just below the surface.

Each time he came to call, she saw a malevolent look. An intense look. A hungry look that frightened her more than the threat of his temper.

"Lady Anne. How lovely you look. Just the sight of you is well worth taking a few hours out of my busy schedule to come to visit. You are indeed breathtaking."

She didn't answer. How could she when his words were so blatantly false?

"May I come in?"

Her muscles knotted with a nervousness that was unfamiliar to her. "Of course, my lord."

Anne stood back to allow him to enter, then turned and walked to the small living room. She sat in the center of the faded settee, leaving him no choice but to sit in a worn chair halfway across the room. "I regret I do not have tea to offer you," she said, folding her hands in her lap.

"That's quite all right, my lady. I didn't come for tea, but to look upon your loveliness and enjoy a few moments of your time."

"How kind." She felt a blush mixed with unease.

"Are you alone?"

"Uh, no," she lied. "Becca will be back any minute. She went to Reverend Talbert's to return some books we'd borrowed."

"The Brentwood library is at your disposal anytime you want. Please feel free to borrow as many books as you'd like. You are always welcome."

"Thank you, my lord." Instinct caused her to lean farther away from him. No matter how desperately she tried, she couldn't ignore the uncomfortable knot that churned in the pit of her stomach.

"I have a great respect for your late brother," he said, leaning forward in his chair. "The holdings I inherited are quite substantial, and from the records I see he did an admirable job of efficiently running both the estates and businesses."

"Frederick was a remarkable man. He was an exemplary individual."

"I hope to follow in his footsteps with equal ability."

She found herself unable to answer. The silence between them became exceedingly uncomfortable. She clenched her hands in her lap.

"Have you thought about your future, Lady Anne?"

She gave him a surprised look. "Given our precarious position, my lord, I have thought of little else."

"Then perhaps I can be of some help."

She raised her eyebrows and studied the confident look on Lord Brentwood's face.

"I've decided it's time for me to consider taking a wife."

Her blood thundered inside her head. Surely he wouldn't consider her for a bride?

She thought of the hungry look she'd seen when he looked at her. The way he held her hand far too long. She was suddenly frightened of him. Terrified of his intent. She would never consider marriage to him. Her mother had been sold to the highest bidder and was miserable her whole life. Anne would never go down that same road. She would starve before she married a man who didn't love her.

"I have certain responsibilities now," the marquess continued, "and as you and I both know from your brother's mistake, it's not wise to be without an heir. I'm afraid I'm the last male Brentwood heir. If something were to happen to me before I could provide a legal heir, the Brentwood name would unfortunately die."

Anne's heart thundered in her chest. She didn't know what was worse—associating the Brentwood name with a man like the new marquess, or not having it in existence at all. His next words pulled her back with a jolt.

"We are not, your family and mine, so closely related that it would be unseemly to form a match between us, being second cousins once removed."

"Please, do not speak of marriage, my lord. Freddie has not even been gone four months. I cannot possibly consider a marriage. Society would not approve at all."

"Society has always made allowances. It would, I'm sure, in your case. Two lovely ladies left all alone with barely enough inheritance to support them. Society would consider a marriage before the year's mourning period was met an essential and wise decision."

"N-no," she stuttered. She rose from the sofa and took several steps away from him. "I will not even consider it."

She thought of spending the rest of her life submitting to someone like Brentwood, and her stomach turned.

"I'm afraid you must, my lady. You cannot go on like this much longer."

"We will be fine. We're quite able to take care of ourselves living as we are."

"That, I'm afraid, is the problem. Things cannot remain as they are."

She stared at him as she tried to wrap her mind around what he was saying. A feeling of dread built inside her until she found it difficult to breathe.

"I have decided to hire a new caretaker. Since this is the caretaker's cottage, I'm afraid you and your sister will have to move."

Anne's heart fell to the pit of her stomach. They were barely getting by as it was. What would they do now?

"Unfortunately, there is not another vacant cottage for you to move into. I'm afraid that leaves you homeless."

The Marquess of Brentwood rose from his chair and walked across the room until he stood inches from her.

Now she knew how an animal felt when being stalked by poachers. She stepped as far away from him as she could.

"There is plenty of room at Brentwood Manor," he continued, "but I can hardly expect you and your sister to live under my roof without tarnishing your pristine reputations. Therefore, I see marriage as the ideal answer to solve all our problems."

Anne faced him with a certain amount of bravado she far from felt. "There are other options open to us. We will find another place to live."

"Do you have the resources to pay the rent that would be required?"

"We'll find it. There is no need for you to worry about us."

"But I do. That is why I offered marriage. I've grown quite fond of you, Lady Anne. Haven't you noticed?"

Before she could stop him, he clasped her upper arms and pulled her against him. He smelled of salty sea air and stale smoke and expensive liquor. She thought she would be ill.

"Every time I am near you, I can hardly keep my hands from reaching out to you, from touching you and holding you. You cannot imagine how I have dreamt of this moment."

"Please. Let me go."

He lowered his head to bring his face closer to hers. "Every night you consume my every thought, my every dream."

"No, please. Don't."

She struggled, but he held her tighter, then brought his lips closer to hers. He was going to kiss her.

"No," she said, pushing her fists against his chest. "I don't want you to—"

His mouth covered hers, stopping her words.

A small, muffled cry echoed inside her head and she struggled against him.

He would not release her. He moved his mouth against hers, his tongue forcing its way through her lips, his touch rough and bruising. She pounded her fists against his chest and fought even harder.

"I'm not sure the lady appreciates your display of passion, Brentwood," a harsh, unyielding voice said from the doorway behind them. "Perhaps you would play the gentleman and allow her to voice her consent before you maul her."

The marquess dropped his hands. He released her so fast she stumbled against the wall.

Anne turned toward the voice. Her gaze focused on the large, imposing man who'd entered her home—Griffin Blackmoor, Freddie's friend. The man who had come to Freddie's funeral hurting more from her brother's death, if that were possible, than perhaps even she.

Brentwood took a menacing step toward the intruder. "What are you doing here, Blackmoor?"

"I came to call on Lady Anne. I didn't realize it would be my good fortune to come to the lady's rescue. Or perhaps I am mistaken." His gaze shifted to hers. "Perhaps the lady would like me to leave?"

"No! Don't go."

"As you wish."

Griffin Blackmoor entered the room as if he owned it and sat on the settee. He leaned back against the cushions and waited quietly.

The Marquess of Brentwood straightened the lapels of his jacket and tugged at his jacket sleeves. "Now is obviously not the time to finish our discussion, my lady," he said, then made his way to the door. "I will return in a few days. When you have had time to think over my proposal."

Without a by-your-leave, the marquess stalked from the room. He slammed the cottage door behind him and was gone.

Anne leaned against the wall and clutched her hands around her middle. Her body refused to quit shaking. She took several deep breaths and when she was more in control, she turned her gaze to where Blackmoor sat. Their gazes locked and Anne experienced a strong connection to him. She attributed that feeling to their common tie to Freddie.

She took in Blackmoor's appearance. The cut of his suit and the pristine whiteness of his shirt exhibited a subtle wealth. His hair was overly long, as it had been the day of Freddie's funeral, but unlike that day, today he seemed more in control of himself. His cravat was not perfectly tied, but he struck a handsome figure that made him a man to notice. Today more than before he resembled the retired military officer Freddie had admired.

She focused on his features, his broad shoulders, towering height, and long muscular legs. His forehead was wide, his cheekbones high. The strong cut to his jaw gave him an intimidating appearance.

He was clean shaven, which revealed the hard angles of his face. They hinted at a dark, brooding emptiness. The taut flesh at his cheeks sank to shallow hollows, as if he'd recently lost weight he didn't need to lose. And yet each of these attributes placed him in a unique category of his own.

He presented a striking air, strong, powerful, the type that made women overlook any obvious flaws he might have. Anne did not need to be told Griffin Blackmoor's flaw. She recognized it.

He was a drunkard.

Although he was not overly inebriated at the moment, she still could tell he'd had more than his share of liquor. She would always recognize the signs: the look, the smell, the speech. She'd lived with it her whole life.

"Are you unharmed, my lady?" His question brought her back to the present.

"Y-yes," she stuttered, trying to make her voice work. "Thank you."

"Just what proposal was the marquess speaking of?"

She took a deep breath. "A marriage proposal."

"Do you need to think over your answer?"

"No. Even if I were looking for a husband, which I'm not, the marquess would be the last man I would consider. No offense, sir, but deferring to any man would be impossible for me."

He paused for a moment as if to think about her words, and when he spoke, her blood turned to ice.

"Then I'm afraid you are not going to like my proposition any better."

Anne had to remind herself to breathe. When she did, she was filled with a fury that made her tremble. She marched around the sofa and stood before him with her hands on her hips. "I'm not interested in finding a husband, Mr. Blackmoor. In fact, I am adamantly against it. My sister and I will get along just fine without either of us being tied to a man."

"Your sister and you will not get along fine, and you know it. How much longer do you think Brentwood is going to let you stay here? Especially if forcing you to leave means you will become more dependent on him?"

She blanched. How did he know?

"How long do you think you are going to be able to put food on your table when you don't have the money to buy it? Freddie hasn't even been gone four months and you've already pawned the first of your mother's jewels to get by."

She took a step backward. "How did you know?"

He didn't answer but raked his fingers through hair the color of deep, rich coffee. Before the waves fell back into place, he rubbed his head at his temples as if he did not feel well.

"Why are you here?" she asked.

"I have come to help you. Freddie was my best friend. I owe him."

"No, you don't. Becca and I will find a way to survive without your help."

"I wish that were true." He turned his head and focused his dark gaze on her. "Unless, of course, you intend to accept Lord Brentwood's proposal?"

64

"Not even as a last resort. I will take care of Becca on my own."

"There is only one way for you to accomplish that. Whether you want to or not, Lady Anne, you are going to have to marry in order to support your sister."

"No!" She pounded her fist against her skirt. "It seems I just had this same conversation with Lord Brentwood. I will tell you exactly what I told him. I have no intention of ever marrying. And I for certain have no intention of marrying you."

He arched his brows. "As I have no intention of marrying you, either."

Anne stopped. Her surprise was too great for her to continue.

"No offense intended, my lady, but I would rather face a firing squad than take a wife. Even you."

His words could have offended her, if she didn't feel the same. "Then what are you talking about?"

"I am talking about taking you to London for a Season, and letting you select someone with whom to spend the rest of your life. Someone who can give you all the advantages that come with titled wealth. Someone of your own choosing."

She laughed. "Mr. Blackmoor, if I can't afford to put food on our table without pawning some of our inheritance, I can assure you, I would have an even greater difficulty outfitting myself to attend months of endless balls and parties."

"I will provide whatever you need. I am not without funds—substantial funds. I will cover all your expenses while you are in London."

She stared at him in disbelief. "Why?"

"Because it's what Freddie would have wanted."

His words contained no emotion. They were issued with a definite lack of gentleness that shocked her. And yet there was a softness about him. Something special about the way he seemed. She'd noticed it when he walked into the room the day of Freddie's funeral.

There was something about the strength of his carriage, his hooded blue eyes, and the haunting depth of his sadness. Everything about him drew her to him, pulled at her. She wanted to comfort him, as if he hurt as much as she.

"I do not want to marry."

"You said as much."

"Then why are you forcing this?"

"Because you have no choice. At least my option gives you the opportunity to choose your own mate, perhaps even someone you will eventually come to love. Choosing your own husband will give you a chance at happiness."

"And if I am not willing to take the risk?"

"You have to. Your sister cannot afford for you to be a coward. Even if you can be satisfied with a life so barren and lacking, are you willing to condemn Lady Rebecca to the same fate?"

A piercing sharpness stabbed through her chest. "How dare you."

"I dare because I care what happens to you and your sister. Just as Freddie would care if he were here." He fisted his hands at his side, then wiped the fingers of one hand across his brow to take away a thin film of perspiration.

His complexion seemed paler than when he'd arrived, and when he raised his hand, it shook noticeably.

"Are you all right?" she asked, fighting the urge to touch his forehead to check for fever.

"I'm fine." He stood beside her. "Brentwood will not stop his advances. Today was just the first."

She shook her head but knew he was right.

"You are alone and unprotected here. Let me help you."

"Why?"

"Because I owe Freddie. His last thoughts were of you. His last words were a plea for me to take care of you."

"And you feel obligated?" When he didn't answer, she turned away from him and looked out the window. She saw nothing but Freddie's handsome face staring back at her in the glass panes. "You are not obligated to do anything, Mr. Blackmoor. You can go away from here with a free conscience. I will not accept anything from you."

"If you want to do what's best for your sister, you will."

A thousand thoughts raced through her mind. She searched for an answer, but there wasn't one—at least, not one she thought she could live with.

Nor was she able to look into Blackmoor's face when she spoke. "When they brought Freddie's body home, I tried to hate you. When I heard a robber had killed Freddie, but you had lived, I asked myself, why? Why would God take Freddie from us when we need him so desperately, and spare you?"

"Did you come up with an answer?"

"No. Except that there is a reason for everything, and some of the answers God keeps only to Himself."

He smiled—the first smile she'd seen on his face. "I doubt God had a hand in any of this, my lady. I doubt God has noticed my existence for a long time. As I have not noticed His."

She looked at him and could not help but wonder what had happened to make him so bitter. Perhaps she was better off not knowing.

"I don't want to marry like this," she said with all the conviction she felt deep in her soul.

"I know."

"Do you see any other way for me to provide for Becca? Any way at all?"

"One. You could put Lady Rebecca in your place, put her on the marriage mart. Even though she is just fifteen, I am sure you could find some wealthy nobleman whose preference runs toward the very young. Then you would be spared the trials of taking a husband, and could live off your sister's generosity for the rest of your life. From what I remember, Lady Rebecca shows promise of becoming quite a beauty. It would be easy for her to make a wealthy match."

The air caught in Anne's throat and she took a step backward in shock. He smiled again, a thin forced smile she did not want to look at.

"I didn't think so." He paced the room as if the four walls were suddenly too confining.

She clenched her hands until they hurt. "What is your plan, sir?"

He stopped. "As you know, my brother is the Earl of Covington. Being neighbors, he also considered Freddie a friend, and has agreed to help you. He and his wife have extended an invitation for you to be a guest at their London town house. They have agreed to introduce you to Society. You have until the middle of June, until the Queen's birthday celebration, to make your choice. Then my brother and his wife plan to leave for the summer months and go to the country."

"But that is barely three months away."

"Do you see that as a problem? I would think three months more than ample time to find a suitable husband who meets your qualifications. Unless, of course, one of those qualifications happens to be love."

She swallowed hard and fought the painful pressure against her chest. "No, Mr. Blackmoor. I would never be foolish enough to make love a qualification. The only suitable husband would be one who makes no demands of me, does not notice or care if I am in attendance, and is wealthy enough to provide Becca a handsome enough dowry so she can afford the luxury of choosing a husband she imagines she can love."

"As you wish. I'm certain there is someone out there who will fit your order to perfection."

She closed her eyes and fought the sinking dread already swelling inside her.

"How soon can you be ready to leave?"

"Becca leaves for school tomorrow. She has missed enough of the term already." She swallowed hard. "I can be ready the day after."

"Very well. I suggest you say your good-byes tonight. The sooner you are away from Brentwood, the safer you will be. I will bring some carts and men in two days to move your belongings. I will also send a carriage and a chaperone to escort your sister back to school. They will arrive midmorning."

She opened her mouth to say something more, then realized there was nothing more to say. Freddie's death left her with no other choice but to marry. It was the only way to provide for Becca.

"I will be ready."

With a curt nod, Blackmoor turned, then walked to the door. Twice on his way out he reached out his hand to steady himself against the wall. When he reached his horse, he lifted himself into the saddle with an ease that belied his large stature, and rode away.

From the drawing-room window, Anne watched him leave. Midway down the lane, he stopped, then again a little farther. Both times he reached into his jacket pocket and removed a flask. He lifted the container to his lips and took a drink.

She shook her head. An overwhelming sense of regret and sadness filled her. She'd hoped and prayed she'd been wrong. She'd hoped she'd misinterpreted his nervousness, his perspiration, and his trembling hands for something other than what she feared it meant. But she hadn't.

Griffin Blackmoor was a drunkard.

Just like her father.

# Chapter 7

✤

Anne stared out the window of the carriage Griffin Blackmoor had brought for her, and tried to calm her taut nerves. The voice that controlled her fear screamed to have the driver stop so she could go home. Until she remembered—she no longer had a home.

She swallowed hard and took a deep breath. Each London town house they passed meant they were that much closer to their destination. That much closer to beginning her search for the husband she didn't want. She thought of Becca, already back at Lady Agnes's School for Young Women, and realized she had no choice. Her sister's future depended on her.

Their good-bye had been teary and filled with trepidation, but the look of excitement on Becca's face when she climbed aboard the carriage showed how eager she was to return to her friends. It would be a relief to leave behind the gloom that had blanketed them since Freddie's death.

Anne's carriage slowed, then turned another corner and slowed even more. They must be near their destination. Anne looked out the window again, not at the grand houses but at the man riding beside her carriage—the man whose offer had saved her, even if his motives consisted mostly of fulfilling Freddie's dying request and easing the guilt she saw eating away at him.

A strange warmth settled in the pit of her stomach, a confusing emotion she'd first experienced the day of Freddie's funeral. Something she refused to put much thought to. She attributed it to Griffin Blackmoor's physical features.

He was inordinately handsome. He sat a horse with magnificent grace, his powerful arms and legs guiding the large beast with seemingly little effort. The chiseled planes of his face only added to an underlying strength she couldn't help but notice, while his dark hair and sky-blue eyes gave him an even more pronounced air of mystery and unapproachability.

There was a firm set to his features, a look of stern determination. As unwavering as the expression she imagined on soldiers before a battle, a look that matched the hollow emptiness in his gaze. A look she only expected to see on a man facing the gallows.

He lifted the flask she'd seen him drink from often on their journey, and tipped it high. It must be empty. With a painful expression, almost one of regret, he stared at the container, then threw it into the bushes.

The carriage came to a halt in front of a town house in the better part of London, and he lowered himself to the ground. He wasn't drunk, and yet he wasn't exactly sober.

A servant opened the carriage door, then stepped to the side while Mr. Blackmoor helped her alight. He towered over her. His height, which should have been intimidating, was instead somehow comforting. She placed her hand on his outstretched arm and felt the hard muscles beneath her grasp; then she looked up. Their gazes locked, the jolt to her emotions unexplainable.

"You have nothing to fear, Lady Anne. Adam will take good care of you."

She lowered her gaze. "I'll try to get this done as quickly as possible so I am not an imposition."

He raised his eyebrows and cast her a sidelong glance. "There is no hurry."

"I regret Freddie made such a demand on your friendship," she whispered as they made their way down the walk. She did not want to be overheard. "Once I'm settled, you may walk away with a clear conscience."

He stopped, the look on his face hard. "Only dead men have the luxury of a clear conscience, my lady."

His words shocked her. She could not think of anything to answer him, so she turned her head and moved with him down the walk and up the steps that led to the Earl of Covington's town house.

She thought he staggered on the first step and she tightened her grip on his arm to keep him steady. But perhaps she'd been wrong. If he noticed, he gave no indication.

The door opened and a butler wearing the Covington maroon-and-silver livery admitted them. He took their coats and hats and handed them to a waiting maid.

"Fenwick, would you inform the earl and countess their guest has arrived?" Mr. Blackmoor said.

"My lord and lady are on their way down, sir. I am to take you and my lady into the sitting room, where refreshments are waiting." Fenwick led the way through the spacious foyer.

Rich oak paneling and beautiful marble floors enhanced the room, while elegant tables laden with fresh-cut flower arrangements added a homey feeling that was welcoming. When they reached the third door on the right, Fenwick stepped back for them to enter.

Anne couldn't stop the quiet intake of her breath when she saw the beautiful room, done in shades of rose and blues, set off by deep oak woodwork.

A servant followed them into the room, carrying a tea tray and a plate of sandwiches and cakes. "I will return later," Fenwick added, pointing for the servant to place the tray in the center of a nearby table. "Then show you to your room after you've had some refreshment. Lady Covington thought perhaps my lady would like to rest a bit before dinner is served."

"Thank you, Fenwick," a deep voice said from behind them.

Anne turned to see the Earl and Countess of Covington enter the room. She tried not to stare, but it was impossible.

She'd seen the earl before, of course. They were neighbors, although Lord Covington and Mr. Blackmoor had never visited Brentwood Manor. Because one never knew what condition their father might be in, Freddie went to visit them.

Today was the first time she'd had to compare the two brothers. The difference between them was striking. She hadn't noticed it when she'd seen the two of them at Freddie's funeral, but she could not help comparing them now.

Mr. Blackmoor's hair was a deep mahogany while the earl's was blond and thinning on top. They were both handsome in their own distinctive ways, and had the same startling blue eyes, but the earl's gaze had a penetrating hardness that was absent in Mr. Blackmoor's. There was also a certain aloofness in the earl's countenance that Anne found more off-putting.

"Lady Anne," the earl said. "Welcome to our home."

"Thank you, my lord. It was so kind of you to invite me."

The earl nodded, then turned to the petite blonde woman at his side. "Allow me to introduce my wife, the Countess of Covington. My dear, may I present Lady Anne Carmichael."

The Countess of Covington stepped forward. Anne greeted her formally with a slight curtsy, then breathed a sigh of relief when the countess smiled. Her smile was warm and friendly, and it immediately put Anne at ease.

"It is a pleasure to have you here." The countess grasped Anne's hands and held them. Her gesture was sincere. Anne would find it pleasant here, at least for as long as it took to find a husband.

"Thank you, my lady."

"And, please, you must call me Patience. I insist."

"And, please, call me Anne."

The countess nodded, then turned her attention to Mr. Blackmoor. She crossed the room until she stood next to him. "Griff," she said, reaching out to him. She took his hands in hers. "How are you?"

Lady Covington turned her cheek to accept his kiss. "It has been entirely too long, you know. It's about time you came back to us. You will have to put forth a massive effort to have me forgive you for staying away so long."

"I will do my best, my lady. I would never wish to disappoint you."

"And you won't. I care for you far too much to let that happen."

Anne saw the genuine affection on the countess's face. She also saw the worry in her eyes.

"Please, everyone. Do sit down and I'll pour tea."

Groupings of sofas and chairs were arranged in small clusters throughout the room. They sat in one of those clusters, except Mr. Blackmoor, who took the cup of tea the countess handed him and made his way to the window.

The earl turned to watch his brother. There was apprehension in his gaze, perhaps concern. It was difficult to tell. The earl did not appear to show much emotion.

Anne wondered if he knew how much his brother had had to drink already today, and if that's what distressed him.

The countess kept the conversation flowing with practiced ease. She spoke of how busy London was at this time of year, and the many things there were to see, the many things she had planned for them to do. Their conversation, though, could not hold Anne's attention. She concentrated more on how the cup of tea shook in Mr. Blackmoor's hands. At the glassy look in his eyes. At his sallow, drawn complexion.

"I hope you don't mind?" the countess said.

"Mind?" Anne replied, making her way back to the conversation.

"I was saying that we will have another guest for dinner tonight. A very good friend of ours, Dr. Samuel Thornton, who will be staying with us for a few days. I hope you don't mind?"

"Of course not. That should be quite pleasant."

The earl and his brother exchanged glances. Anne thought at first Dr. Thornton's presence might be significant, but Mr. Blackmoor only turned his head and drained the liquid in his cup in one swallow. He drank it with the same desperation she'd seen when he'd emptied his flask. She somehow knew he wanted the liquid in his cup to be something stronger than tea.

When their tea was finished, the countess rose. "I'm certain you would like to rest awhile before dinner. I'll have Fenwick show you to your rooms."

As if by magic, Fenwick appeared at the door.

"Thank you so very much, my lady," Anne said. "You have been most generous, and I am exceedingly grateful."

"Nonsense. I look forward to having you as our guest. Tomorrow I must introduce you to our three sons. Timothy is nearly five, and Matthew three, and Simon not quite a year. For now, though, I'll let you retire to your room. I'm sure you'll want to rest after such a long trip. Dinner is served at eight. I'll have someone call you in plenty of time to dress."

"Thank you again," Anne said, then walked to where Fenwick waited for her. When she reached the door, she stopped. She could feel Mr. Blackmoor's gaze on her, watching her. She turned. "Thank you, Mr. Blackmoor," she said. "For everything."

"It is nothing," he said, then turned his back to her and stared out the window. It was as if he'd hardened himself to any display of kindness. Any show of concern.

Anne followed Fenwick up the stairs to her room. When she was alone, she lay on the bed and closed her eyes. She wanted to push Griffin Blackmoor from her mind. To forget how much he disturbed her.

There was no connection between the two of them other than the promise he'd made to Freddie. His obligation to her was over. Now it was up to her to do what was necessary, up to her to find a husband who was wealthy enough to provide for her and Becca. A husband who would not expect her to be the perfect wife, or love him, or cherish him, or care for him. Above all else, the man she chose as her husband would never be someone who wanted the liquor in a bottle more than his wife or his children.

Griffin Blackmoor's dark, handsome face appeared in her mind's eye. She quickly shoved his image away. He was the last man she would ever risk taking as her husband. He would demand too much of her. He would take too much from her.

She'd never seen another human being who needed someone to love him more than he did.

Never seen a man who resembled her father more than he did.

\* \* \*

He couldn't do this.

He'd barely made it through dinner without throwing the china to the floor and storming from the room to find a drink. His hands shook so badly he'd spilled his glass of water twice and upset his cup of tea more times than he could count. He needed a drink.

"This is ridiculous!" he said, pacing the floor like a caged animal. "I don't need to do this." He spun around to face Adam and Dr. Thornton. "I can stop anytime I want."

"Can you?" the doctor asked.

Griff didn't dignify the question with an answer. Of course he could.

Except right now he wasn't sure. He'd already gone without a drink longer than he had in months and was nearly frantic for even one swallow.

"It's going to get a hell of a lot worse before it's over," the doctor said, sitting with his legs outstretched before the fire. "This is only the beginning."

Griff closed his eyes and took a deep breath. They'd gone to the study after they had finished eating under the pretext of having an after-dinner brandy. That was a joke. There wasn't a drop of liquor in the whole damn house. He knew that for a fact. He'd searched every inch of Adam's town house for one. He was desperate.

He clenched his fingers around the glass of water Adam had given him. His hands shook like a leaf in a windstorm. He was cold and clammy one minute and hot and sweaty the next. If he could just have one drink, he'd be better. He knew he would.

"Do you want to know what you're going to have to face, Mr. Blackmoor? Or would you rather go into this blind?"

Griff looked at the doctor Adam had hired to get him through this. "Neither," he answered. "I'd rather not go through this at all, but my brother has left me with no choice."

Dr. Thornton set his glass on the table and stood. "Then I'm afraid trying to help you is a waste of my time."

"Samuel, please," Adam interrupted, and the doctor sat back in his chair.

Griff kept his gaze leveled on the doctor. He was younger than Griff had expected him to be, twenty-four or twenty-five at the most. And he was a great deal more handsome than any doctor Griff had ever seen before. At least Patience and Freddie's sister must have thought so. Neither of them had been able to take their eyes off him during dinner. He was quite amiable, but there was a tough side to his nature Griff couldn't ignore.

"What do you mean, helping him will be a waste of your time?" Adam asked.

"We've found that patients who have a deep desire to cure their alcohol dependency have an excellent chance of succeeding. Those that do not fail nearly one hundred percent of the time."

"What does that mean, Samuel?" Adam asked.

"It means if your brother doesn't want to be helped, nothing you or I do is going to work. He's the only one who can want to be cured badly enough to make it happen." The doctor intensified the look he gave Griff. "Do you, Mr. Blackmoor?"

Griff turned his head and stared at the flames flickering in the fireplace. Did he want it badly enough? He closed his eyes and struggled to find the answer.

He was tired of not knowing where he was most of the time. Of not knowing who he was, or where he was going. Or where he had been.

He was tired of the lost days and nights, and waking up in strange places and not knowing how he'd gotten there. Of being so sick he thought he would die before he had his first drink, then downing enough until he no longer cared.

Of not being able to remember Freddie's face, or Julia's voice, or Andrew's laughter.

He was tired of it all. Just plain tired. A pain burned like fire in his gut. He sighed. "What am I facing? I'd rather know."

Dr. Thornton straightened in his chair. "All right. Here's the worst of it. You already know the first signs. You're suffering from them right now. You are desperate for a drink and don't think you can survive if you don't have one. You are nauseous and you can't stop your hands from shaking. First you're hot, then you're cold, and your head hurts so badly you're afraid it might explode at any moment. That will only get worse. You'll shake until you can't even stay lying on a bed. We'll tie you down if we have to. The nausea will intensify, along with the sweating. You'll be so hot you'll think you're burning up. And the pain will be so powerful you'll pray you'll die."

"Will I?"

Samuel Thornton didn't answer for several long seconds. "Not if I can help it."

"How long will this last?"

"If you're lucky, three days, maybe four. If you're not, it might be a week. By then, all the symptoms will have lessened and will eventually go away. All except one."

Dr. Thornton looked at Griff with more conviction. "You will never lose the craving for a drink, Mr. Blackmoor. You will always want one. But once you take your first drink, you'll be back to the point you are right now. Worse. The next time, it will be even harder to stop. Eventually, the liquor you can't live without will kill you."

Griff swiped the back of his hand across his forehead. The room was like an oven. He felt like hell.

"This will not be easy, Mr. Blackmoor. I won't lie to you and tell you it will. You have to want to stay sober a hell of a lot more than you want to be drunk."

Griff turned his gaze to Adam and found him watching him. A tightness clenched in Griff's chest. Dear God, he wanted to be the man he used to be. The loving, caring man he'd been when he still had Julia and Andrew. And even after. After he'd lost them. When he hurt so badly he wanted to die. Even then he'd still found the courage to go on.

Then he'd gone to war and had come home a man who had seen too much and endured too much but who could, if he tried hard enough, forget most of it some of the time, some of it most of the time. But all that changed when Freddie had died. Freddie had been one death too many. The death that should have been his own.

"Decide tonight, Griff," Adam said. "Before Lady Anne gets too settled."

Griff stiffened. He could do this. At least until she chose a husband. How hard could it be, after all? It wasn't that he couldn't stop drinking anytime he chose to; he just didn't want to. But he would. Until Freddie's sister had made a match.

Griff looked at the unyielding expression on Adam's face and tried to appear in control. But the unbearable pain thundering inside his head and the roiling of his stomach made pretending he was in command impossible.

Bloody hell.

He wiped the sweat from his face and paced the room. "I've got to get out of here." He stopped. Even he heard the panic in his voice, a terror that bordered on desperation. "I'm going upstairs."

"There's a room ready for you in the east wing, at the end of the hall," Adam said. "Fenwick will show you up. Dr. Thornton and I will be up shortly."

Griff paid little attention to what Adam said. He stalked to the door and walked away without a look back. His stomach lurched and his vision blurred. How ironic. He was going to spend the week going through hell in order to wash away the liquor he'd consumed in excess over the last four months. But right now, he'd chop off his right hand if only someone would give him a drink.

At least one.

# Chapter 8

❦

Anne lay in the dark, unable to sleep. She'd already spent two and a half days in London. Each day had been a whirlwind of activity. Lady Covington had been wonderful, taking her to one of London's most famous modistes each morning to select designs and material for the new gowns she would have made. Then they stopped at the milliner and the shoemaker. When they finished, they took their packages home, ate a light lunch, and rested a short while; then at precisely five o'clock, the most advantageous time to be seen, they went for an open carriage ride through Hyde Park.

Patience had secretly hinted that this would ensure invitations to the most prestigious events where Anne could meet the créme of London's eligible young men—which, she reminded herself, was the reason she'd come to London.

She stifled a shiver.

She had not seen Mr. Blackmoor since the first evening they'd arrived. Perhaps he'd gone back to the country. No one said, and Anne didn't ask. She didn't want to know where he'd gone. At the same time, she did. She wanted to know everything about him. That she wanted to know everything about him frustrated her.

On the surface, the countess had at first seemed reserved, always the epitome of decorum and refinement. Underneath, Anne found her to be charming and witty. She thought they could easily become friends. The earl, however, remained a mystery. Anne had the impression that something was terribly wrong.

She saw him very seldom. He ate dinner with them each evening but spoke little and excused himself early. The worry lines on his face said something was not right. The look he and his wife exchanged every time he entered the room confirmed it.

Anne reminded herself that perhaps she imagined a problem. At dinner that evening, the earl had promised he would be in attendance for the dinner party to which they had accepted an invitation for later next week.

Next week.

Anne threw back the covers and sat on the edge of the bed. Her search would begin Friday.

Patience informed her that she'd received an invitation to a tea hosted by the Duchess of Wallingsford next Friday afternoon. Then there would be the dinner party at the Marquess of Edington's that evening. Although the countess did not expect there to be a huge number of males attending either event, she assured Anne that such small gatherings would be an excellent opportunity to begin her process. She also assured her that by the middle of next week, she would have invitations to more events than she would have time to attend.

Although the countess never openly mentioned Anne's reason for coming to London, it was obvious she understood the purpose. She was here to select a prime candidate to be her husband.

Blood rushed like ice water through her veins.

She jumped from the bed and shoved her arms into the sleeves of her robe. There suddenly was not enough air to breathe. The wonderfully spacious room was not big enough for her. She had to escape these four walls.

She lit two branches of the candelabra on the table by the door and slipped out of her room. Perhaps she would go to the library and search for a book to read. Something to occupy her time, to shift her thoughts from why she'd come to London. Something different to concentrate on other than her search for a husband.

If only there were a different way to guarantee Becca a secure future. But if there was, it was a mystery to her.

She walked down the narrow hall, careful to take the back way so she wouldn't wake anyone. Positive she wouldn't encounter anyone in this part of the house at this hour, she held her candle high as she made her way to the stairs.

If she hadn't been so lost in thought, she probably would have seen the Earl of Covington approaching, but she wasn't paying attention.

On the small landing where the stairs from the floors above connected with the stairs going down, she nearly collided with Covington as he raced down the steps. She covered her hand over her mouth to stifle her squeal of fright, then leaned against the wall while her heart thundered in her breast.

"I'm terribly sorry, my lord," she whispered by way of an apology, but she wasn't sure the earl heard her. His eyes were wide with alarm. When he spoke, the worry in his voice added to her concern.

"Would you help me? Please. I need your help."

The shock she suffered from coming upon him in the dark changed to concern. Then to fear. "Of course. Is something the matter?"

"It's Griff."

"Mr. Blackmoor?"

"Yes. Please, come with me."

She nodded her assent.

The earl took the candelabra from her hand and led her up the stairs from which he'd just descended. They went down a long hallway to the east wing.

She hadn't been in this part of the house before.

"I'm sorry to involve you in this." He kept his hand on her elbow and led her down another long, narrow hallway. "But I don't know what else to do."

"Of course," she assured him. She tried but couldn't come up with a reason Mr. Blackmoor might need her. Then she heard his voice. The tone was strained and harsh. From this distance, he almost sounded hoarse, as if he'd been calling out for hours. She heard it again.

"What's wrong with him?"

"He's...sick. He's getting so very weak. I'm afraid he might..."

Blackmoor called again.

"What is he saying?"

"Julia. He's calling out for his wife."

Anne's heart skipped a beat. "His wife?"

"Yes. She drowned four years ago, but he—he's not himself right now. I was on my way to get my wife. Dr. Thornton thought if someone answered him, another female perhaps, he would think it was her and calm down. Will you do it?"

Anne nodded.

Before she had time to prepare herself, the earl flung open the door and ushered her inside.

Three candles lit the room, keeping it shadowed as if it were a sickroom. The lighting was too dim to see the figure on the bed clearly, but when the earl set the candelabra on the bedside table, she got a close look at him.

She covered her mouth with her hands to stop the cry that wanted to escape. Oh, heavens, she couldn't believe the change in the man who'd brought her to London.

Griffin Blackmoor lay on the bed, his face as pale as the sheet beneath him. A heavy film of perspiration covered his face, his bare chest heaved with exhaustion.

Dr. Thornton wiped his skin with a damp cloth while he tried to hold him steady. But the harder he held him, the more Mr. Blackmoor struggled.

The sight of him desperately fighting to escape was almost more than she could bear. Anne thought her heart would break.

He thrashed from side to side on the narrow bed. Undoubtedly the reason for the heavy cord strapped across his waist. His legs were tied to the bed, but that didn't stop him from struggling to escape his bonds. He cried out his pleas as if demons only he could see tortured him.

"Julia!"

"Please, my lady. Answer him."

Anne was unable to move let alone speak.

Dark bruises dotted Blackmoor's arms, no doubt from where the earl and Dr. Thornton had tried to restrain him.

His hair was matted to his scalp and the growth of stubble on his face made him appear...demented.

"Julia! Where are you?"

He pulled against the bonds holding him with greater desperation. He was frantic with fear for the woman called Julia.

"Please," the earl whispered again. "Tell him you're here."

"Julia. Answer me! Please. Oh, please."

"Just tell him that you're here, my lady," the doctor whispered. "He needs to think his wife is safe."

"Julia!"

Her legs trembled beneath her as she took a step closer to the bed. "I'm here, Mr.—Griff."

She hadn't spoken very loud, but the air in the room crackled with silence. He stopped thrashing and held perfectly still.

"Julia?"

"Yes, Griff. It's me. I'm here."

"Oh, thank God," he cried out. His voice was filled with emotion. "I thought you were dead."

"No. No. I'm right here."

"Where's Andrew? Is he all right?"

She lifted her head to look at the doctor and he nodded emphatically.

"He's fine, Griff. Don't worry about Andrew. Just worry about yourself and getting better."

Anne stepped closer to the bed and reached for the wet cloth the doctor had in his hand. She wiped the perspiration from Blackmoor's face, then brushed his hair from his forehead.

"Oh, Julia. I was so scared." His breathing came in ragged gasps. "I couldn't find you." His words came out faster and faster as he became more agitated. "I thought I'd lost you." He tried to rise, but the doctor's hands tightened around him. The Earl of Covington's hands held him from the other side. "Don't leave me. Promise you'll never leave me."

"No, Griff. I won't leave you."

His hand moved at his side as if he were searching for her. As if he wanted to touch her to make sure she was real.

She couldn't do this, let him touch her, hold his hand, twine her fingers with his. She looked up and saw the frantic desperation in the earl's eyes. The dark concern in the doctor's.

"Julia, where are you?" His hand moved in search of hers.

She didn't want to feel the heat of his warm flesh next to hers. It would make him too real. It would connect him to her closer than she wanted to be. But she couldn't stop herself. She reached for him and held his hand in hers.

A thousand jolts of something she could not explain rushed through her body. "I'm right here, Griff. Just stay with me and I'll help you. Day by day. One day at a time."

She held his hand while she wiped the sweat from his brow.

"Oh, Julia. I love you."

The air caught in her throat. "I know, Griff. I love you, too."

# Chapter 9

✤

*A*nne sat on a stone bench in Lord Covington's garden and pretended interest in the book she'd selected from the earl's library. But she couldn't feign interest in mere words when she had the real-life memories that refused to leave.

It had been nearly a week since she'd sat with Mr. Blackmoor. For two days and two nights she'd gone to him at various times when he was the most distraught, and pretended to be his dead wife. For two days and nights she begged him to stay with her. Promised that if he stayed, she'd help him. Day by day. One day at a time.

That's what he needed to hear. Those were the only words that calmed him. But those words bound her to him in a way that refused to lessen.

It was wrong of her to continually think of Mr. Blackmoor. Wrong of her to remember so much about him. Since those days and nights, he'd been a dream that wouldn't go away. A dream that appeared each time she closed her eyes. Sometimes even when her eyes weren't closed.

A noise from down the path interrupted her and she turned her gaze. The Earl of Covington walked toward her.

"I'm glad I found you," he said when he reached her bench. "I want to thank you. I know asking you to help

Griff this past week was a great imposition, one hardly appropriate for a lady of quality. But I was desperate and—"

"How is Mr. Blackmoor?" She stopped the earl from explaining something that was obviously uncomfortable for him to talk about.

"Much better today. He was able to eat a little broth for lunch and was out of bed for a while this morning."

"I'm glad."

"He's even threatening to leave his room," he said with a slight smile. "He says the walls are too confining." The earl looked to the ground. "I don't know if you realize what was…wrong with Griff, but—"

"Yes, my lord. I do." Anne closed her book and placed it in her lap. "My father went through the same torture when he tried to quit drinking. Unfortunately, his efforts failed. He wasn't strong enough to stop."

The earl lifted his gaze and stared at her, his face filled with regret. "I'm sorry. I didn't know."

She looked away to the pretty flowers just beginning to bloom. "Not many people did. We were fortunate he stayed in the country as much as he did and away from Society's eyes."

"Griff was not always like this. It wasn't until your brother was killed that he…got worse."

"I see."

"I'm confident that he won't return to his former ways once he's cured," he said, as if trying to convince himself at the same time he was trying to convince her. "Dr. Thornton assures me he has an excellent chance."

"I hope so." Anne didn't feel nearly as confident. Her father had proved to her every day of his life how impossible it was not to take another drink when your body wanted liquor more than it wanted air to breathe. She'd seen firsthand the grip alcohol had on Griffin Blackmoor the days and nights she'd pretended to be his wife. The times when being with him shifted her world on its axis. That had been nearly a week ago.

A week since she'd sat with him. A week since she'd held his hand, told him she was his wife. Told him she loved him. She hadn't been able to erase from her memory every detail of those times.

She still heard him call for his dead wife, Julia. Still felt his hand clench hers. Still felt the hard muscles on his shoulders, arms, and chest when she soothed his burning body with cool cloths. She remembered the rugged planes of his face when she wiped the sweat from his brow, the bristly stubble when she touched his cheeks and jaw, and every magnificent inch of him beneath her fingertips. A hidden part deep inside her still burned with a yearning she refused to acknowledge.

"He doesn't remember I was there, does he?"

"No. He remembers nothing from that night or the next two days when you sat with him. Nothing after the time he went upstairs the night you arrived."

She nodded, absently rubbing her thumb along the smooth leather binding of the book in her hands.

The earl straightened his shoulders. "Lady Covington reminded me again at lunch that she had accepted invitations to a tea this afternoon at the Duchess of Wallingsford's and a dinner hosted by the Marchioness of Edington later in the evening. Do not worry that you will have to go unescorted. I promise to be at both."

"You do not owe me for what I did, my lord. It is enough that you have given me refuge and have offered to sponsor me in Society. It would be impossible for me to find anyone to marry without—" She stopped, unable to go on. "If there's anything more I can do to repay you for what you have already done, you have only to ask."

"I am certain there is not. From now on we will—"

The earl's gaze lifted to a movement coming from the terrace and she turned her head to see Mr. Blackmoor coming down the walk.

"Griff! Bloody hell, man. What are you doing out of bed?"

Griffin Blackmoor walked toward them, tall and so very distinguished looking. His dark hair was still longer than was fashionable, yet it suited him perfectly. He was clean-shaven now and had a shirt and jacket to cover the parts of his body she tried without success to forget. He seemed much improved, although his face was still pale and his eyes had not regained their luster. Even recovering from several days in bed, he was, without a doubt, the most handsome man she'd ever seen.

"I couldn't stand those four walls any longer, Adam. I thought I would sit outside for a while."

"Dr. Thornton said you were to stay abed a full two weeks. It's only been one week."

"One was enough." He locked his gaze with Anne's and nodded in greeting. "If I had known you had such pleasant company, I would have come earlier."

"Good afternoon, Mr. Blackmoor. Would you care to sit?" She moved her skirt to make room for him.

"Yes. Unfortunately, I am not as strong as I thought. I have been…ill."

"Yes. Lord Covington told me you were stricken with an ailment after we arrived. Traveling can sometimes do that. I hope you are much improved."

"Yes. I'm much better now." He sank down on the stone bench and breathed a shaky sigh. "Have you settled in adequately?"

"Yes." She tried to ignore how his nearness warmed her flesh through all the layers of her clothing, but failed. "Lord and Lady Covington have been most generous. They have been the perfect hosts. Yesterday I met the earl's three sons. They were all perfect gentlemen."

"I am looking forward to seeing them." He smiled. "Let's see. Simon should be nearly six months old now, right?"

"He will be a year in six weeks' time," Adam answered.

"I see."

Anne wanted to take Griff's hand in hers and hold it like she'd done before. She wanted to comfort him and tell him he would be all right, that in a few days he would be better and would learn all the events that had happened while he was not sober. But she couldn't. She'd learned from her father that tomorrow might be exactly like last week, and the day after like all the others before them, and he would never be sober again.

"Patience and I will be taking Lady Anne to an outdoor tea this afternoon, hosted by the Duchess of Wallingsford. It should be quite the affair. Lady Anne will find it quite interesting."

"Are you looking forward to it?" Griff asked, his gaze riveted on hers.

A warm rush swirled through her body. She wished he would not look at her like that. Having him so near did strange things to her. *If only I hadn't touched him. Held him.*

"That is the reason I came to London."

"There is no rush," he reminded her. "You came to find a man who would suit you. Not to marry the first man to offer for you."

She lowered her gaze. "I am quite aware of what I must do. My requirements are not that difficult."

Mr. Blackmoor frowned. "Adam, perhaps you could make a list of the nobility in attendance and we can peruse it when you return. That way we can eliminate anyone unsuitable and save Lady Anne a great deal of wasted effort."

Lord Covington smiled. "You make it sound like we're hiring someone to fill a post, Griff. Perhaps we should let Lady Anne decide if anyone she meets intrigues her. Or better yet, perhaps we should let her enjoy her first London gathering without added pressure."

Blackmoor's shoulders stiffened and he dragged his hand over his jaw. "I only thought we might save Lady Anne from making a huge mistake if we warn her in advance of any suitor she should not consider."

She felt the heat rush to her cheeks. "I know your concern. You take your promise to Freddie very seriously."

"Yes, and that is why—"

"You don't need to concern yourself," she interrupted, "that I will make any rash decisions. No one is likely to offer for me today, and if they do, I promise I'll refuse them." She rose from the bench. "Now, if you gentlemen will excuse me. I think it's time to get ready for Lady Wallingsford's tea."

She followed the garden path back to the terrace that opened off the drawing room. Her face burned with embarrassment. Discussing her purpose for being here was more humiliating than anything she'd ever done. Especially with a man whose nearness caused her heart to race.

Picking out a husband should be no different than picking out an already-made gown from the seamstress's rack. But she knew that if she did not like the husband she picked out, she could not return him like she could a gown.

She didn't doubt that choosing a husband would be an easy task. She had few requirements. Looks weren't a concern. Neither was a title. All that concerned her was that the man she married had enough wealth to provide Becca with a Season. And that he wouldn't be a drunkard like her father.

Like Griffin Blackmoor.

# Chapter 10

✤

*G*riff had no intention of following Adam's orders to remain in the house and retire early. He refused to give up his search for the man who'd killed Freddie.

Griff waited until Adam's carriage drove away from the house, then took his greatcoat from the cloakroom and left by a side exit. He kept to the shadows as he left the house, hoping to lose the man following him but knowing that wasn't likely. Any of Fitzhugh's men were too good for him to escape their notice.

Griff walked to the nearest corner and hailed the first hackney he saw. He gave the driver an address several blocks away, then stepped inside. The second the cab lurched forward, he relaxed against the squabs and breathed a sigh.

He was still bloody weak. More than once during the last week he thought he might not survive. Ridding his body of the liquor he'd consumed over the last several months was a hell unlike any he thought possible. Only the soft voice urging him to stay with her had kept him from giving up.

He closed his eyes until the cab slowed, then got out when the cab stopped several blocks from his intended destination.

When the horse and driver pulled away, Griff wrapped his fingers around the pistol in his pocket and made his way through the dusky darkness of London's narrow backstreets. He kept in the shadows until he reached a hidden doorway at the end of an alley that very few in the city even knew was there. After a cautionary glance over his shoulder, he leaned forward to work the lock. A few seconds later, he turned the handle and let himself into the building that housed the secret offices of British Foreign Intelligence.

The entryway was unlit, and he stood in the darkness until his eyes acclimated to the lack of light. When he could make out vague shadows, he made his way down the dim hallway. He stopped in front of the third door on his right and stepped inside.

Except for the faint glow from beneath the door on the far wall, this room was as dark as the rest. Griff listened, then walked to Colonel Rupert Fitzhugh's office and turned the handle. He came face-to-face with his former commanding officer.

"I must be losing my touch," Griff said, closing the door behind him. "There was a time you wouldn't have heard me until it was too late."

"You haven't lost anything, Griff. I've been expecting you." Colonel Fitzhugh walked around his desk and relaxed into his chair. "Come in and sit down."

Griff crossed the room and sat in a worn leather chair in front of Fitzhugh's desk. "Which one of your men is following me?" he said, crossing the ankle of his right leg over his left knee.

"Johnston and Turner."

Griff lifted his eyebrows. "Both of them?"

"Just a precaution. It's been well over a week since you've surfaced. They didn't want to miss you."

Griff's breath caught. "I've…had things to do."

"I'm glad. You look a damn sight better than you did the last time I saw you." Fitzhugh shuffled several papers on his desk, then focused on Griff. "Now, why don't you tell me why you're here?"

Griff leveled a pointed glare at Fitzhugh. "As you know, I don't believe the Marquess of Brentwood was killed by a robber. He was killed by a sniper. Someone I think was after me."

Fitzhugh removed his spectacles and laid them on the desk. "That's what you told me several months ago. What proof do you have?"

Griff shook his head. "Just a gut feeling that tells me the shooting was intentional. Since Brentwood didn't have an enemy that would want him dead, my instincts tell me that I was the one the killer wanted. Not Brentwood."

Fitzhugh rose from his chair and walked around the corner of his desk. "Johnston and Turner should be here by now." He walked to a secret door hidden within the bookcase. "They've been watching Covington's town house since you arrived. We'll see if they've seen anything."

"Before they join us, I'd like to ask you a question."

Griff's statement stopped Fitzhugh from opening the panel.

"Do you think there's a chance someone's still out there who wants me dead?"

Griff was desperate for Fitzhugh's opinion, an opinion he valued. His blood rushed through his head while he waited, the pressure building behind his eyes. He wasn't sure which answer he wanted, a no, which would mean he probably wasn't in danger and Fitzhugh never thought he had been; or a yes, which would only confirm that no one was safe anywhere near him. If the answer was the latter, it would be best if he left London before he was responsible for another death.

Griff studied Fitzhugh's hesitation, then felt his gut tighten when the colonel shook his head.

"I don't know. But after the night we met at the docks, I realized we couldn't take any chances. You implied we'd let one of the Russian spies escape."

A wave of unease washed over Griff. "I don't remember everything I said."

"I don't doubt it. You probably have several months you don't remember."

Fitzhugh lowered his hand from the lever that would open the secret door and turned back to Griff. "After that night, Johnston, Hawkins, and Turner have taken turns watching you."

"They were good. I didn't notice."

Fitzhugh laughed. "They could have followed you in a lumber wagon and you wouldn't have noticed. What were you trying to do? Drink England dry?"

Griff shook his head. "Something like that. It didn't work."

"I'm damn glad you finally failed at something."

Fitzhugh turned back to the bookcase and lifted the lever. A secret door opened, and Barry Johnston and Matt Turner walked in.

"Good evening, Captain," they said to Griff. They took turns shaking his hand.

"Good evening, Johnston. Turner. It's been a long time."

"Too long," they said in unison.

"Colonel Fitzhugh tells me you took turns watching my back. Have either of you seen anything?"

"No, sir," Turner answered. "If someone did try to kill you the night they shot Brentwood, they haven't tried again."

Griff raked his fingers through his hair. "Maybe I've lost it." He walked over to a large map of London that hung on the wall and stared at the familiar streets and roadways. "Maybe I'm just imagining all of this."

"No, Blackmoor," Fitzhugh said from behind him. "If you don't think that the man who killed the marquess was a robber, then that's good enough for us. Maybe he realizes you're being watched, and he's waiting until we get lax before trying again."

"Could be," Griff said, although every instinct told him the killer should have tried again before now. There had been plenty of opportunity. "Colonel, do you have the files on the four spies we executed?"

"Not here, but I can get them for you."

Griff nodded. "I'd like to see them."

"Come back tomorrow. I'll have them by then."

Griff turned to the two fellow agents. "Thank you," he said to Turner and Johnston. "And tell Hawkins when you see him. I appreciate it."

"Anytime, Captain."

Griff moved to leave, but Johnston's words stopped him.

"Don't worry, Captain. We'll watch your back, like you watched ours."

Griff nodded, then walked out of the office and down the narrow alley. When he reached the opening, he stopped to look in both directions. Around the corner was his club, Waterman's. It was too early to go home yet. Adam and the ladies would not have returned from the Edington dinner. He could go there and sit for a while. Have a drink. Just one.

He turned the corner and saw the subtle lights glowing from behind the familiar beveled glass doors. He took a step closer, then stopped. Dr. Thornton's words came back to haunt him. *You will never lose the craving for a drink, Mr. Blackmoor. You'll always want one. But once you take your first drink, you'll be back to where you are right now. Worse. The next time, it will be even harder to stop. Eventually, the liquor will kill you.*

Griff swiped his hand across his jaw. He didn't doubt Adam would send Anne away if he took even one drink. His threat was the leverage he held over him. But it wouldn't work.

He could stay sober until she found a husband. He told himself he didn't want a drink that badly. That he could just walk away from his old life without a look back.

He looked again as the door to Waterman's opened and two men he recognized stumbled out. He could do this—go without a drink one more day. But, bloody hell, it was hard. He wanted a drink. In fact, he wanted more than one.

That thought scared him to death.

*Just stay with me and I'll help you. Day by day. One day at a time.*

He walked down the street in the opposite direction, taking the long way home. When he reached the earl's residence, Fenwick opened the door. The pensive look on his face was filled with concern. Was he worried that Griff had been drinking?

"Good evening, Mr. Blackmoor. How was your evening?"

"Fine, Fenwick. I needed to go for a walk."

Fenwick studied Griff a moment longer, then a smile lifted the corners of his mouth. "I'm glad to hear it, sir." The butler lifted Griff's jacket from his shoulders and folded it over his arm. "Although perhaps it would not be a good idea to let His Lordship find out you left for the evening. He might not agree that you're strong enough to leave the house yet."

Griff smiled. "Perhaps you're right. It might be better if we said nothing."

Fenwick nodded his agreement. "Are you ready to retire, sir?"

"No. I think I'll wait for the earl in his study. Would you tell him I'm up when he returns?"

"Of course, sir. May I get you some tea while you wait?"

"Yes, thank you. That would be fine."

Griff took a chair before the small fire burning in the fireplace and rested his chin upon his steepled fingers. It bothered him that Colonel Fitzhugh didn't think whoever had killed Freddie had a connection to the four spies they'd executed during the war. There wasn't a finer officer in Her Majesty's service than Fitzhugh. Griff trusted his opinion even above his own. Still, there was a reason the sniper had come after him. But if it wasn't related to the spies he'd had a major role in capturing and executing, what else could it be?

The bullet that had killed Freddie that night hadn't been fired from a robber's gun. Of that Griff was certain. What other explanation could there be but that the bullet had been intended for him, and Freddie had stepped in the way to protect him? But why hadn't the killer tried again?

Griff got to his feet and walked to the window. He stared out at nothing while Fenwick brought tea and poured him a cup.

"Thank you," he said, taking the cup from Fenwick. Griff looked down at the dark liquid swirling in his cup and took a sip. What he wouldn't give for something stronger.

Griff pushed that thought to the back of his mind. He couldn't want a drink that badly. That would mean he was a…

Thankfully, the door opened and he didn't have to face what his mind told him. He turned and watched his brother and wife and their guest enter the room.

"Hello, Griff. I didn't expect you to still be up."

"I—" His gaze rested on Lady Anne's face and he couldn't stop a smile from forming.

She was beautiful. The satiny fabric of her midnight-blue gown shimmered in the firelight.

A narrow strand of pearls was her only jewelry. The delicate strand rested on her porcelain skin just above the rise of her creamy breasts, which were, in his opinion, revealed to excess by the low cut of her gown. He wanted to cover her exposed flesh. One would think she was making an effort to draw attention to her body, to all the attributes with which she'd been blessed—which, of course, she was. How could he not have noticed before?

Their gazes met and held. Griff tried to look away but couldn't. In the span of just a few interminable seconds, a blazing heat rushed through his body and seeped to every extremity. His breath caught as rapid little pockets of air struggled to find their way into his lungs. Thankfully, she turned her head to the side, releasing their locked gazes.

Only when she looked away did he notice the rosy hue to her cheeks, as if she, too, thought the room overly warm.

"I wasn't tired," he finally said. "I wanted to hear how your evening went."

"It was marvelous," Patience said. The excitement in her voice was impossible to miss. "Lady Anne was the belle of the dinner. She had such a group of admirers surrounding her that one could hardly get to her for the crush."

Griff raised his eyebrows as he fought the tension that pulled inside him. Why was he bothered? This was what he wanted. This was the reason he'd brought her to London. He should be glad she'd been received so enthusiastically.

"Wonderful," he said, turning his gaze back to Lady Anne. Her cheeks remained a rosy hue, which only added to her appeal—and his frustration.

"Well, it's been a long day," Patience said. "I think Lady Anne and I will retire. Tomorrow night we've been invited to the Countess of Fillington's. It promises to be another late night. If you'll excuse us."

"Of course," the earl answered.

"Good night, Griff," the countess said before she left.

"Good night, Patience. Lady Anne."

"Good night, Mr. Blackmoor."

Griff took one last look at Anne before she was gone. She was, without a doubt, a beauty.

Adam closed the door behind the two women and sat in the chair next to Griff's.

Griff barely waited until he was settled before he asked, "So, did she catch the notice of anyone in particular?"

"Yes," Adam answered, drinking from his cup of tea. "You should have seen it. Baron Jamison's son, Bradley, nearly tripped over himself trying to be the first to be introduced to her."

Griff shot him an angry look. "Bradley Jamison is a pup. He isn't old enough to be out of the schoolroom yet. What was he doing ogling her?"

Covington laughed. "The same as every other eligible male in attendance. Harvey Barnes, and the Earl of Portsmouth, and Lord Franksly, they all tried to be first to gain introductions."

"Lord Franksly? You can't be serious. He doesn't have a penny to his name. And the Earl of Portsmouth? I thought he was dead."

Adam laughed. "He isn't that old, Griff."

Griff didn't like the smirk on Adam's face and told him so. "You can wipe that grin off your face, Adam. I asked you to escort Freddie's sister around so she could meet someone who'd fit her needs. Not to have her lusted after by every male in London who wouldn't recognize quality if it ran over him. Or only wants to steal a kiss."

"It wasn't like that at all, Griff. Lady Anne truly had a wonderful time. She met several interested suitors, and added a little variety to the same old faces we see at all the events. Tomorrow will be even better."

Griff didn't doubt it would. He also didn't doubt that this time he'd be there to pick and choose the men Anne would meet. Obviously, marriage had dulled Adam's talent for spotting someone who would make Anne a good match. Griff would be much more particular. He didn't intend to let just anyone have her.

# Chapter 11

✣

The crush gathered around her at the Fillington ball was suffocating, yet Anne kept the smile on her face while the Marquess of Candlewood told a humorous story he'd heard while having tea with his grandmother. When he finished, Anne laughed, as was expected.

The marquess was quite charismatic, tall and extremely good-looking, with golden blond hair and pale-blue eyes. He was also personable, she supposed, but that was it. Nothing more. As was Mr. Camdorn, Baron Fillmore, the Earl of Pendron, and the Marquess of Lancheister. They each paid her court during the evening, asking for the customary dance or two, offering to fill her punch cup, or suggesting a walk in the garden. Which of course she refused.

But not one of them interested her, and it was his fault entirely. Griffin Blackmoor's.

She snapped her fan against her skirt in an uncustomary show of temper. When she lifted her gaze, she found Patience watching her.

Patience turned to the Marquess of Candlewood and Lord Mechon, then gave them one of her smiles. "Would you mind getting us a glass of punch?"

They both hurried to do her bidding, and Patience led Anne to the side where they could be alone. "Is something wrong?"

"Oh, no," she said, seeing the frown on Patience's face deepen. "Everything's perfect."

"You seem uncomfortable."

Anne smiled. "Perhaps I am just a little. This is all so new."

"You don't like them, do you?"

"What?"

"The crowds, the parties, playing the belle of the ball. All the attention you are receiving."

"Is it that obvious?"

Patience patted her hand. "I'm certain I'm the only one who's noticed so far. Everyone else thinks you are reveling in this newfound popularity."

"I simply feel so exposed. As if everyone knows the reason I'm here."

"Nonsense."

"It would not be more noticeable if I had worn a sign reading, 'Wanted: Husband with sizable fortune to provide for destitute aging spinster and her younger sister.'"

"Don't, Anne. You're not that old, and your situation is no different than anyone else's here. Just look around you. Most of the ones still unattached are seeking the same thing. A husband with an impressive title, or a wife with a sizable dowry."

"But I don't have an attractive dowry. I'm penniless."

"I'm certain that will not matter. There are any number of unattached young men who are not seeking a large dowry." Patience squeezed Anne's fingers. "There are other reasons people marry, you know."

Anne looked into Lady Patience's eyes, searching for confirmation that there could be more. "Is love a possibility?"

The countess hesitated, then smiled. "That remains to be seen."

"Did you and the earl marry for love?"

"No. But many marriages begin without love, then change."

Anne thought of how stiff and formal the Earl and Countess of Covington appeared in public. Even in private, there seemed little difference—the earl seldom shedding his austere exterior, the countess always the epitome of decorum.

Anne thought of what her future might hold. She didn't want her marriage to begin without love. Her mother had lived her whole life desperate to win her husband's love, then lost her will to live when she failed. She didn't want to live the same fate.

"Don't worry, Anne. Enjoy yourself tonight and perhaps, when you least expect it, you'll find that perfect match. Everyone in the room is in awe of you already. How could they not be? You look absolutely stunning."

Anne fought the wave of guilt. Even though it was less than the customary six-month mourning period for a sibling, Patience had talked her out of wearing mourning colors. "It's the gown. I had no idea when we chose the material that it would make up so grand."

She ran her fingers over the beautiful peach silk moiré and sighed. The gown was remarkable on its own, but what made it even more so were the three wide lace flounces overlaying the peach, each one gathered at various lengths around the skirt by large peach bows. The exposing, off-the-shoulder bodice was trimmed with the same lace.

Anne suddenly felt very bold and daring—and beautiful. She smiled as Candlewood and Lord Mechon came toward them, each carrying two glasses.

"Here is your punch," Candlewood said, holding out a glass. Lord Mechon handed Patience a glass at the same time.

Anne thanked the men and took a swallow, grateful to find the liquid still a little cool.

She was introduced to even more strangers as the group of men and women surrounding them increased in size. There were so many that it was doubtful that she would remember their names after tonight—or wanted to. The shallow men and tittering women simply reaffirmed her distaste for city life. The crowds made her uneasy, the packed ballroom was too confining, and the false laughter assaulted her ears.

She waved her fan in front of her face to cool her burning cheeks. She prayed she could find a way to escape from the confines of the crowded ballroom.

If she hadn't been so uncomfortable with her surroundings, she might have realized sooner than she did that he was close by. But she didn't.

There'd been no sounding alarms or gunshots fired to warn her. Only the goose flesh that rose on her arms and the ghost of a whisper that ran down her cheek as an indication that he was near. These were all the warnings she needed.

Before the person next to her mentioned his name, Anne was aware that he was watching her.

Her heart picked up speed, but she refused to turn to face him. She decided to pretend his presence wasn't important, that she didn't care that he'd come to watch her every move. Just as she tried to forget that it was impossible not to compare every male she met to Griffin Blackmoor—and find them all lacking.

Anger welled inside her, anger directed more at herself than at him. She was here to find someone suitable who could be her husband, not have her thoughts muddied by visions of a man she would never consider, a man she'd rarely seen sober since he'd walked into her life.

She turned her thoughts back to the crowd around her. She laughed at their conversations with greater enthusiasm, spoke with more animation while discussing the opera with the Marquess of Candlewood, and batted her eyes when he paid her the most flattering compliment. Just as she'd seen a few of the other debutantes do.

"Would you care to dance, Lady Anne?" the marquess asked, holding out his arm.

"I would love—"

"I'm sorry, Candlewood. This dance is promised to me."

Blackmoor's deep, rich voice sent a shiver of apprehension down her back. She turned to face him, to tell him with a glance she didn't appreciate his interference. He barely noticed as he focused his challenging glare on the Marquess of Candlewood.

"Is that so, my lady?" Candlewood asked, refusing to back down from Blackmoor's effrontery.

She hesitated. She couldn't allow them to argue over her, couldn't allow them to cause a scene. "Yes. I'm afraid it is, my lord. I'm sorry. I had forgotten."

She lifted her gaze. The look on Blackmoor's face brimmed with smug self-confidence. Her blood roared in anger.

She placed her hand ever so lightly on his outstretched arm. She wanted to dig her fingernails into his skin to show him how furious she was with him. She had never been so outraged.

She refused to consider that her agitation might also be caused by his nearness. Instead, she convinced herself that the sole reason for her outrage was the high-handed way he'd manipulated her in front of everyone.

He led her to the dance floor. The minute he turned her in his arms, she glared at him with a look she hoped would singe his dark hair. He'd cut it since she'd last seen him.

"That was unconscionably rude, Mr. Blackmoor," she hissed, refusing to walk into his outstretched arms.

"Yes, it was."

"Then why did you do it?"

He smiled. "Because dancing with the Marquess of Candlewood would have been a waste of time."

"How dare you."

"I dare because I intend to help you find someone suitable to marry." He paused. "Candlewood isn't suitable."

Their gazes held, and Anne's heart thrummed in her breast as sporadic shivers raced down her arms. She fought to quash her reaction to the fact that he held her in his arms.

"Do you intend to stand here arguing while the rest of the couples dance around us, or would you care to join them?"

She looked around the room and saw several pair of eyes watching them. He pulled her close to begin the dance—a waltz.

"Why did you force me away from the group I was talking to? I thought that was the objective of my coming to London." She spoke softly so no one could hear her. "I thought you wanted me to acquaint myself with every eligible male."

When he spoke, his voice was hard, with not the least softness in it. "Not the Marquess of Candlewood."

"Why? He seems quite pleasant."

"I'm sure he is, as well as charming and funny and very handsome. He is also very self-assured, and is fortunate enough to have more than an adequate amount of wealth to make himself quite the catch. But any woman foolish enough to marry him will have to share her husband with a great number of other women, including the mistress he keeps in grand style on Derby Street."

"You can't know that."

"Everyone knows it. Unless, of course, you wouldn't mind your husband servicing half the women in London on a regular basis."

Anne's cheeks burned.

"Ah. I see you would."

He firmed his hold around her waist and executed a tight turn on the floor in rhythm to the music. He was an excellent dancer, and her heart raced from the excitement of being in his arms.

She didn't want to feel such a connection to him. She wanted to step away, to release herself from the grip that heated her skin through the material of her dress, searing her flesh like a branding iron and weakening her knees. At the same time, she wanted him to pull her closer so she could feel the hardened muscles of his shoulders and back. She wanted to press her cheek against his fashionable black tailcoat and silver brocade waistcoat, and breathe in the maleness of him. She wanted to lift her hand to his cheek and run her fingertips over the strong line of his jaw and his thick, full lips as she'd done when she'd cared for him.

She wanted there to be one other man in the room who could set her on fire the same as he did. But she knew there was not.

"There are other men in attendance," he said, jolting her mind back to the present. "Any of them would be a better choice."

"Then what do you think of Baron Fillmore?"

"Too young."

"The Earl of Pendron?"

"Too broke."

"The Marquess of Lancheister?"

"Too boring."

She struggled to break free of his grasp. He would not let her. Instead, he twirled her to the side of the room and out the double doors that led to the terrace.

Cool air hit her like a slap in the face and she twisted out of his arms and stepped away from him.

"Is there anyone in attendance who would meet with your approval?"

"I'm certain there are any number of men who would be suitable." His nostrils flared slightly and his chest rose and fell. "You have just made the acquaintance of the wrong ones."

"Perhaps I should let you choose for me," she said without thinking. "Since you are such an excellent judge of character."

A grin lifted the corners of his mouth, causing the two creases on either side to deepen most seductively.

"Perhaps I should."

"Over my dead body," she whispered through clenched teeth. "If you want to play matchmaker, sir, I suggest you experiment on yourself. I'm sure there are any number of eligible young females who could be forced to take your name. Perhaps if you paid them the slightest attention, you could find yourself a suitable wife and leave me alone."

She had wanted to lash out at him, to say whatever would punish him for causing her such confusion. Her words had somehow hit the mark.

The smile faded from his face and his eyes turned even darker. "I'm afraid not, my lady. I have no desire to marry. That is one risk I never intend to take again. You, unfortunately, do not have that choice."

A cold chill washed over her. She'd been unforgivably cruel. "Why are you doing this to me?"

He swept a hand across his brow. For the first time, she noticed the light sheen of perspiration that covered his face. He shouldn't be here. He wasn't recovered enough, and attending a ball was too big a temptation. Champagne and brandy flowed like water. For a man just resigned never to drink again, this was the last place he should be.

"I'm doing this because I promised Freddie I would take care of you. I have an obligation to fulfill, and I don't intend to let you make a decision you'll regret for the rest of your life."

The effect of his words landed in the pit of her stomach like a hollow ache. What a fool she'd been. What an idealistic, muddleheaded romantic. She deserved to feel such betrayal, to feel hurt. If only she hadn't sat at his sickbed and held his hand—and told him she loved him.

"You need not concern yourself with my welfare, Mr. Blackmoor. I am quite capable of taking care of myself."

"I feel it my duty to warn you—"

She turned on him. "You have done more than is expected of you, sir. I have agreed to find a husband—and I will. The moment I do, your obligation will be at an end. If you will excuse me now."

She stepped around him and returned to the ballroom. She kept her back straight and her chin high as she made her way to where Lord and Lady Covington stood. "Is something wrong?" Patience asked, the look in her eyes understanding more than Anne wished to reveal.

"No. Everything is fine."

"Griff?" the earl asked, looking at a spot just behind her. He'd followed her. How dare he.

"Everything is fine," he answered.

But everything wasn't fine. Anne felt trapped. She needed to escape.

"Oh, there is the Marquess of Candlewood," she said, looking to the opposite side of the room. "If you will excuse me, I promised the marquess a dance before I was interrupted."

She gave Griff a defiant glare as she stepped past him. It was an effort to keep from visibly shivering at the hostile look he gave her in return. Let him be angry. If she had no choice but to marry against her will, it would at least be to a man of her own choosing. Not someone Griffin Blackmoor and his guilt-ridden conscience picked out for her.

* * *

He needed a drink.

What the hell was she trying to prove?

He watched as she stood in the middle of the ballroom, the most beautiful woman there, her upswept hair exposing her long, graceful neck, the mass of mahogany curls cascading down her back while delicate peach ribbons twined through the tendrils. She looked elegant, enchanting. Thoroughly kissable.

He'd never seen anyone more beautiful—far too beautiful, and far too naive to be let loose alone in London Society. Anyone with half a brain could see how innocent and unsuspecting she was. How had Freddie kept her locked away for so long?

One look at the way Candlewood and the rest of the men ogled her told him she didn't stand a chance. And the way she was dressed didn't help. Her gown was much too low, her breasts far too exposed to be considered decent. He would have to speak with Patience tomorrow and insist she have a talk with Lady Anne. Exposing that much of her exquisite body would only lead to trouble.

Just as letting that womanizing Candlewood hold her hand was dangerous. Bloody hell, she was courting disaster.

And all that after he'd warned her about the marquess. What made her do something so foolish?

Griff couldn't stand by and watch her. He needed to leave before he said or did something to embarrass them both.

He left the Fillingtons' town house and stepped out into the crisp nighttime air. He needed to walk. He needed to clear his mind. But how could he when all he could think about was the way she'd looked tonight. The way she'd felt in his arms when he'd danced with her, the way he'd felt when she was near him.

She was far too precious to let just anyone have. He would make sure whoever she married was perfect.

# Chapter 12

In the last six days, Griff had dismissed one duke, three marquesses, five earls, seven barons, and countless other of London's nobility with lesser titles he could not recall. And he was about to add four more to his list.

The Covington morning room was as crowded as a receiving line at a ball. Patience and Lady Anne sat on a floral settee in the spacious salon, while he and Adam and four suitors faced them. In attendance today were Baron Pendencarn, who sat in a chair on Griff's right, and Lord Benchley, on a chair next to the baron. The Earl of Welleby sat to Adam's left, and the Marquess of Tanhouse next to the earl. Griff sat in his customary place next to Adam on the sofa, drinking tea and eating delicate little sandwiches as if the two of them had nothing better to do with their time.

Bloody hell! What a bore.

Since the Fillington ball nearly a week ago, there had been a steady stream of admirers at the door. Patience had played chaperone for so many carriage rides through Hyde Park, Griff was certain they were going to erect a shrine in her honor. And he and Adam had consumed so much tea and eaten so many of those damn little cakes and sandwiches, he wouldn't think twice about selling half the estates he'd inherited for a thick piece of roast mutton.

And of the scores of admirers who'd showed interest in Lady Anne, there wasn't one of the titled imbeciles who was worthy of her.

"Perhaps you would care to accompany me on a carriage ride through Hyde Park this afternoon," the Marquess of Tanhouse said, a hopeful expression on his face.

"Of course. That would be wonderful."

Griff sat forward in his chair. "From the look of the clouds gathering outside, I'm afraid this afternoon might bring rain. Perhaps another time."

All eyes turned to look out the window—all except for Anne's. Her hostile glare locked with his, and the expression on her face hinted at a warning he refused to acknowledge.

"I think Mr. Blackmoor might be right," the dejected marquess said. "It does look like rain."

"Then perhaps Lady Anne would like to accompany me to the Countess of Williamhan's musicale instead?" the Earl of Welleby interjected, looking pleased with himself. "A little rain never stopped a musicale."

The earl laughed overenthusiastically at his little joke. Griff could see by the light in her eyes and the slight nod of her head that Anne intended to accept the invitation. "I'm certain Lady Anne would love to attend," he offered for her. "I'll make sure to free up my schedule to accompany her."

"There's no need for you to go to such trouble on my account," Anne said with a lethal smile that hinted of syrupy sweetness. "I'm quite certain Lady Patience will send one of the staff to chaperone. Or perhaps you intend to go yourself, Patience, and I could go with you?"

"It's no trouble," Griff interrupted. "I don't mind. I've always enjoyed Lady Williamhan's musicales."

"I could not possibly let you inconvenience yourself so," Anne spoke, her glare shooting painful pinpricks toward him.

There was a bite to her voice that Griff chose to ignore. "Don't bother sending a carriage, Welleby," he said over her protest. "I'll see Lady Anne and Lady Patience there myself."

The Earl of Welleby nodded, but disappointment was clear on his face.

"Have you been to Covent Garden yet?" Lord Benchley asked, his enthusiasm obvious. Both he and Baron Pendencarn made moon eyes at Anne as if her only competition was the sun in the sky. Since both of them were nearly bankrupt, their attention to Anne was obvious. They'd no doubt heard of the more than generous dowry he'd placed on her.

"No," Anne answered, setting her teacup back in the saucer. "But I hear it is wonderful."

"The theatre just recently reopened after the fire." Benchley sat forward in his chair. "*Les Huguenots* is playing. Mother and I have reserved a box for next Thursday evening. Perhaps you, and Lord and Lady Covington, of course, would care to—"

"I'm afraid Lady Anne has already made plans for next Thursday." Griff gave the baron a look that usually wilted the starch out of even the most determined of her suitors. Unfortunately, the argument he received did not come from Benchley, but from Anne.

"I believe you are mistaken, Mr. Blackmoor." There was an undeniable tinge of acid in her voice. "I'm certain we are free that evening."

"May I be so bold as to suggest you are mistaken?" He leaned back against the cushion and tried to appear more relaxed than he felt. The look the two of them shared resembled two bulls locking horns.

"And I'm positive I know my own calendar. I am quite capable of making plans of my own."

An uncomfortable tension filled the room. Several long seconds stretched by while Patience lowered her gaze to her hands. The marquess and the earl looked around the room as if the pattern in the wallpaper held their fascination. Baron Pendencarn fidgeted nervously with the ruffles on his shirt while Lord Benchley repeatedly cleared his throat.

"You are already engaged that evening, Lady Anne," Griff repeated, struggling to keep his voice soft and factual. "You have accepted—"

"I would appreciate it if you would allow me to speak for myself."

"Of course. I just did not realize you had changed your plans to attend the Duchess of Stanfields's ball." He made sure his voice contained a hint of conciliation.

"I'm afraid Blackmoor is correct," Lady Patience said. She was undoubtedly trying to soothe the troubled waters churning in her parlor.

Anne's cheeks turned a delightful shade of rose.

Bloody hell, but she was a beauty. Today she wore a gown the faintest shade of alabaster, with delicate pink flowers embroidered throughout the material. Her dark, mahogany hair was loosely pulled back, and delicate tendrils cascaded around her face. She looked almost too pretty to be real. No wonder every male in London searching for a bride was beating a path to her door.

"Oh, I had forgotten," she said, flashing him another angry look. "That is the same evening."

"Perhaps it will not be a total loss," the Earl of Welleby said, placing his empty teacup on the table beside his chair. "I hear the duchess has procured that renowned pianist, Van Seffeld, to provide entertainment for the evening. Quite a coup, too, since he's playing for the Queen that very morning."

There was a moment of awed silence, then the Earl of Welleby sat back against his chair. "I also have an invitation to attend the duchess's ball. Perhaps I will be fortunate enough to find an empty chair next to you during the performance."

Griff opened his mouth to give a reason why he was sure the chairs on either side of Anne would be occupied, then clamped his lips together when she flashed him a look that brimmed with violent threats.

"That would be delightful," she answered, smiling ever so sweetly at the earl.

Thankfully, the conversation turned to more general topics. For the next fifteen minutes, they spoke of the weather, the beautiful flowers just coming into bloom, and the crush of carriages forming the five-o'clock parade through Hyde Park. All bland and inconsequential matters that occupied them until the customary time allotted for afternoon visits expired. The guests made their excuses, then left.

Griff breathed a sigh of relief. This afternoon had been a damned circus.

When the room finally emptied of their guests, he crossed one ankle over the other knee and sat back against the cushions. When he looked up, he noticed all eyes in the room were focused on him. "What?" he said, looking from Adam to Patience, and finally to Anne. "Is something wrong?"

"You know very well there is," Anne said. The hostility in her voice matched the fire in her eyes. "You were unconscionably rude. Again."

He noticed the clenched hands she held in her lap and the pursed line to her beautiful full lips, and felt a slight twinge of guilt.

"Do you have to practice at being obstinate and disagreeable whenever I have guests?" she continued. "Or is your irritability something that comes naturally?"

He shrugged his shoulders as if he didn't have the slightest idea what she meant.

"You were overly critical, and most of your objections were totally unjustified," she added.

"I was not *that* disagreeable."

"Yes, you were. You were horrible, sir. I swear you would have found something objectionable if Prince Albert himself had come to call on us."

"Of course I would have. His attention to you would have made our queen quite unhappy, and no telling what bad tidings would have befallen us."

"You are impossible."

Griff smiled. "Not impossible. Perhaps a little difficult, but only because—"

She gave him another searing glare that stopped his words. "If you will excuse me, I need to go for a walk in the garden."

"Would you like me to—"

"No! I would like you to stay far away from me." She rose, then walked across the room with an angry swish of her skirts.

"Don't stay out too long, Anne," Patience said. "We're invited to the Earl of Framingham's ball tonight and will need to get ready soon."

"I won't," she answered, then opened the door.

And was gone.

There was an uncomfortable moment of silence when Griff's brother and sister-in-law looked accusingly in his direction. The tension thickened until Griff wanted to squirm in his seat. Thankfully, Adam broke the silence.

"Are you going to the Framinghams', Griff?"

"I had intended to."

"Perhaps you might want to find your own way tonight. I'm not certain your company will be appreciated."

Griff couldn't keep the surprised look from his face. "Perhaps I should go speak with her," he said, staring at the door where she'd exited.

"Only if you intend to offer up an apology or two," Adam said, lifting his eyebrows in the familiar way that was as good as a command.

"You think I need to apologize?" Griff couldn't hide his surprise.

"You definitely crossed the line this afternoon, Griff," Patience said behind a shy smile. "Even worse than yesterday. I'm afraid just an apology may not be sufficient. I'm afraid you may need to grovel."

"Grovel?"

"Yes, grovel."

Griff considered Patience's warning. Surely not. "Thank you for your advice, my lady," he said, lifting Patience's hand and kissing it. "I appreciate your concern."

Patience's words echoed in his head as he made his way to the door. He knew he'd been rude and overbearing, but bloody hell, how could he be anything but? None of the jackals paying her court were worth the effort it would take to throw them out the door.

He still hadn't found one he would let her marry.

\* \* \*

"I prefer to be left alone," Anne said stiffly when she heard his boots hit against the stones on the garden path. "And even if I did want company, your presence would be the last I would let take up space anywhere near me."

"Patience said I needed to apologize. I see she was correct."

"Apologize! If you think you can fix the abominable way you behaved with a simple apology, you are greatly mistaken."

He at least had the good sense to look remorseful. "Well, actually, Patience said I would need to grovel. I see that was closer to the truth."

"You could grovel from here to Westminster and back, and it would not excuse the way you behaved this afternoon. How dare you treat my guests with such rudeness and blatant disregard! You have no right to tell me with whom I can associate and with whom I can't. You have no right to intimidate them so."

He pointed to the end of the stone bench where she was sitting. "May I?"

"No." She scooted to the center of the bench so there was no room for him beside her.

His next word surprised her. Or maybe it was the way in which he said it. "Please."

With a sigh of frustration, she acquiesced and scooted as far to the opposite side of the bench as she could. She moved her skirt so he had room to sit. But she refused to be polite to him. After the way he'd behaved, he didn't deserve it.

"It's a beautiful afternoon, isn't it?" he asked, looking at the clear blue sky above.

"It's been a horrible afternoon, and it's entirely your fault."

"You aren't going to make this easy, are you?"

"No. You don't deserve it."

He breathed a deep sigh and sat up straight. He kept his shoulders rigid.

For several long minutes neither of them spoke. Suddenly, he rose from the bench and took a step away from her. With his back to her, he looked out onto the blooming flower beds. His voice, when he spoke, wrapped around her like a soothing balm. His words reached inside her breast and cradled her heart.

"I'm afraid I'm not good at apologizing. Even worse at groveling. If you found my behavior rude, suffice it to say I was only trying to point out the shortcomings in the men vying for your attention. Choosing a husband is a very serious decision. Due to the time limitations you are under, I thought it prudent to aid you to the best of my abilities. If you found my behavior offensive, I will apologize for that. But I'm afraid that is all for which I will offer an apology."

He stopped and Anne stared at him open-mouthed. She wanted to stay angry with him, heaven only knew he deserved it. But how could she when his voice rang with a sincerity that tugged at a place deep inside her breast?

She studied him. He clasped his strong hands tightly behind his back. His proud stance remained rigid, the contour of his broad shoulders exhibited a strength she ached to be able to rely on. She lifted her chin and her eyes caught the shimmering hues in his dark hair as the bright sunlight bathed it.

Anne clenched her hands in her lap to keep from reaching out to rake her fingers through his thick waves. Oh, she remembered the feel of it from when she'd sat with him. From when she'd held him.

Then he turned to face her.

Deep creases etched his forehead, his concern evident in his gaze. The tempo of her thundering heartbeats increased.

"Am I forgiven?"

Anne swallowed past the lump in her throat. "Only if I have your promise you will never behave like that again."

"Oh," he said.

He held her gaze and something shifted deep inside her where she thought her heart might be.

"You are going to make this difficult, aren't you, my lady?"

"You're the one who has made things difficult, Mr. Blackmoor."

"But surely it was obvious that none of the gentlemen vying for your attention were acceptable?"

"Acceptable to whom? You?"

"No. To you."

She sucked in a sharp breath. "But I have to marry someone. You know that as well as I. How else can I provide for Becca, and see that she makes a good match? How can I do that if you discourage every male from showing an interest in me?" She rose from her seat and stepped toward him. "I have been here nearly three weeks already. I don't have much time left. I can't impose on the earl's generosity forever."

"But none of the gentlemen here today were right for you. Surely you could see that?"

"I don't know what I see anymore. Please, Mr. Blackmoor. Don't make this any more difficult than it is. Let me find a husband on my own. You've fulfilled your obligation to Freddie simply by bringing me to London. You aren't responsible for anything else."

His eyes turned dark. Any hint of softness she thought she'd seen in his features faded from his face. With a look of resignation, he gave her a stiff nod.

"Very well, my lady. If that is how you want it, then that is how it will be."

"That is how it must be, Mr. Blackmoor."

Their gazes locked for several moments; then he turned and walked down the path toward the house.

# Chapter 13

✤

*H*er evening at the Framingham ball promised to be anything but enjoyable. Griffin Blackmoor and the earl stood amid a small group of fashionably dressed men on the opposite side of the room. Griff hadn't bothered her once all evening.

Anne didn't understand it, but for the first time since she'd arrived in London, she felt alone. Abandoned.

Not once did he give her a disapproving glare when she danced with someone he didn't approve of. Or even lift his dark brows in a questioning frown when someone he didn't think was suitable marriage material approached her. It was as if he didn't know she was there.

She liked this latest attitude far less than the overprotective interference she'd objected to before. She suddenly felt as if he'd deserted her.

She took in a deep breath and shook off such a ridiculous notion. How could she think he had abandoned her when she was the one who had demanded that he leave her alone?

She turned to find the Earl of Welleby standing in front of her.

"I can't guess who the person occupying your thoughts so completely might be, but I find I envy him your attention more than I can say."

Anne lowered her gaze, afraid she might turn her head to look at Griffin Blackmoor and give herself away. "It was no one. I was just lost in thought."

"Well, if I might tear you away from such ponderous musings, may I have the pleasure of this dance?"

Anne smiled. "I would be delighted."

The earl was tall and good-looking, with reddish hair and steely-gray eyes that held little warmth. She took his offered hand and, for his sake, tried to pretend she enjoyed his company.

She smiled as he twirled her around the floor and kept up the conversation as much as possible. But every time they moved to where Griff was in sight, she couldn't help but look in his direction. And each time, a painful knot tightened in the pit of her stomach because he hadn't looked at her once. He even stood with his back to her, as if dismissing her from his sight.

"You seem flushed, my lady. Would you like to step outside for a breath of air?"

"What?"

"I asked if you would like to step outside for a breath of air."

"Oh, yes. That would be nice."

The earl led her out onto the terrace, then to the far corner where a short cement railing cordoned them off from entering the garden.

Colored lanterns of yellow and orange and green decorated the terrace, but the spot where they stood was just beyond the last lantern and more in the shadows than in the light.

"I have waited all evening for a chance to have you to myself," the earl said from beside her. "You are, without a doubt, the most beautiful woman here."

"Thank you, my lord, but I hardly think—"

"No, do not deny it. All others pale in comparison."

Anne stepped to the side to put more room between them.

The earl inched closer, then reached for her hand.

His hands were hot and sweaty. His touch made her uncomfortable.

"I knew we shared something special the first time we met. Do you remember where that was?"

"Of course," she said, pulling ever so slightly to free herself. The way the earl rubbed his thumb over her fingers and against the top of her hand bothered her. "We met nearly two weeks ago at the Countess of Fillington's ball."

"And I have not been able to think of anyone but you since then. You enchanted me with your beauty, captured my heart with your warmth, and totally enthralled me with your graciousness. You have me at your mercy, my dearest Lady Anne. I beg you to allow me the honor of speaking to Lord Covington and announcing my intentions."

Anne felt a cold wave of apprehension wash over her. "No!"

He pulled her closer against him. "Please. I won't take no for an answer."

"I'm sorry, but we don't know each other. You can't possibly think that—"

His hot breath washed against her cheek and his hands moved over her shoulder. This was hardly the sort of conversation she wanted, hardly the confrontation she was prepared to handle.

"It's not sudden," he whispered against her ear. "I have prayed for a chance to tell you how I feel. A time when Mr. Blackmoor would give us a moment of privacy, and now I have it. I can't waste even one second of it. I fear you have captured my heart, my lady, and it will cease to beat if you deny me."

Before she could stop him, he brought his mouth down to hers and kissed her.

His mouth was warm and wet, his touch disgusting. The harder she pushed against him, the harder he pressed his soft lips against hers, crushing against her until she wanted to scream.

"I hope I'm not interrupting," Griffin Blackmoor's deep, penetrating voice said from behind them.

The Earl of Welleby dropped his arms from her shoulders and faced the intruder. "I'm afraid you are, my good man. Lady Anne and I were enjoying the beautiful evening."

"Then I must have misinterpreted what I saw. It didn't look like Lady Anne was enjoying herself in the least." He took one step toward them, then another. "I think I will ask the lady if she was enjoying your attentions, and if she tells me she did not appreciate your advances and you are still here, you can be sure you will never enjoy another beautiful evening for the rest of your very short life."

"If you think you can bully me into—"

"Lady Anne," Griff said, taking another step toward them. "Would you like me to go back into the house so you and the earl may continue to enjoy the evening?"

Before she could choke out a sound or even shake her head in answer, the earl was gone.

Griff stepped up to her and clasped his fingers around her upper arms. "Are you all right?"

She tried to tell him she was, but her body refused to stop shaking. Her chin trembled so violently she couldn't release one word from her mouth.

She refused to cry in front of him. She was the one who'd insisted she could do this on her own, that she did not need his interference. But how could she concentrate on another man when she couldn't think of anyone but him? When she didn't want to talk to, dance with, or look at anyone but him? When the reason she'd come out to the garden with the earl was to get away from Griff, so it wouldn't hurt so much when he ignored her?

Her vision blurred and one traitorous tear trickled down her cheek before she could swipe it away.

"Ah, hell," she heard him mumble, then he took her in his arms.

Anne wrapped her arms around his waist and held on as if he were the only safe harbor in her stormy world.

"If you get my new silk cravat wrinkled and wet, my lady, I will hold you accountable."

"I won't, sir," she whispered, breathing in the masculine scent she'd come to love so. "I'm not crying. I'm only angry."

"I'm glad."

He held her with a great amount of tenderness. He rested his chin on the top of her head.

"You were a little fool for coming out here with the earl," he whispered in her ear. His warm breath was a soothing balm over her flesh. "Don't you realize what could have happened?"

She knew she should pull away from him, should step out of his arms and the comfort he afforded her. Griffin Blackmoor was the last man on the face of the earth she should let hold her. The last man she should trust with her heart and her future. He was exactly what she swore she would never want, the kind of man she would never allow to become important to her. A man she couldn't trust to stay sober from one day to the next.

But she couldn't step away from him. He was the man her heart ached to have hold her and touch her and kiss her.

She lifted her head and looked into his face. What she saw in his eyes startled her. He was as frightened of what was happening between them as she was.

He kept his gaze riveted on hers a moment longer before he clamped his hands on either side of her face and lowered his head.

"Ah, hell," he whispered again as his mouth covered hers.

A warm heat spread through her and settled in a spot low in her stomach. Her knees grew weak.

He kissed her tenderly, touched her softly, then deepened his kiss.

She kissed him back in her inexperienced, untutored way, knowing she lacked a knowledge she wanted desperately to have. But he didn't seem to mind. He tipped her face to the side and kissed her again. She wrapped her arms around his neck and accepted what he offered.

A soft, almost gentle moan echoed in the darkness and she realized it had come from him. She didn't know what power he possessed over her, but she would have agreed to anything when he kissed her like that.

"Oh," she whispered, her breathing ragged and gasping. Her blood thundered against her ears and her heart pounded in her chest. She couldn't breathe. And still she wanted more.

He kissed her again, then lifted his mouth from hers. His gaze lowered, then locked with hers. A frown deepened across his brows. "We shouldn't have kissed." His voice was hoarse. "It was a dreadful mistake."

"Kissing me was that terrible?"

He turned his back on her. "Yes," he answered.

Anne reached out her hand to the railing to steady herself. His single word hurt more than she thought possible.

"It might be best if we don't go back inside together," he said from the shadows. "Are you all right, or should I send Patience out here to you?"

"No," she answered, pressing her fist against her stomach. The ache she experienced was the result of a painful lesson. She would never let a man do this to her again. "I am fine, Mr. Blackmoor. You are an excellent teacher. A little harsh in what you hoped to prove, but an excellent teacher. I have learned a lesson I will never forget."

Without looking to see his reaction, she stepped around him and walked away. On legs that trembled beneath her, she made her way through the ballroom.

Anne found Lady Patience discussing the latest fashions with the Duchess of Weston, and joined in. She forced herself to smile, and glanced occasionally at the terrace doors, but didn't see him again.

That was just as well.

\* \* \*

He was gone when she rose the next morning. The Earl of Covington called her into his study to inform her that Griff had moved to his own town house late last night and would not be returning.

The earl said Griff had given no explanation other than it was time for him to go home and that he trusted her good judgment in choosing a husband.

She accepted Griff's decision the only way she knew how—with a calm, serene outward appearance. She vowed to devote every second of the next weeks to finding a husband who would put a roof over her head and provide a generous dowry for Becca.

If she searched diligently enough, she was certain she could find a man who was desperate enough for a wife.

One who wouldn't care if she no longer had a heart to give him.

# Chapter 14

✤

$\mathcal{G}$riff made his way down the dark, deserted London streets. When he was sure no one was following him, he turned down the familiar narrow alley that would take him to the office of British Foreign Intelligence. He had left as soon as he received the message from Colonel Fitzhugh asking to meet him.

When he reached the well-concealed entrance, he opened the door and entered. After locking the door behind him, he walked down the hallway to the colonel's office. He knocked twice, then waited and knocked again before opening the door.

"I'd almost given up on you," Fitzhugh said, laying his spectacles on the desk and rubbing his eyes.

"I wanted to make certain I wasn't followed." Griff sat down in the chair facing Fitzhugh's desk and stretched out his legs.

"Were you?"

"No. Sometimes I think this is all my imagination. Maybe it *was* a robber who killed Freddie, and I've spent too much time working intelligence to tell the difference between an ordinary robbery attempt and something else."

"And maybe not."

Griff focused his attention on the colonel. "What have you learned?"

"Nothing I'm certain means anything, yet something I wish I'd never discovered."

Griff took the sheets of paper Fitzhugh handed him and moved his chair closer to the desk so the glow from the lamp would light the words enough to read what they said. He skimmed the report first, then went back and read it slowly. A lump formed in his chest with every sentence.

"I don't believe this."

"Neither do I," Fitzhugh said, breathing a deep sigh. "At least I don't want to, but if this information is right, it opens the door to a lot of questions. And a lot of conjectures."

"Why didn't we know this before?"

"I don't know. Maybe he lied. Maybe he didn't want anyone to know."

Griff looked at the information one more time, thinking that if he stared at it long enough, it would change, that the words would disappear that told them that one of the intelligence agents they'd executed as a spy was Jack Hawkins's brother.

Griff raked his fingers through his hair. Jack Hawkins had been a fellow agent with him. He'd saved his life more than once. He'd jumped in front of an attacking Russian soldier and been injured himself. He couldn't believe that same man was capable of trying to kill him. Or that he'd been the one who'd killed Freddie.

"What do you want me to do with this?" Fitzhugh asked.

Griff looked at the paper one more time, then held it over the lamp until it caught fire. "Nothing. Do you think if Jack Hawkins wanted me dead, I'd still be alive to wonder when he was going to do it right? He's too good. He wouldn't have missed me and killed Freddie instead."

"But we executed his brother as a spy, and *you* were the one who captured him and brought him in."

Griff bolted from the chair and paced the cramped room. "But Hawkins wouldn't play it out like this. If he wanted revenge, he'd have had it by now."

"Maybe he's getting his revenge. Maybe he's methodically killing anyone you get close to."

A feeling of dread sucked the air from his chest. He couldn't believe Jack Hawkins hated him that much, and yet...Griff *had* been responsible for his brother's death. Blood was often a much closer bond than even patriotism.

Griff took a deep breath. With a shaky sigh, he focused on Fitzhugh. "I want you to pretend you never saw that report. I won't have a good man's reputation questioned because of my gut instincts. Hawkins's never done anything to make us question him. I'm not going to start now."

"What if you're wrong?"

"I'm not. Hell, other than the bullet that killed Freddie, there hasn't even been another attempt. Maybe I'm being paranoid."

"And maybe the other agents following you have kept you alive."

Griff felt like he'd taken a sucker punch to the gut. "It isn't Hawkins. I know it isn't."

Griff walked to the door and lifted the latch. "I don't want Hawkins to know we found out about this."

"Very well. But watch your back," Fitzhugh warned.

He gave Fitzhugh a smile. "Johnston, Turner, and Hawkins are doing that."

Griff left Fitzhugh's office and made his way to the quiet street, where only an occasional carriage carrying some late-night revelers home from a ball or party intruded on his thoughts. He didn't want to think that Jack Hawkins could have killed Fespoint and Freddie. Just like he didn't want to think about Anne. But he couldn't stop himself. He wondered what she was doing, where she'd been, who she'd been with.

It had been nearly a week since he'd seen her. Perhaps she'd already found the man she intended to marry. The breath caught in his throat.

He walked slowly, not caring how soon he got home. There was nothing waiting for him in his empty town house, nothing except memories of the way Anne had looked the last time he'd seen her—and an ever-present craving for a drink.

He pushed that thought from his mind and concentrated on Anne. He could still feel her in his arms, still feel her lips pressed against his, and her arms wrapped around his neck as if she never wanted to be separated from him.

Bloody hell! If only he'd never kissed her. What a fool he'd been. But he'd wanted her so badly he hadn't been able to stop himself. And she'd wanted him. It was obvious by the way she answered his kisses. In the way she held him, and touched him, and moaned when he deepened his kiss.

But when the kiss was over, a ton of guilt pressed down on him until he couldn't breathe. How could he have been so selfish to take advantage of her like that when he knew nothing could come of it? When he knew loving him was a death sentence for anyone foolish enough to take the risk?

Julia, Andrew, Fespoint, and Freddie had already given their lives because of him. They were all dead and it was his fault. And now he'd taken an even greater risk and involved her.

It had been wise to move out of Adam's town house. The sooner she found someone and was safely married, the sooner he could resign himself to having lost her.

He made his way up the steps to his town house and let himself in the door. He'd instructed his butler, Childers, not to wait up for him. He preferred to be alone. He wanted to sit in the dark and gather strength from the soft, gentle voice he remembered from the days he'd spent driving the liquor from his body. He knew he'd been hallucinating, but it was almost as if Julia had been there, holding his hand, talking to him, taking care of him.

He made his way to his study and sat before the lifeless embers in the grate. It was times like these that he allowed himself to think of the past. Times like now that he opened the door to the precious people from his past—the special people he'd lost. There had been too many.

He closed his eyes and struggled to remember the person he'd loved most—Julia. His heart ached when he thought of her, and that ache refused to go away. Dear God, but he missed her. She'd been his wife. He'd loved her.

But her memory seemed to fade with each passing day. There were even times when he feared he'd lost her.

She'd been gone four years now, and sometimes it was difficult to remember what she'd looked like.

The face he thought he would never forget was now a blurry memory. And her features were being replaced by a picture of Anne's smiling lips and laughing eyes.

# Chapter 15

❧

*A*nne sat on the end of the sofa and kept a smile on her face for the sake of pretense. She joined in the conversation frequently enough not to draw attention to herself, but not more than was required of her.

The room was full again today, five suitors who'd come to beg a moment of her time and request either the honor of a dance at the next ball or an afternoon ride through Hyde Park. The attention she received even after all these weeks still astounded her. She never thought she'd be so popular. She was still puzzled that she was.

There was nothing extraordinary about her. She wasn't a great beauty and she wouldn't come to her marriage with any landholdings or accumulated wealth. She had only the gowns Mr. Blackmoor had purchased for her.

Anne stiffened her shoulders and focused again on the suitors who'd come to pay her court. She wasn't going to question her good fortune or her acceptance since coming to London. Time was running out. She needed to find a husband soon.

She acknowledged their invitations, one and all. How was she to find a husband if she had no one to choose from? How was she to find a husband if she allowed herself to crawl into hiding like she wanted?

The emptiness in her chest ached more painfully. Memories haunted her continually. All she had to do was close her eyes and she would see his dark, handsome face in front of her, feel his arms around her and his lips pressed against hers. How had this happened?

How had she fallen in love with him when he was the last man on earth she wanted to love? How, when he obviously disliked her so much? It wasn't something she'd planned, something she'd let happen intentionally. If only she hadn't let him kiss her, hadn't kissed him back. If only she hadn't gone to him when he was ill—hadn't talked to him and held his hand and told him that she loved him.

If only she hadn't come to care for him so much. If only she had a home to go to where she could hide until this didn't hurt so much. If only...

But there were no more *if onlys*. There were only the facts. And the fact was, Griffin Blackmoor regretted kissing her. He'd found it so distasteful that he'd moved out of the earl's town house so he wouldn't have to look at her or be around her or be reminded of what he'd done.

She looked at the five men sitting across from her. Lord Benchley was here again today, as well as the Marquess of Candlewood, Baron Fillmore, and Lord Jamison. And again, for the first time since that first week, the Earl of Portsmouth had come.

The earl was older than the others, perhaps a score and more, but he was still very handsome. He seemed a quiet gentleman with a sharp mind and a pleasant personality. His hair was graying, which gave him a distinguished look, but his eyes still contained the sharpness of youth. They were filled with a natural humor she didn't often see. He was tall, and there was not an ounce of excess flesh around his middle.

Anne felt very comfortable around him, and she had to admit that the qualities he offered her would not challenge or threaten her. He was someone whose company she could learn to enjoy. Perhaps she might eventually learn to appreciate him in a special way.

Griff would not approve of him.

"My lady, you have another guest. The Marquess of Brentwood."

Anne watched the man who now held Freddie's title enter the room.

There was a slight commotion while the five guests who'd been there longer than was polite said their farewells and left. Then, only Brentwood stood before them.

He greeted Patience first, then stepped in front of her. He held her hand longer than necessary and Anne couldn't stop herself from pulling her fingers from his grasp. A stabbing of discomfort pierced her.

"My dear Lady Anne." He took the seat directly across from her, where he couldn't help but focus on her every move. "I have been extremely concerned for your welfare. I called the minute I arrived in London to be assured that you were well."

She smiled. "As you can see, I am doing splendidly. Lord and Lady Covington have graciously opened their home to me and have invited me to stay with them for the Season."

"Do you have plans after that?"

She felt her cheeks warm. She refused to admit her quest to find a husband. "I haven't decided."

"I did not mean to offend, my lady." He looked remorseful. "I am simply anxious. You and your sister are my only living relatives. I couldn't live with myself if I thought that you were in need and I hadn't come to your aid."

"Let me assure you, Lord Brentwood," Patience said, placing her hand over Anne's. "Lady Anne is not in need. She knows she is more than welcome to stay with us for as long as she wishes."

"How gracious of you and your husband." He returned his gaze to Anne. "I wish you would have told me that you were coming to London the last time we spoke. I would have been more than happy to let you stay in the Brentwood town house."

She shook her head. She couldn't imagine spending even one night in the house that used to belong to Freddie—the house where the new earl might appear at any moment.

"As a matter of fact," Brentwood continued, sipping on the tea Patience had poured, "I realized there are a number of items that might be of value to you. Mementos and personal keepsakes that your brother kept at his London residence. I would like you to have them."

His words gave her pause. "Thank you, my lord. That is very gracious of you."

"Nonsense. I am only staying in town a few more days. Perhaps you could come tomorrow afternoon and gather anything that is of value to you, and I will have it sent here before I return to the country."

She looked at Patience, then back at Brentwood. "I would be most grateful. Perhaps tomorrow at three?"

Brentwood nodded. "I will expect you then." He placed his cup and saucer on the table in front of him and rose.

"Before I take my leave, I would beg a few minutes of your time in private, Lady Anne. Perhaps a walk in the garden would not be inappropriate."

"I—I don't—" she stammered.

"Please. It is important."

She gave Patience a look that told her to come to her rescue if she was gone too long. "Very well. For just a moment."

She rose and walked with him out to the garden. They strolled down the flowered paths in silence for a while before he said anything.

"I know we did not part on amiable terms before you left the country, my lady, and I want to apologize for my actions that day. They were inexcusable. My only explanation is that I was overcome by your charm and beauty, and was not myself. I deeply regret my forwardness and promise I will never behave so rudely again."

He stopped near a bench and waited for her to sit. She reluctantly sat. She did not like having to look up at him. It was a very intimidating experience.

"Although I handled our conversation very badly before, the one thing about our last meeting I do not regret was that I asked you to be my wife."

"Lord Brentwood—"

"Please, hear me out. I know your reason for coming to London is to procure a husband. In your position that is indeed a wise course to take. However, as I explained before, I am in need of a wife, and have found myself quite taken by you. I beg you to reconsider my offer and agree to marry me."

"I couldn't possibly accept—"

"Please, don't make too rash a decision. I realize the staggering dowry that goes with your hand is almost a hindrance, but you can be assured that I have no interest in the money. It is only you that I want."

The breath caught in her throat. "My dowry? But I do not have a dowry," she whispered. "You know what I was left."

Brentwood gave her a look that indicated he intended to call her bluff. "Everyone knows how much Mr. Blackmoor put on your hand, Lady Anne. Such an amount would entice half the male populace of London Society who are searching for a bride."

She clasped the edge of the stone bench to keep her balance. "Mr. Blackmoor provided me with a dowry?"

"Enough to make you the catch of the Season."

She felt the blood rush from her head. No wonder she'd received such attention. The thought almost made her laugh. Not only did Blackmoor not want her, but he thought she would be such a valueless commodity that no one else would be interested in her either. Not unless she came with a hefty purse.

"I know how very fond you were of your country estate," Brentwood continued. "By marrying me, you would be assured of remaining in your childhood home forever. I am the perfect choice, Lady Anne. I already believe the two of us are well suited to each other, and in time, will develop a certain fondness that will be quite pleasant."

Anne felt as if her head were going to explode. She wanted nothing more than to rub her fingers against her temples and pretend none of this was happening.

"Lord Brentwood," she began, keeping her voice pleasant yet firm. "Let me first state how flattered I am by your offer. There is nowhere on earth for which I hold greater fondness than Brentwood Manor. I grew up there. Every memory from my childhood is connected there. Which is exactly the reason why I could never spend the rest of my life there. It contains too many memories."

"Then we can live somewhere else."

"No. Brentwood Manor is yours. It is a wonderful home, a place where the wife you choose can make a life for the two of you. Where the two of you can raise your children, and look forward to your grandchildren."

"But you and I—"

"No, Lord Brentwood. There is no *you and I*. I am flattered by your offer, but I will not marry you."

The look in his eyes turned hard. A stabbing of wariness raced through her. For a moment he appeared dangerous.

"There is nothing I can say to change your mind?"

"No. I will not be swayed in this."

His face turned red. The veins at the side of his neck stood out. "I will bid you a good day then, my lady."

"I am sorry, Lord Brentwood. My intent was not to hurt you. Perhaps it would be best if I did not come to your town house tomorrow," she said when he turned away from her.

He stopped but did not look at her. "No. Please come. I intended to leave for the country later tomorrow afternoon. I will change my plans and leave first thing in the morning to avoid the embarrassment of meeting again. I will inform the butler that you will arrive at three o'clock to pick up your personal belongings. Take whatever you want."

"Thank you, Lord Brentwood."

His hands remained fisted at his side. "Good day, my lady."

She sat on the bench a long time after he left, fearing she would be ill.

Mr. Blackmoor had offered a sizable dowry for her. It was no wonder the drawing room was filled each day with suitors. But none of them were interested in her. They only wanted the money that would come with her.

The pressure in her chest weighed with painful heaviness, and she hurt more at that moment than she had hurt since they'd brought Freddie's body home. If Griffin Blackmoor were here now, she wasn't sure what she'd do. But she was certain he would not survive it.

At first she thought she might cry, but her eyes remained dry. The time for tears was past. She was too numb to feel any more pain, too numb to wish for her life to be different.

"Are you all right?" Patience asked when she reached the bench where Anne still sat. "Lord Brentwood did not seem pleased when he left."

"No. He offered me marriage and I refused him."

"I see."

"May I ask you a question, Patience? Something I'd like you to keep just between the two of us?"

Patience hesitated a moment, then answered. "If it is that important."

"It is." Anne needed to know. She had to find out if there was one man, just one, who had vied for her hand who did not need the money.

"Of all the men who have called on me in the past few weeks, is there one of them who is wealthy in his own right?"

Patience hesitated as if to consider an answer to Anne's question. "I'm not sure I can answer that, Anne. Adam would be a much better source to find out finances than I am."

"I do not need to know how much they are worth. Only if they have enough wealth to support me."

"Well, they are not all on the verge of bankruptcy, if that's what you are asking. It's just that some of them are supposedly more solvent than others. A handsome dowry would benefit all of them, I believe. With the exception, of course, of the Earl of Portsmouth."

"The earl does not need money?"

"Good heavens, no. He is as rich as Croesus and could probably buy and sell each of the others in the room today ten times over."

"So if the earl were looking for a wife, the size of her dowry would not influence him one way or another?"

Patience shook her head. "I would venture that the earl wouldn't care if his bride came to him in rags."

"Thank you," Anne whispered.

She finally knew what path she would take. The only path Blackmoor had left her.

# Chapter 16

❧

Griff paced the room like a trapped animal. "No, Adam. I won't do it. You take her."

"I can't. The prime minister is holding a special meeting to discuss overseas trade regulations. I have to be there."

Griff slapped his hand against his thigh. "Find someone else."

"No!" Adam pounded his fist on the top of his desk. "I agreed to keep Lady Anne under my roof and sponsor her in Society. My promise did not absolve you from any association with her. You are obligated to do at least this much."

Griff started to turn away, but Patience's gentle voice stopped him.

"Please, Griff. There is no one else I would trust. I've already explained how upset Brentwood was when he left yesterday. It is imperative that you accompany Lady Anne to get her personal items from her brother's house."

Griff walked to the window and braced his hands on either side of the frame. "I'm certain Lady Anne would rather go alone than have me anywhere near her."

"She needs you, Griff," Patience said. "It will be hard enough just going to her brother's town house so soon after his death. Going through his personal belongings will be even more difficult."

"You don't know what you're asking," Griff said on a sigh. "We didn't part on exactly the best of terms."

Patience walked across the room and placed a hand on his arm. "I gathered as much. There is a sadness in her eyes that wasn't there before you left. I've tried to get her to confide in me, but she refuses."

Griff dropped his head between his outstretched hands. "I was afraid she was beginning to care for me."

"And that would have been so terrible?"

Griff turned. "Do you think I want to risk another person's life?"

"It's not your fault Julia drowned, Griff." Patience's voice contained compassion and understanding. "It was an act of nature. There was nothing you could have done to save her."

"I could have left her at home. She didn't want to go with me, but I forced her. And now she's dead."

Patience brushed a tear from her eyes. "So you punish yourself every day because you didn't die with them? Because you are alive and they aren't? Have you ever thought that there might be a reason you survived? That there is a reason you didn't die during that storm? A reason that you survived the war, even though you took every risk imaginable? That you survived after you returned, even though you tried to drink yourself to death? That maybe there is someone here and now who needs you alive? Have you ever thought that it might be the person you're trying to ignore?"

"I can't chance caring for someone, then losing them." His voice was little more than a whisper. "I can't go through that pain again."

"Then I feel sorry for you, Griff. There are no guarantees against pain in this life. But if you do not let yourself love, you will have put your heart in an empty box and sealed it shut. You will have missed out on every blessing life can grant you."

"And I will have spared myself the pain. You don't know, Patience. You've never lost someone you thought you could not live without."

"No. And I pray I never do. I know losing Julia and Andrew was horrible, Griff. But you can't spend the rest of your life punishing yourself and pushing away anyone who gets close to you."

"Falling in love is not a risk I'm willing to take. Not with Anne."

"Do you think you're the only one taking a risk? The only one who has something to lose if you risk your heart? You aren't. This isn't easy for Anne, either. I think you're right. I think she does care for you. Much more than she wants to. What kind of a risk do you think she's taking, losing her heart to someone who throws her gift back in her face?"

"I'm doing what I must in order to protect her."

Adam entered the conversation. "No, you're not. You're refusing to admit how you feel because you're afraid."

Griff focused on Adam's unwavering gaze, but not without a great deal of effort. He didn't like what his brother said because his words were true. He was afraid. Afraid to risk his heart and have it broken.

"Whether you like it or not," Adam said without any softness, "Lady Anne is *your* responsibility. If you care for her at all, you won't let her go through this alone."

Griff turned away from where Patience stood by her husband. Adam was not going to budge on this. "What time did Lady Anne intend to leave?"

"A quarter to three."

"Then we'd best get this over with. I have a feeling it won't be pleasant for either of us."

Griff walked through the door, dreading the first meeting with her. He knew he'd hurt her, but he'd had no choice. How else could he stop what was happening between them? How else could he protect her from thinking she could be happy with him, when she probably wouldn't live long enough to find happiness?

He opened the door to the parlor, ready to face her indifference. Ready to steel himself against the shadowed hurt and sadness he knew he'd caused. He was not, however, ready to challenge the raw anger he saw on her face, nor to battle the fire that blazed in her eyes when she glared at him.

"Griff has graciously offered to escort you in my place, Anne," Adam announced from the doorway. "I have an obligation I cannot ignore, or I would take you myself."

Her cheeks flushed with color, her jaw clenched with determination. "Mr. Blackmoor doesn't have to trouble himself. I'd rather wait until it's convenient for you to escort me, my lord."

Griff tried to ignore the frigid chill that engulfed the room and not let her words affect him. He kept his voice steady and showed as little emotion as possible. "That's not necessary, my lady. I'm here. We might as well get this over and done today. Adam tells me Brentwood will be out of the house. From the first meeting you had with him in the country, and your meeting with him here yesterday, I think it's best he's not around when you are."

"I would rather go alone," she answered.

"That's not a possibility."

"Then it's not necessary for me to go. I'm sure there aren't that many items of importance."

"Would you like me to accompany you and Griff?" Patience asked, her words a conciliatory offering.

Anne turned away from him. "Yes, please. If I must go today, would you mind?"

"No. Not at all."

Griff braced his shoulders. "Very well. The three of us will go. Adam," he said, turning to his brother, "have a couple of your men meet us at Brentwood's with a wagon."

Adam nodded, then issued the order to Fenwick, who stood just beyond the door.

"Are you ladies ready, then?" he asked, not letting his gaze linger on her any longer than necessary. The sight of her made his heart pound in his chest. The defiant look in her eyes issued a warning. This Anne was not the warm, accepting woman he'd held in his arms and kissed the last time he'd seen her. This woman was furious. She'd been hurt too deeply and wanted to lash out at him.

They walked to the foyer where Fenwick and a maid waited with bonnets and light wraps for the ladies. Even though he made certain he was there to escort her down the steps, she walked ahead of him and made her way to the waiting carriage without any help.

She accepted a footman's assistance and climbed the two steps into the carriage. Once inside, she insisted that Patience sit beside her. He sat alone on the opposite side.

He did not know which was worse. Having her sit beside him, where her nearness would drive him to distraction, or having her sit across from him, where he had nowhere to focus his gaze but on her beautiful features, her long, graceful neck and upturned nose. And her white-knuckled hands fisted in her lap.

She didn't look at him once. Neither did she join in the stilted conversation Patience tried to initiate. Instead, she kept her head turned and her eyes riveted on the passing scenery.

When at last the driver pulled up in front of the town house, Griff hastily exited the carriage to escape the explosive tension inside the small enclosure.

"I'm sorry, sir," the driver, Carney, said when Griff exited. "I couldn't pull the carriage up in front of the house because of the vehicles already blocking the street. One of the houses nearby must be entertaining. I had to park on the opposite side."

"That will do, Carney. We can manage the short distance across the street."

He held out his hand when the ladies descended. Patience exited first. She gave him a sympathetic smile, then walked out of sight around the carriage. Anne came next. He knew if she could have managed the steps in her wide, cumbersome skirts without his assistance, she would have done so. She would have done anything to avoid having to touch him, or look at him, or be near him.

He couldn't let her continue like this. The next few hours were going to be difficult enough without the barrier she'd erected between them.

"Anne?" he said, before she reached the side of the carriage.

She stopped but did not turn around. "Did you need something, sir?"

"I don't want it to be like this between us." He stepped closer to her.

She turned, her anger obviously boiling near the surface. "And how would you like it to be, Mr. Blackmoor?"

Patience had already crossed the street and they were alone. He wanted to console her but had no answer. He didn't know how he wanted it to be between them. But whatever it was, he did not want it like this.

"None of what happened the other night was your fault. You did nothing for which to feel ashamed."

"Ashamed? You think what I feel is shame?" She fisted her hands even tighter at her sides, if that were possible, and took a step toward him. "I have one question I would like you to answer, Mr. Blackmoor, and it has nothing to do with the kiss we shared."

He looked into her eyes and fought the urge to take her in his arms and hold her. He wanted to tell her he wished he hadn't hurt her, but he didn't get the chance. Her next words hit him like a battering ram that slammed into his gut.

"Just how big a dowry did you think it would take to force someone to marry me? How much money did you offer to ensure that someone would be desperate enough to take me off your hands?"

The air left his lungs. How the bloody hell had she found out about the dowry? What fool had told her?

He struggled to find the right words. "I didn't provide the dowry because I thought you couldn't attract suitors who would want you, but because I wanted to show Society how valuable I considered you to be."

"And that is why you kept the dowry a secret from me? Because you thought I would be so impressed by your opinion of my worth?"

"I kept it a secret because of what is happening right now. I knew you wouldn't understand what I'd done and would misconstrue my intentions."

She took one step closer to him. "Misconstrue your intentions? I think I understand them quite accurately."

She stopped long enough to gather her control. "You don't have to worry, sir. I don't need your dowry. I have no intention of taking one pound from you. You have provided me with the chance to find a husband. Your obligation to Freddie is paid in full."

"The dowry is already set. It will go to whomever you marry."

"No! Even though you are convinced I cannot manage without your help, I intend to find a husband on my own. A husband who does not want the dowry you heaped on me. You can be assured your money will not have paid for the man I marry."

She turned to leave, then stopped. "One more thing, Mr. Blackmoor. I know you consider kissing me a dreadful mistake. But just know, I regret what happened between us a thousand times more than you. But not because I thought it was so terrible. You see, I kissed you because I thought you were worth the risk. And I paid dearly for my error in judgment. You took something from me I will never get back. A part of me I didn't even realize I was guarding with such care, or realize I would miss so desperately when it was gone."

"I'm sor—"

"Don't you dare say you're sorry!" She slashed her hand through the air. "I don't want to hear any more inept excuses to absolve your guilt-ridden conscience. I have lived with the regrets long enough. You can, too."

With that, she turned and walked away from him.

He followed but not too closely. There was no use stopping her. There was nothing more for him to say.

If he hadn't been so angry with himself, he would have paid closer attention to their surroundings. He would have noticed the carriage that barreled down the cobblestoned street toward them sooner. He would have seen it before it was practically on top of them. Would have been able to reach her before it was too late.

"Anne!"

He dove for her, barely missing being run over by the wheels of the black carriage himself. But he couldn't reach her in time to pull her out of the way.

The carriage didn't run over her, he was sure it hadn't, but he knew she'd been struck. Perhaps by one of the horses.

He heard her scream of surprise, then saw her being tossed through the air. She landed with a hard thud.

She lay in the street, her body curved at an odd angle, like a broken doll.

"Anne!" He fell beside her on the cobblestones. Her head was turned to the side, her eyes closed. A red welt already marred her perfect features, where her face had hit the cobblestones.

Griff touched her cheek, then put his face next to hers. Her breathing was shallow, but warm, moist air hit his cheek. She was still alive. He felt her arms and legs and ribs to check for anything broken but found nothing.

"Griff! Anne!" Patience raced across the street and knelt beside them. "Is she all right?"

With trembling fingers, Griff brushed the hair from Anne's face. "I don't know. She's not conscious. She must have hit her head." He removed her bonnet and placed his hand at the back of her head. Warm, sticky liquid oozed through his fingers.

He ripped his cravat from around his neck and pressed it behind her head. "Carney," he ordered the driver who'd come running up behind him. "Pull the carriage close. We have to get her home."

"Yes, sir."

Griff heard the sound of heavy boots racing toward him and looked up.

"I'm sorry, Griff. I lost him."

Griff stared into Jack Hawkins's face. His expression was unreadable. His chest heaved from exertion.

"I saw the carriage coming but was too far away to warn you."

"Did you recognize him?"

Hawkins shook his head. "No." He looked down at Anne. "What can I do?"

Griff picked her up in his arms, trying not to notice how much blood had soaked his cravat. "We have to get her home. Follow us?"

Hawkins nodded, then helped Griff lift Anne into the carriage. The minute the door closed, the carriage took off with a lurch. Griff cradled Anne close to him. He was desperate to have her near him.

The trip home seemed to take an eternity, but within minutes, they were there.

"Send someone for Dr. Thornton, Fenwick," he ordered as he carried Anne up the stairs. "And tell him to come as quickly as possible."

Patience climbed the stairs close behind him, and raced ahead to pull the covers back on Anne's bed.

Griff gently laid her on the bed, then looked up at a pale Patience. "We'll need water and cloths and a clean nightgown. Then tell Fenwick to find a bottle of brandy. She may need it when she wakes."

Patience raced from the room to get what they would need.

Griff tossed his bloody cravat to the floor then hastily undid the tiny buttons on the bodice of her gown. She didn't move. Griff wasn't even sure she was still breathing. If only she would move, or moan, or make a sound. Anything. Then he wouldn't be so afraid.

He worked frantically, pulling the buttons off as his anxiety for her increased. At last the bodice of her gown was open, revealing her smooth, creamy breasts trapped beneath the corset. He reached for the laces.

"What are you doing?" Patience said, rushing back into the room, her cheeks flushed a bright red.

"We need to get her clothes off," Griff said, placing a fresh cloth against the back of her head.

Patience ran across the room and called for two maids to help her. "You can't stay here while we undress her, Griff. Leave long enough for us to put her in a clean gown."

Griff hesitated, then breathed a heavy sigh and gave in. "Hurry, Patience."

"We will."

Griff left the room. The minute they finished, he raced back to her side.

She was dressed in a clean, white cotton gown with pink embroidered flowers on the bodice. A thin blanket covered her. She was breathing but still unconscious.

"When do you think she'll wake?" Patience asked, the worry in her voice echoing the terror building inside him.

"I don't know. It can be like this sometimes with a hard blow to the head."

He took another cloth and dipped it in water, then held it against her forehead. She was pale and so horribly lifeless. "Annie," he whispered in her ear. "Can you hear me? I want you to wake up. Can you open your eyes?"

He stroked his fingers down her cheek and kept the damp cloth against her forehead. He was cold inside, as cold as he'd ever been in his life. As cold as fear could make a person. He brushed his lips against her cheek and talked to her. Finally, the door opened, and Dr. Thornton entered. He stopped at the side of the bed.

"What happened?" He touched Anne's forehead with his hand, then placed his fingers against her neck.

"She was struck by a carriage. She has a cut on the back of her head, but I think the bleeding has stopped."

"Let's take a look."

Thornton removed the towel Griff had pressed against her, then turned her head so he could examine the wound. "Griff, why don't you step outside for a moment while I examine Lady Anne."

Griff hesitated, but Patience placed her hand on his shoulder and squeezed. "Go on outside, Griff. Dr. Thornton will call if he needs anything."

"I'll be right outside the door."

"That's fine," the doctor said, already starting his examination.

Griff walked into the hall and dropped his head to his hands. Why hadn't he seen the carriage coming? Why hadn't he paid more attention to what was going on around him? How could he have forgotten how dangerous it was for anyone to be near him? Griff wasn't sure how he'd manage if Anne didn't survive.

The wait took an eternity, but finally Patience opened the door. Griff rushed into the room and went to Anne's side.

"We're going to have to put a few stitches in that cut," Dr. Thornton said. "Help me turn her over, Griff."

Griff carefully lifted her. She suddenly seemed very fragile. The doctor cut the hair around the gash, then pushed the threaded needle through her flesh. Griff's mind echoed a fervent prayer with each stitch.

When Thornton finished, Griff laid her back down and covered her with the blanket.

"Other than her head," Dr. Thornton said, putting a pillow beneath her, "she doesn't seem to be injured. Just a scraped knee and a bruise on her hip where she must have hit the cobblestones."

"When will she wake up?"

The doctor shook his head. "I don't know. Maybe in an hour. Maybe a day. There's no way of knowing."

"So, now what?"

"We'll watch her. We should know more by tomorrow."

"Tomorrow?"

"I know it's difficult, but sometimes these things take time."

Griff touched his fingers to Anne's face.

"She'll be fine now, Griff," Dr. Thornton said, checking his patient again. "I suggest we all have a cup of tea. Lady Covington, perhaps one of the servants can sit with her until we return."

"No. I'll stay." Griff looked down on Anne's pale complexion. He couldn't leave her.

"Very well," Patience said, as if realizing it was useless to argue with him. "I'll have one of the maids stay here with you."

Griff nodded as the maid Dolly busied herself on the other side of the room.

"Griff," Patience said from the doorway. "I nearly forgot. That young man who followed us home from the accident is waiting downstairs."

"Send him up. I'll talk to him here."

When they left, Griff pulled a chair beside the bed and sat down. He reached for Anne's hand and held it, gently rubbing his thumb over her fingers. "I'm right here, Anne. I won't leave you. You rest now and when you're ready, you can open your eyes and yell at me all you want."

He placed his hand on her forehead and gently brushed her hair from her face.

"Griff?"

Griff turned as Jack Hawkins entered the room. Was this the man who'd fired the bullet that had killed Freddie, and hired the carriage that ran Anne down? His blood boiled when he thought it might be, but he didn't want to believe it. He couldn't. This was the man who'd saved his life twice during the war.

When Jack Hawkins stopped at the foot of the bed, Griff got up from his chair and went to where he stood.

"How is she?" Jack asked.

"Still unconscious. I keep thinking that if I talk to her, she'll hear my voice and wake up."

Jack Hawkins nodded.

"Did you see anything, Jack? Anything that might give us a clue as to who tried to run me down?"

"No. I was too far away. I didn't see the carriage move until it was too late."

Griff clenched his hands into tight, angry fists. "Damn! Why doesn't the bastard just kill me and have it over?"

Jack Hawkins didn't answer Griff but stared down at Anne's still body lying beneath the covers. After a long silence, he took in a huge breath that expanded his chest and turned so he was eye to eye with Griff.

"Griff?"

Griff took in the serious expression on Jack's face.

"I don't think you're the person anyone wants to kill." Hawkins lowered his gaze to where Anne lay on the bed. "I think the driver ran down the person he intended to hit. I think someone wants the lady dead."

# Chapter 17

✤

*J*f there was ever a time in his life that he wanted a drink, it was now.

Griff bolted from the chair where he'd sat for the past eight hours and paced the room. The drapes were open and the light from the full, bright moon shone through the windowpanes onto the bed where she lay.

He wasn't sure he could sit here without a drink in his hand hour after bloody hour without knowing if she would live or not, without knowing if she would ever wake. He wanted just one drink so he could make it through this. Then he would need a second drink, and a third, and even that would not guarantee he could forget the terrified expression on her face when she saw the carriage careening toward her. A drink would not help him forget her frightened scream, or the sight of her fragile body being thrown through the air and landing on the cobblestones. There wasn't enough liquor in the whole of England to make him forget the terror that raged through him.

*Just stay with me. I'll help you.*

The soft, whispered words that had been his comfort since he'd stopped drinking echoed in his mind. He held her hand as if he could make those words come true for her.

Except for the few minutes it had taken him to wash and change out of his bloodstained clothes, he'd refused to leave her bedside. Patience had sent up a tray of food earlier, but he'd hardly touched it. Even Adam eventually gave up trying to bully him into eating or getting some rest.

Jack Hawkins's words raced through his head. *I don't think you're the person anyone wants to kill. I think the driver ran down the person he intended to hit.*

Griff lifted her delicate hand in his. That couldn't be true. Who would want Anne dead? Who could possibly want to harm her?

His mind went back to Jack Hawkins. What if Griff had judged him wrong? What if the report was true, and Hawkins wanted revenge because Griff had been responsible for his brother's death? What if Hawkins had been the driver of the carriage and Anne had gotten in the way? His made-up story about the driver wanting to hit Anne would certainly add confusion about what Griff thought he saw, and steer the attention away from Hawkins.

"Anne," he whispered again, gently brushing back a wisp of hair that had fallen across her forehead. "Ah, Annie."

The pressure in his chest grew painfully tight and he looked at her gentle features. No. There was no way anyone could want to hurt her. Just like her brother, she didn't have an enemy in the world. It was him. He was the one the killer wanted. As he'd been the one the killer had been after when Freddie had been shot.

Griff knew it would not end until either he or the killer was dead. And anyone who got in the way would get hurt. He never should have put her in such danger.

An icy chill raced through his veins. Could that have been the reason she'd been run over? Because someone thought she was important to him? Because someone hated him so much that they would kill anyone close to him? Like Freddie? Like her?

His breath came out on a shuddered sigh. Surely not. Surely no one was that cold-blooded. But he knew it was possible. And if making him suffer was the reason Anne had been run over, he had to make sure he kept as far away from her as possible. And Adam, and Patience, and the boys. He did not want to think who might be next.

He rose to his feet and paced the room, struggling to keep his fear at bay. As soon as he was sure she was all right, he would leave her. He would stay in the open to make himself a target. With Fitzhugh's help, they would ferret out the killer. If he survived, he would decide then what to do. *If* he survived...

He raked his fingers through his hair and tried not to think about the future.

"What time is it?"

Griff's heart skipped a beat, and he turned toward the bed. She was awake.

"The clock downstairs just struck three. You've taken quite a long nap, my lady."

"Were you worried I would sleep away the rest of my life?"

He sat in the chair and gathered one of her hands in his. "Silly of me, wasn't it?"

"Yes," she answered, but her voice sounded weak. "Hardly worth the effort."

"I will be the judge of that. Can I get you anything?"

"Some water. I'm terribly thirsty."

Griff picked up the glass Dr. Thornton had left on the bedside table, then placed his hand behind her shoulders and helped her up. She moaned in pain the minute he lifted her.

"I hurt all over."

"I know. Drink this. It will make you feel better."

"What is it?"

"I don't know. But Dr. Thornton said you were to drink it the minute you woke. He said it would help the pain."

"I think my head is going to split open," she whispered, touching the side of her head, then grimacing as another wave of pain hit her.

"Drink it, Anne."

He lifted it to her mouth and helped her tip the glass until all the liquid was gone. "Now, lie back down and stay still. But don't go to sleep. Dr. Thornton said under no circumstances were you to go back to sleep. Are you still awake?"

"Yes," she said with her eyes closed. "I'm awake. But it hurts too much to keep my eyes open."

"Then close your eyes, but don't go to sleep."

She mumbled something he couldn't understand, but he was so thankful she was awake, he didn't care. She repeated it anyway.

"What happened to me?"

He hesitated. "How much do you remember?"

"I'm not sure. I remember our argument, and walking away from you. And then...there was a carriage coming down the street. I couldn't get out of the way soon enough."

"You were thrown to the side of the road and landed on the cobblestones. You hit your head. Dr. Thornton had to sew the cut in your head."

Her eyes flew open. "Did he have to cut my hair?"

"Only a little. As long as you wear your hair loose, no one will notice."

She breathed a sigh of relief. "That is vain of me, isn't it?"

He laughed. "Yes, terribly. But I'll excuse you this once."

"Thank you." She relaxed against the pillows and closed her eyes. "Have you been here the whole time?"

He sat back in his chair. "Yes. I drew the short stick."

"How unlucky of you."

"It's all right. I couldn't sleep anyway."

"Griff?"

"Yes." He leaned forward to straighten her covers. His fingers brushed against hers and a warm shot raced through him. He pulled his hand away and sat back.

"You must not blame yourself."

He stiffened. "I don't know what you mean."

"Yes, you do. You're blaming yourself for what happened."

"And how do you know it wasn't my fault?"

"I just do."

"Did you see anything that might help us recognize the driver?"

"No. By the time I realized what was happening, the carriage was nearly on top of me. I remember thinking it was aiming for me on purpose. I know it couldn't have been, but I remember thinking it."

Griff closed his eyes and breathed deeply. He needed to leave before he took her in his arms and held her. He needed to walk away before something else happened to her. He could never forget that no one was safe around him. "I should tell Patience that you're awake. She's terribly worried."

"No. Don't wake her yet. I imagine she's exhausted and needs the sleep."

"You know it's not proper for us to be alone together."

"Then why did they let you stay here?"

He smiled. "I think perhaps I frightened everyone away."

She smiled, then closed her eyes again. "Don't worry. Although your reputation as a rake is quite justified, I doubt even the worst of Society's gossips will credit you with taking advantage of someone barely conscious."

"I suppose you're right. Does this mean you are no longer angry with me?"

"I'm still furious." Her voice was heavy and her words were slurred. "But something is different with you, and I don't understand what it is."

"You can blame it on the blow to your head, my lady. It causes strange thoughts to enter your mind."

"I doubt that's it," she answered, her voice even more slurred than before. "I dreamt I heard you talk to me."

He hesitated. "Did you?"

"Yes."

"Do you remember what I said?"

"Not all of it," she slurred. "I dreamt you were telling me to wake up."

"I was. You aren't going to go back to sleep, are you?"

She opened her eyes but did not look at him. "No. I'm awake. I have one or two points I would still like to make."

"And they are?"

"I want you to take back the money you settled on me."

"And if I refuse?"

"I will not accept your money, Griff. I am not such a terrible catch that I will only find a husband who will marry me for the dowry you provided."

"That wasn't my intent. I only wanted the world to know your value. Providing you a dowry was the only way I knew how."

"That's not what it seems. When I find someone who will take me, I want to know it was not your money that purchased him for me."

"Do you have someone in mind?"

She turned her head and looked at him. Their gazes locked for a long minute before she turned away. The expression in her eyes was a little sadder than before. "Perhaps. Are you going to interfere?"

He swallowed past the lump in his throat. Dear God, but he hurt. Like someone had just ripped his heart from his chest. "No. I will leave the choice to your good judgment and wish you all the happiness in the world."

He rose from his chair. "I'm going to get Patience now. She'll never forgive me if I don't tell her you are recovered." He walked to the door, the ache in his chest almost greater than he could stand. "Don't go back to sleep before she gets here." He opened the door to leave, but her soft voice stopped him.

"You aren't coming back, are you?"

He paused with his hand on the latch. "No. It's not safe."

"Safe for whom?"

"You, Anne. And me."

He wanted to leave, but something kept him there. There was a question he needed to ask. "Would you answer me just one question before I leave?"

He couldn't look at her. Didn't want to see the relief in her eyes if she was glad he was leaving. Or the sadness if she didn't want him to go.

"Yesterday you said the reason you regretted kissing me was not because it had been so terrible, but because I took a part of you that you didn't realize you had been guarding with such care. Something you didn't realize you would miss so desperately when it was gone. What did I take from you, Annie?"

For a long time she didn't answer. When she did, her voice was soft and she sounded terribly, terribly tired.

"It was nothing, Griff. Nothing I cannot learn to live without."

Griff couldn't bring himself to press her further.

"Good-bye, Anne," he whispered.

He walked out of the room and shut the door behind him, closing himself off from the one person whose loss he would never get over.

# Chapter 18

❋

She hurt like she never thought it was possible to hurt. The cuts and bruises from the accident three weeks ago were long gone, but not the ache deep inside her heart—the ache that Griff had caused when he had walked away from her without a backward glance.

She cursed him. She cursed herself. Why had she allowed this to happen? Why had she fallen in love with him? He was exactly the kind of man she swore she would never trust with her heart—a man like her father, who would always want a drink more than he wanted a wife and a family. For all she knew, he'd gone back to drinking already. Her father had never been able to stop for more than a few weeks at a time.

Knowing that it had been so easy for him to walk away from her—not once, but twice—was what had given her the strength to accept the Earl of Portsmouth's proposal when he'd asked.

Thanks to Griff, it was impossible to marry for love.

Portsmouth seemed a kind and gentle man. Perhaps she would find happiness of a different nature. He would give her children to love and care for. He'd made no secret of it. He had three grown daughters from his first marriage, but he wanted an heir, a son. She would give him his heir, and a house full of children besides. Being his wife would give her the security she wanted. And with the earl's wealth and position, Becca was assured a good match.

Anne laid down the embroidery she was working on and walked to the parlor window to look out over the garden. Patience had gone to a tea at Lady Wimpley's, but she had stayed home. The Earl of Portsmouth was scheduled to come later this afternoon to discuss the terms of the marriage with Adam, and they thought it best if she were here in case there were any points that needed clarifying.

It sounded so cold, and she supposed in a way it was. But then, neither of them was marrying for love. The earl had made that plain before he'd asked her to be his wife.

He still loved his first wife, and even though she'd been gone for more than five years, he hadn't gotten over her and said he probably never would. Just as she was sure she would ever get over Griff.

In time, she prayed things would be different. She couldn't imagine living with such pain for the rest of her life.

Anne leaned her shoulder against the window frame to watch a squirrel scamper about in the garden, but jumped with a start when the door behind her flew open.

The force of the heavy oak door being opened, then the loud crash of it being slammed shut startled her. She turned to face the intruder.

"What the bloody hell do you think you're doing, Anne?"

Her gaze locked with Griff's.

He stood on the other side of the room, his hair mussed, his face shadowed as if he hadn't shaved yet today. His eyes blazed with blinding fury. His anger was palpable.

He wore no jacket or cravat, and his white linen shirt hung loose at the neck in a casual, unkempt way. He was ruggedly handsome, and she was reminded again of how much he meant to her. Her heart leaped with excitement before it resumed a rapid beating.

"Tell me you don't intend to marry him. Not Portsmouth! Tell me I heard wrong. That you wouldn't do something so foolish."

She lifted her chin. "I *do* intend to marry him, Mr. Blackmoor. And I do *not* consider the match foolish."

"He's an old man."

"He's not that old."

"He will never love you. Anyone who knows him knows he's never gotten over his first wife's death. He'll never love you!"

"Perhaps I don't need love."

"You do! You need love as much as you need air to breathe. You won't survive without it. I know you won't."

"How do you know that?"

"I know because I've held you. I've kissed you. And you've kissed me back. I know what we shared. That one kiss barely released the tip of the vast emotions you have stored inside you. The passion you have buried needs to be given to someone."

"No! That kiss was a mistake. You said so yourself. I don't need anything more than what the earl can give me."

"And what is that?"

"A home. Children to love. The ability to provide a good match for Rebecca."

"That's not enough!"

"It will have to be!"

"No! There is so much more. You have to marry a man who can unlock your heart and release the emotions you have never let people see. A man who can make you burn with his touch and set you on fire with his kisses."

"Stop it!"

He crossed the room and grabbed her by the shoulders. He held her close. "You will never feel anything for him, Anne. He's cold, with the zest for life already burned out of him. You need someone who can show you the wonders of love. The rewards."

She struggled to get out of his arms, but he wouldn't release her. "Don't do this, Anne. There's so much more."

"No. I will be content with what he can give me. A love that sets your flesh on fire only happens in fairy tales. It doesn't happen to plain, ordinary people like me. I'll be happy with what the earl can give me. It will be enough."

He pulled her hard against him. "Ah, Annie. No. You deserve more. So much more."

"Griff, don't. It's no use. It's too late for us. What we did before was a mistake. You said so yourself."

"I know," he said on a breathless sigh.

He looked at her mouth as if it were the forbidden fruit, then clamped his hands on either side of her face.

"And I'm about to make an even bigger mistake."

He brought his mouth down on hers and kissed her hard. The gentle passion she remembered from the last time he'd kissed her was not there this time. He ground his mouth against hers with a frantic desperation she understood. It matched her own desires.

Why did his kisses have to be like this, all turmoil and chaos and violent thunderstorm? Why did his arms have to be the only arms that burned her flesh and made her feel safe? Why was Griff the man to whom she wanted to give all that she had to offer, with whom she wanted to spend the rest of her life?

She opened her mouth beneath his and he deepened his kiss. He penetrated her warmth and she met him, her tongue touching his, battling his, mating with his.

Some of the pins in her hair fell to the floor as he raked his fingers through her loose curls, caressing her scalp, holding her closer to him. And still he kissed her deeper, until she was on fire.

Every inch of her burned, from the tip of her head to that mysterious spot deep in the pit of her belly. She was hot as if the gates of hell had opened, and that is where she was afraid she was going.

His touch frightened her. His kisses terrified her. Yet she knew she could not stop him. She did not want to stop him.

She felt his touch on her arms, and her back, and lower, pulling her hard against him. His lips touched her cheek, and her neck just below her ear. Her gown slipped from her shoulder and he kissed her there. Cool air struck her and his warm mouth kissed her flesh at the top of her breast, stopping when her confining chemise would let him go no further.

She wrapped her arms around his neck and held him to her, begging him to show her what it could be like.

He brought his mouth up to hers again and kissed her, deeper than before. With more desperation than before.

How could it be like this? She couldn't breathe. She was too weak to stand. And she didn't have the ability to put two coherent thoughts together. She couldn't do anything but hold on to him and run her fingers across his muscled shoulders and chest.

"Griff! What the bloody hell are you doing?" Adam's voice raged from behind them.

Griff lifted his mouth from hers and stiffened beside her.

She couldn't stop the tiny gasp that escaped her.

Neither of them could breathe. Their gasps were ragged and harsh.

"Are you all right?" he whispered, then ran his fingers over her hair to smooth it.

She nodded.

He dropped his hands from her and turned to face their intruders. When he turned, Anne got her first look at the men on the other side of the room—Griff's brother, Lord Covington, and the Earl of Portsmouth.

Covington wore an angry scowl. The Earl of Portsmouth's face was an unreadable mask.

For several long minutes, no one spoke. The Earl of Portsmouth was the first to break the silence.

"I'm afraid we have a problem, Covington. You failed to mention that the woman I had asked to take as my wife was involved with your brother. Who, I might add, spent numerous weeks living under your roof."

The muscles in Adam's jaw clenched. "I assure you, Portsmouth, the lady's reputation is beyond reproach."

"Is it?"

"That's enough," Griff said, his voice low and angry.

Portsmouth stiffened, his demeanor taking on a hint of anger. This reaction was the first emotion she'd seen from him.

"You will have to excuse me," he said. "The display I witnessed when I walked into the room hardly assures me that my intended is the paragon of virtue I was led to believe she was."

Portsmouth turned his attention to her, scanning her from the top of her head to the tip of her toes. She knew her hair was tangled from Griff raking his fingers through it, and her gown was still slightly askew, with a button near the top gaping open. Her cheeks burned like fire and her lips felt swollen and abused. She had no doubt she looked thoroughly wanton. Used.

Portsmouth pulled his gaze away from her and turned to Adam. "You understand anything we discussed earlier is no longer valid." The tone of his voice held a strained emotion.

"Of course," Adam replied.

"I consider the matter closed, and bid you good day." He turned to leave, then paused at the door. He turned to address Griff. "I will anticipate word of your upcoming nuptials. I'm sure you will not want to wait for the reading of the banns."

She saw Griff nod and felt a heavy rock fall to the pit of her stomach.

The earl walked out of the room, and Adam followed.

"No, Griff," she started to argue when they were alone. "We don't have to—"

"Shh. It's too late."

"No. It's not too late. We can—"

He held out his hand to stop her, then pulled her in his arms and held her to him. "God help you, Anne. You are mine to protect now."

# Chapter 19

*The storm tossed the ship over the water like a little toy boat. Each angry wave smashed against the hull like a battering ram. Water came at him from every direction, and with each assault, Griff felt a fear unlike any he'd ever known before. He'd been in his share of storms, but this was by far the worst.*

*He made his way to the wheelhouse, hanging on to anything fastened down. One violent wave after another slammed against him, threatening to throw him into the watery brine.*

*"Blackmoor! Is that you?" the captain's voice bellowed through the roaring winds.*

*Griff grabbed on to the railing and made his way across the slippery deck to where Captain Morton struggled with the wheel. "Yes, Captain. It's me."*

*"I need your help. I've given the order to abandon ship. Alert all the cabins in your section and bring your wife and son on deck. We're putting the passengers in lifeboats."*

*"Is it that bad? I thought the winds showed signs of letting up."*

*The captain paused. "They are, but we're taking on water. A huge hole, starboard side."*

*Griff took a deep breath. The ship was going down. His thoughts raced to Julia. He had to get to her and Andrew. It was his fault they were here. He'd forced her to come with him even though she was terrified of sailing.*

"How much time do we have?"

"My guess is about an hour. We'll wait as long as we can to lower the boats and hope the wind dies down even more."

Griff nodded his understanding, then hugged the railing as he made his way back to the hatch that would take him below. Unrelenting rain pummeled his face and body, stinging his flesh. He stumbled down the stairs, then pounded on each door to order the passengers to go topside.

When he reached the cabin across from his own, he pounded on the Dowager Countess of Marchon's door and warned her and her maid to gather their wraps and go on deck. Then he stumbled across the hall to his own cabin and threw open the door.

The sight of his wife huddled in the corner, clutching little Andrew so tightly the lad could barely breathe, tore his heart from his chest. Wide-eyed terror flashed from her beautiful blue eyes. Her purple lips trembled violently and her whole body shuddered with near uncontrollable fright.

"Julia. Come here. We have to go on top."

"No!" She clutched Andrew closer and burrowed farther into the corner.

Griff staggered over to them and pulled his wife's stiff arms from around their son. "Everything will be all right, sweetheart. We just need to go up on deck. The captain has another boat for us."

"No! I won't go up there. We'll be washed overboard."

"No, we won't. I'll be with you. I won't let anything happen to you."

"No!"

Griff didn't give her time to argue. He threw a blanket over two-year-old Andrew to protect him, then wrapped an arm around his wife. He forced her across the room and out the door.

*She fought him every step of the way, but finally they made their way to where the crewmen were lining passengers to board the lifeboats.*

*"Is everyone up from your area, Mr. Blackmoor?" the captain yelled.*

*Griff looked around and saw everyone from their section of the ship except the dowager countess and her maid.*

*"No! The dowager countess."*

*"I can't spare anyone to get her," the captain shouted. "The men are busy with the lifeboats."*

*Griff had no choice. "I'll go."*

*"No!" Julia screamed, digging her fingers into his flesh. "Don't leave me, Griff. You promised."*

*"I'll be right back, Julia. I have to get the countess. She can barely walk."*

*"Griff! Don't leave me!"*

*Griff placed Julia over by the railing where one of the stewards was lining up passengers. "Stay right here, Julia!" he ordered, kissing little Andrew then handing him to her.*

*"I'm afraid, Griff! I want to go home."*

*"I know." He held her and Andrew close for a moment. "We'll be home soon."*

*She was terrified. He saw the panic in her eyes, heard it in her voice. She had an irrational fear of the water. The whole trip had been agony for her. He swore when they reached England, he would never ask her to step foot on another ship again.*

*"Don't leave this spot, Julia. I'm going to get the countess and I'll be right back."*

*"No, Griff! Don't leave me!"*

*"I'll just be gone a minute. Stay right here. You'll be safe." He took a step away then turned back to her. "I love you, Julia. I won't let anything happen to you. I promise."*

*Griff found the dowager countess and her maid halfway up the narrow stairs.*

*The moment they stepped on deck, a loud explosion shattered the air. The ship shuddered, and splinters of wood rained down on them. They were going under!*

*With renewed determination, he led the dowager and her maid to where the last of the passengers were loading. He handed them over to the captain, then turned to get Julia and Andrew. The spot where he'd left them was empty.*

*"Where's my wife and son?" Griff yelled at the captain.*

*"I don't know, sir. I haven't seen them since you left."*

*Griff bolted for the passageway that would take him below. He knew she'd gone back to hide.*

*"Julia!" he screamed.*

*Griff tried to make his way to the stairs, but with the ship tilting at such an angle he couldn't make any headway. They were going under!*

*"Julia! Come here!"*

*"Griff! Help me!"*

*"Julia! Come here!"*

*"Help me," she cried again, but it wasn't Julia's voice he heard. It was Anne's.*

*"Help me, Griff!"*

*"Anne!"*

*Griff heard another loud boom, then looked up as a huge section of one of the yardarms crashed down on him and everything went black.*

Griff woke with a start and bolted from the bed. His legs trembled beneath him and he grabbed onto the poster at the foot of the bed to keep from falling.

He couldn't breathe. He gasped for air but still felt the panicky suffocation of Anne's cries while the water rushed in around them. He swiped his hand over his face, then reached for a towel and wiped away the chilling sweat that covered every inch of his body.

It was a nightmare. The same nightmare as before, only this time it wasn't Julia, but Anne who was drowning. And he couldn't save her.

Griff pitched the towel angrily to the floor, then walked to the other side of the room. He threw open the window and stood in the darkness to let the cool night air wash over him.

When would the nightmares end? How long would he be tormented by Julia's death? By Andrew's?

Griff tried to come to grips with the turn his life had taken. He tried to tell himself that he wouldn't be responsible for another person's death, but he nearly had been. Anne had nearly been run down because of her association with him.

Griff reached for a glass of water to wash away the bitter taste of fear. He threw the liquid down his throat, then smashed the glass in the lifeless fireplace. He wanted a drink. He wanted to find a bottle of brandy and lose himself in the fiery liquid.

He looked at the decanter of cool, clear water. Water couldn't drown out Julia's and Andrew's last cries for help. Water wouldn't give him the courage to say the vows that would make Anne his wife. Water couldn't make him pretend that marrying him wouldn't put Anne in danger.

He didn't want a wife. He couldn't protect a wife. With Anne, the risk was even greater. Someone had already tried to harm her and they would try again. And again. Until they succeeded.

He dragged his hand over the day-old stubble on his jaw. He knew what Anne expected from a marriage, what every new bride expected. He couldn't give it to her. He couldn't be a loving husband to her until he was sure she was out of danger. He couldn't give her a child until he knew he could keep it safe.

He clenched his hands until his fingers ached. She would be his to protect, watch over, and keep safe. His to make sure she came to no harm from whoever wanted him dead. But he couldn't keep her safe. Just like he hadn't been able to keep Julia and Andrew safe.

Gnarled fingers of dread clamped around his heart and squeezed until he wanted to cry out in pain. He couldn't live with the death of one more person he loved.

He walked back to the open window and let the cool air wash over him. He stared into the darkness and prayed he'd see an answer to the problems he faced, an easing of the fears that plagued him. What he saw, however, was something more frightening.

His gaze focused on a movement in the shadows across the street. Someone was there. Someone was watching his house, waiting for him.

He would end this here. Now!

He grabbed the clothes that lay across the chair and dressed as quickly as he could. He pulled on his boots and grabbed the pistol he kept in the drawer in the table by his bed, then raced out the door.

Griff walked down the street at a slow, steady pace. He kept his body in plain sight so he would be an easy target.

With each footstep his litany was that the man following him was the killer, and that he would finish this game he was playing before Anne was hurt—or worse.

Griff wasn't sure how long he'd walked, but he knew it had been an hour or more. The sun was beginning its ascent. The golden orb blended muted shades of pinks and purples and blues and oranges together in unequaled perfection. The hour was perfect for an assassination. It was light enough now for the killer to see him clearly. Light enough for Griff to recognize the killer and finally know who wanted him dead.

Suddenly the hair on the back of Griff's neck stood out in warning. He was close. Griff could feel him. Something moved to his left.

Griff ran after him. He caught a glimpse once, then nothing. He raced faster but had to stop when he lost him.

Griff stood still, listening. He concentrated on the quiet sounds around him. He heard nothing but the soft clopping of his own boots against the cobblestoned streets. But the killer was still there. Watching. Griff could feel him.

*Do it. Dear God, let it be over.*

He continued his way down the street. His heart thundered in his chest. His mind raced like a wild man's. He knew to any passing stranger he'd appear a demented creature, but he didn't care. He only wanted it over.

*Do it!*

He neared Adam's town house. How he'd gotten there he didn't know, but the tree- and shrub-lined walk came closer. Only a few more feet and he would no longer be in the open. Only a few more feet and the killer would not have a clear shot. Griff slowed, then stopped.

*Do it!*

Nothing happened. No gunshot exploded in the air. No bullet slammed into his body.

Griff uttered a vile curse, then braced his hands against the shiny, black iron gate that surrounded Adam's town house. After several minutes, he lifted his gaze.

A curtain at the front window moved. He'd been spotted, but he didn't want to go in. He would wake the household, and this was hardly the hour to cause a scene. Everyone was most likely resting for what promised to be a very long, exhausting day.

Today was the day he and Anne would marry.

Griff turned, then followed the path that would take him back to his town house. His feet moved as if his boots were lined with lead. Yet he was desperate to distance himself from her. He needed time to convince himself that he could do this.

He needed a drink.

He made his way down the street, past a row of fancy town houses, then through the working section of London. Past a milliner and a boot maker, then a bakery, and finally an ale house. He stopped. Just one drink. He only needed one.

He tried the door. It was locked.

He pounded until the proprietor appeared.

All he wanted was a bottle. Just one.

# Chapter 20

❧

There was a great commotion at the front of the house, and Griff looked up. The sound of Adam's thunderous voice echoed in the foyer. His heavy boots thudded across the marble floor as he marched toward the study. Adam threw open the door, then stopped short when he saw him.

Griff looked down at the full glass of brandy cradled in his hands.

"Not today, Griff," Adam whispered. "It's her wedding day. Give her at least today."

Griff took in his brother's disheveled appearance. "You look like hell," he said. "Hardly the customary look for a member of the *ton*." Adam's clothes were askew, his hair uncombed, and his boots did not match. He looked so out of character, so unlike the earl, that Griff wanted to laugh.

"I dressed in a hurry."

Griff smiled. "I saw Fenwick at the window and knew he would go for you."

"He waited for you to knock." Adam walked across the room and sat in the chair opposite Griff. "He said you left without coming up the walk. He thought perhaps whatever got you out at such an hour might have been important."

"It was nothing." Griff turned the glass in his fingers. He concentrated on the amber liquid. Bloody hell, but he wanted to drink it. He wanted it so badly his hands shook. But he hadn't tasted it. It had taken every ounce of courage he had, but so far he hadn't lifted it to his mouth and drunk any of it.

Adam watched him. "If there is anything I can do…"

"No. Everything's fine."

"I'm a good listener."

Griff lifted his gaze. "Are you?"

"Yes."

"Do you know how badly I want this?"

"I can only guess."

Griff released his grip on the brandy and sat back in his chair. "Last night I had a dream. Well, actually, it was more of a nightmare. A very vivid nightmare. One I've had often.

"In my sleep, I relived the day Julia and Andrew drowned. I heard her screaming for me to save her. I couldn't get to her, but that is not unusual. In my nightmares I can never reach her." Griff slid his chair back from the desk and rose. "Except last night her voice changed, and it wasn't Julia crying out for me. It was Anne, and I couldn't save her. Anne was drowning and I couldn't reach her."

"It was a nightmare, Griff. You and Anne aren't aboard a ship, or anywhere near an ocean. You're only nervous because you're getting married."

"It's not water that might kill her."

"You don't know that."

"I didn't intend for this to happen. That's why I brought her to London. So she could find a husband of her own choosing."

"That no longer matters. The two of you were drawn to each other from the start. Anyone could see that."

Griff shook his head. "She told me once that she would never marry me because the risk was too great. I'm sure she hasn't changed her mind."

"Staying away for the last three days hasn't helped, Griff. You could have at least spent a little time with her. It might have made things easier."

"Perhaps. How is she?"

"Nervous, I think. Angry. Patience says she reveals about as much as you. It's hard to tell."

Griff pounded his fist against the corner of the desk. "How could I have let this happen? How could I have taken advantage of her like I did?"

Adam smiled. "If what Portsmouth and I saw when we walked in on you is an example of your attraction to each other, neither of you can accept full responsibility for what happened. The lady appeared to be an equal partner in what was going on."

"She will make some man a hell of a wife," Griff said, looking absently out the window.

"That man is you, Griff. And you will make her a hell of a husband."

Griff sat back down behind the desk and ran his finger around the rim of the glass. He stared at the liquid as if it were gold. "Do you think she'll go through with the wedding?" he asked, turning the full glass in his hand.

"Why don't you ask her yourself?" Anne's soft voice said from the doorway.

Griff's head snapped up and his gaze focused on her. "What are you doing here?"

"I heard Fenwick wake Lord Covington and tell him he thought he should come over here right away. I thought something might be wrong, so I dressed and followed him."

"Nothing is wrong. You should go home."

She stared at him. Her gaze eventually dropped from his face to the full glass of liquor in front of him. "Are you going to drink that?"

"I...don't know," he answered honestly.

She swayed on her feet. "Well, decide before you come to say your vows. I need to know which one of us you choose."

Before Griff could answer, she turned and walked out of the house.

Griff went to the window and watched to make sure she made it safely to her waiting carriage, then turned back to his desk. He stared at the full glass of brandy for several long seconds, then picked it up and threw it into the cold hearth.

"You had the right of it," Adam said with a smile on his face. "She will make some man a hell of a wife."

Griff poured the rest of the bottle onto the ashes. "Only if I stay alive long enough to enjoy our marriage."

\* \* \*

Griff made his way down the London alley. It was almost time for his wedding, but first he wanted to talk to Fitzhugh. He needed to know if he'd learned anything new.

Griff couldn't believe that Anne was the target, but he didn't want to take the chance that she would be an innocent bystander and get hurt in an attempt on his life.

As soon as the ceremony was over, Griff intended to take her to Covington Manor. She would be safer in the country. There would be no parties, teas, or balls to attend where anyone could step out of the crowd with a knife or a gun, or come up behind her to push her into a busy street as a carriage rolled past. In the country, she would not be able to leave his sight without him knowing where she was.

He reached the hidden entrance, then knocked and opened the door. This time, Fitzhugh's secretary greeted him. He immediately rose from his desk to tell Fitzhugh he was there.

"I was a little surprised to get your message, Griff," Fitzhugh said, looking up when Griff entered. "I hardly expected you to have time to see me today. Word is you're getting married this morning."

"Never let me be the one to cast doubt on what you hear on the street."

"Is something wrong?" Fitzhugh asked with a frown.

"Who is following me today?"

"Johnston. Why?"

"I have a second tail."

"Are you sure?"

Griff arched one eyebrow.

Fitzhugh held out his hand, palm outward. "All right. That was a stupid question. Did you see him?"

"No. I saw one tail on my left. I'm assuming that is Johnston. Someone else is on my right. He stayed back farther, almost as if he knew this was my destination."

Fitzhugh rose from his chair and paced the few feet behind the desk.

"This isn't the first time I've had more than one person following me," Griff added.

Fitzhugh stopped pacing and braced his hands on the top of the desk. "Hawkins came to see me last week. He found out we'd investigated him and wanted to know why."

"What did you tell him?"

"Not much. Not enough to satisfy him, but maybe just enough to make him suspicious."

"Does he know we found out about his brother?"

"I don't know. He didn't mention it." Fitzhugh picked up a folder from his desk. "I read his report from the day Lady Anne was hit by the runaway carriage."

"It wasn't a runaway," Griff said, his temper firing.

"Very well. Hawkins believes the carriage that tried to run her over was not after you. He's convinced she was the one the driver wanted to hit."

Griff stood. "That isn't possible. There's no way anyone could want to harm her. Unless it's to punish me."

"All right. Let's assume that's true. Do you realize what that means?"

Griff swiped his hand over his face in frustration. "Of course I do. That means she's not safe anywhere near me."

"So what are you going to do?"

"I'm leaving for Covington Manor this afternoon. I can protect her more effectively there. I can watch out for myself better, too."

"Is there anything I can do from here?"

"Just keep an eye on Hawkins for me." Griff slammed his hand against the wall. "Damn! I can't believe he's behind this. We've been through too much. He saved my life over there!"

"But you are responsible for his brother's death. You arrested him. You were responsible for his execution."

Griff nodded, not wanting to think what it might mean if Hawkins was the one trying to kill him. He was good, one of the best agents they had during the war. It was a miracle Griff wasn't already dead. If Hawkins was after him, he should be. Unless…

Maybe Hawkins knew he could cause a deeper hurt if he killed Anne.

A cold chill raced down Griff's spine. The thought that Hawkins wanted to kill Anne scared the hell out of him. He wouldn't let anything happen to her.

"Let me know if you find out anything," Griff said when he reached the door. He didn't wait for an answer, but twisted the knob to let himself out.

"Griff."

Griff turned.

"Congratulations. I wish you all the best. You deserve it."

Griff thanked Fitzhugh, then left.

Let whoever it was kill him. He didn't care. But he wouldn't let anything happen to Anne. He couldn't. He cared for her too much.

\* \* \*

Anne stood before the long mirror and looked at the reflection that stared back at her. She couldn't believe she was getting married today. That she was marrying Griffin Blackmoor.

*I need to know which one of us you choose.*

In her mind's eye, she saw his long, narrow fingers wrapped around the glass of brandy. She wouldn't marry him if he'd picked it up after she'd left. She wouldn't have a marriage like her mother's, loving a man who was never there for her, who could never love her as much as she loved him. It would be better to live the remainder of her life alone.

The weight inside her chest hurt even more. Why had she fallen in love with him? Why hadn't she been strong enough to stop him before he'd kissed her? Strong enough to walk away from him before he'd held her? Now it was too late. It didn't matter how big a dowry he heaped on her; her reputation was ruined. No one would have her now.

Anne brushed her damp palms over the pale-blue gown she'd chosen in which to be married. She turned when the door opened and Patience entered.

"Oh, Anne," Patience said, clasping her folded hands to her breast. "You are absolutely beautiful."

Anne felt her cheeks warm. "All brides are beautiful on their wedding day."

"Just wait until you see the look on Griff's face when he sees you. Then you will know."

"Somehow I doubt he'll see anything except that he had no choice but to marry me." Anne walked over to the window and lifted the heavy curtains. "Is he here yet?"

*I need to know which one of us you choose.*

"Not yet, but it's still early. Surely you're not worried?"

"No." Anne dropped the curtain and sat on the stool. Patience came up behind her and rearranged the delicate flowers in her hair. "He'll be here," Anne said more to herself than to Patience. "Can you imagine Mr. Blackmoor not fulfilling his responsibility?"

Patience smiled. "No. He is very much like Adam in that respect."

Anne lifted her gaze. She looked at Patience's reflection in the mirror. "Are you happy, Patience? Does the earl make you happy, or are you merely content?"

Bright circles of pink covered Patience's cheeks. "Both, Anne. I am deliriously happy and I am ever so content. I am in love with my husband. And I am loved in return."

Anne dropped her gaze to her hands. She was suddenly embarrassed.

"Does that surprise you? Did you think that because our marriage was arranged, it would be impossible for us to be happy?" Patience laughed out loud. "Or did you assume because Adam is so staid and formal in public, ever so much the earl at all times, that he remains so behind our bedroom door?"

Anne looked up. Patience's face brimmed with happiness, with the youthful blush of a woman who knew secrets the rest of the world could only guess at.

"Let me assure you he does not. Adam is the most affectionate of husbands." Patience turned Anne around so she did not have to face her in the mirror but looked into her eyes. "Are you worried Griff does not love you?"

*I need to know which one of us you choose.*

Anne clasped her hands tight in her lap. "I'm just being silly. I'm nervous, I think."

"Well, don't be. Griff already loves you. It's obvious to everyone who sees the two of you together." Patience paused, then said, "Can you love him in return?"

Anne's heart skipped a beat. She already did. Even though he was the last person on earth she wanted to love, she was cursed the minute she met him. He was the one who took possession of her heart when she held his hand and wiped his brow.

"I think it's too late to keep from loving him."

"Oh, Anne," Patience said, taking Anne in her arms. "Then I know you will be happy with Griff."

Anne smiled, unable to say more.

"Now, you stay here and I'll go down to make sure everything's ready." Patience rushed out of the room. She returned a few minutes later with a huge smile on her face. "Are you ready, Anne? The minister is here and they are ready to start."

Anne's heart raced in her breast and she gasped for air. "Is Griff here?"

"Of course," Patience said on a laugh. "I think you were worried he would not be."

Anne's heart pounded faster. "Yes. No. I mean…I just thought perhaps he might be late."

"No, he's on time. I still wish you would have let us invite at least a few guests."

"No. This is the way I want my wedding to be. We will invite all of London when Rebecca gets married."

Anne took a few steps toward the door, then stopped. *I need to know which one of us you choose.*

She didn't want to ask her next question, but she had to. She had to know. "Patience, is Griff…?" She twisted her hands in front of her. "Is he…?"

"He's fine, Anne. Fine. And I must admit I have never seen a more handsome groom since Adam walked down the aisle at our wedding."

Anne nodded, then followed Patience down the stairs. She walked across the marble foyer, then came to a stop when she entered the morning room and saw him. Her heart skipped a beat. Patience was right. It wasn't fair for one man to be so handsome. Especially the man who would be her husband. And it wasn't fair for the man she was about to marry to feel such regret. She could see it on his face. Feel his frustration.

She knew she should walk to him. Patience was already in the front of the room with the minister. But Anne couldn't force her feet to move. She couldn't take the first step that would change the rest of her life. She took a deep breath, praying for the strength to go to him.

Their gazes locked. The understanding in his eyes told her he knew how difficult this was for her.

He came toward her, stopping in front of her.

"I know this isn't what you envisioned for your wedding day."

She shook her head. "I was never a romantic schoolgirl who dreamt of a wedding day." She looked toward the window. "The sun is shining. Doesn't that promise the bride and groom something?"

He smiled. "Yes. I believe I heard somewhere that it does."

He reached for her hands and she pulled them back. "I'm not sure..." she started. Heaven help her. She wasn't sure she could go through with this. "I don't think—Is this the choice you wanted to make?"

He placed a finger beneath her chin and lifted her gaze to his. "Yes. I cannot promise you my heart, Anne, and perhaps you will never want it. But I can promise that I will do everything in my power to keep you safe and keep you from regretting that you took my name."

"And what would you like me to promise in return?" she asked, sensing the distance he wanted to keep between them. "My heart?"

He hesitated, then answered. "No."

"My love?"

"No."

"Then what?"

He turned his face away from her, unable to hold her gaze.

"Then what?" she demanded.

"Your hand to hold when I lose my way."

Her heart twisted in her breast. "And what if I don't know the way? What if what I have to offer is not enough?"

"It will be."

He held out his hand again and this time she took it. His touch sent a fiery heat spiraling to every part of her body. She didn't want to feel this attraction to him.

She didn't want to remember the way he'd held her to him, and ran his hands over her body, and kissed her lips until she couldn't breathe. She didn't want to ache for his assurance that her life wouldn't be like her mother's. Empty. Lonely. Desolate. That she wasn't marrying a man who loved a bottle more than he loved his wife or family. But she had no choice. She had to take the risk.

She walked to the front of the room and repeated her vows. She promised to love and honor and cherish, until death do us part.

She wanted the words to mean something, but when it came time for Griff to repeat the same vows, he hesitated.

She thought for a moment he wouldn't repeat the words the minister spoke.

The silence echoed in the room with a deafening roar. He took a deep breath and reached for her hand.

*Your hand to hold when I lose my way.*

She wrapped her trembling fingers around his sweating palm and held tight.

# Chapter 21

✤

*G*riff sat opposite Anne as their carriage traveled through the English countryside. He kept his eyes focused out the window, watching for anything that might seem out of the ordinary. If there were a time and a place where they were most vulnerable, this was it. They were basically in the open. He absently touched his hand to the pistol in his jacket pocket, then turned back to his wife.

He hadn't been the best companion on their journey to Covington Manor. His thoughts had been too occupied with keeping his new wife safe. "Do you need to stop?" he asked, breaking the silence. "We could stop to rest if you need to."

"No, I'm fine. Thank you."

This was the first she'd spoken in over an hour, the last time only to answer when he'd asked if she was comfortable.

He pointed to a basket under her seat. "Patience sent along a light lunch and something to drink so we wouldn't have to stop along the way." Adam had provided a meal before they'd left, but he'd noticed she'd eaten very little. "Are you hungry?"

"No. Are you?"

He shook his head.

"Are you watching for something, Griff?" She studied him as if he were a stranger. Perhaps the magnitude of having him as her husband was finally taking hold. Perhaps she couldn't believe she was married any more than he could.

"Nothing in particular. But it's better to be cautious."

"Yes. I've always considered riding with two loaded pistols and three armed guards necessary when traveling through the peaceful English countryside."

The expression on her face said she realized the precautions he'd taken in assuring their safety were not normal for an ordinary trip to the country. So be it. For her own safety, it was best she knew up front the danger she was in. It was best he kept no secrets from her. She would be safer that way. Safer than he'd kept Julia and Andrew. Or Fespoint. Or her brother.

He studied the disinterest she attempted to show and knew it was feigned. "I'm being cautious because you did not step out in front of the carriage that hit you. It swerved into your path. Whether you were the intended victim or I, the attempt to hit one of us was deliberate."

A frown darkened her face. "Do you know why?"

"I'm afraid I am the reason. It has something to do with what I was involved with during the war."

"Which was?"

"Intelligence. I uncovered a group of agents who had infiltrated our regiments. They were executed."

"Then how can they still be a threat?"

"There is a possibility that the attempts may be in retaliation for their deaths."

"But that carriage accident was just one event. How can you draw such a conclusion when something only happened once? If there had been another time, another attempt on either…" The color drained from her face. "There was another attempt, wasn't there?"

He held her gaze. He had known this day would come and was almost glad it was here now. "Yes."

"It was the night Freddie was killed, wasn't it?" Her eyes opened wider, and her breaths came in harsh, shallow gasps. "You think the bullet that killed Freddie was intended for you, don't you? You think Freddie died instead of you?"

Griff turned to watch out the window. He couldn't hold her gaze. He was afraid he couldn't handle the hatred he'd see. "Freddie didn't have an enemy in the world," he finally answered.

"But you did."

"Yes. I did."

"That is why you took such an interest in us. Your reason for helping Rebecca and me was motivated not only out of friendship for Freddie, but to ease your own conscience. That is why you brought me to London. Why you outfitted me in the latest fashions. Why you placed a dowry on me that was guaranteed to attract any number of suitors. You couldn't live with the fact that you were responsible for Freddie's death."

He drilled her with a look meant to intimidate her. "Everything I did, I would have done anyway. Freddie was my friend. His dying words were a plea for me to take care of you."

She did not back down. "How unfortunate for you. I'm sure you found his demand on your friendship a great imposition."

"I did for him what I would have expected him to do for me. I took care of you the only way I knew how."

"I'm sure he didn't mean for you to marry me."

"Perhaps not. That was a decision I made on my own."

"A decision? I think not, sir. It was a mistake. A mistake neither of us should have let happen."

He lifted his eyebrows. "You think either of us could have stopped what happened between us?"

Her cheeks turned a bright crimson. He knew she was remembering the kiss they'd shared as well as the way he'd held her and touched her.

"I wish I would have at least tried."

"You would have been no more successful than I."

She lowered her gaze to her hands folded in her lap. "What are your plans now? Do you intend to lock me away in the country while you return to London to find the man who killed Freddie?"

"No. I intend to wait for him to come to me."

Her eyes opened wide. "You think he will follow us?"

"There is that possibility."

"Then what? Will we make ourselves targets and wait for him to kill one of us?"

"No! Nothing will happen to you. I've already made arrangements to have the grounds of Covington Manor guarded. No one will get close enough to do you any harm as long as you go no farther than the gardens."

"Do you intend to stay where you will be safe, too?"

"I'll do what I have to do. But I must have your word, Anne. You must promise that you will not go beyond the gardens until I am sure everything is safe."

"You mean until either you or the killer is dead."

"That will probably be the outcome. I will try not to distress you by making you my widow so soon after making you my bride."

"I'll hold you to that, Mr. Blackmoor. I have no intention of wearing black, even for you."

"I'll keep that in mind." He returned his focus to the scenery outside the window.

For a long while they were both silent. When she spoke again, her voice held a resolve he knew she could achieve at will.

"We must be nearly there. I recognize this area."

"We've just crossed the border onto Covington land. That copse of trees is the boundary line between our two estates."

"Is this where we will live?"

"Yes. I am the steward of Covington Estate. We will live here. Adam and Patience prefer to reside at Wellington Estate, another Covington holding. It's not too far from here, so it will be convenient for us to visit often."

"Did you know that Freddie left me a small parcel of land on the border between Covington Estate and Brentwood Estate?"

"Yes. Your solicitor explained that he did, although I can't imagine why. That area is worthless."

"Is it near here?"

Griff's heart skipped a beat. "Yes, it's to the east of here. But you are never to go there."

"Why?"

"Because it's dangerous."

"But surely—"

"No," he said more sharply than he intended. Fear that something might happen to her sent a wave of raw panic racing through him. "The rocks are littered with caves that flood when the tide comes in. Anyone trapped there will drown before they can get out. You will never, under any circumstances, go anywhere near the cliffs. Do you hear me?"

Two bright-red circles dotted her otherwise pale complexion. "Yes, sir. I hear you."

Griff saw the proud lift to her chin and heard the defiance in her tone. He'd recognized this strength when he'd seen her at Freddie's funeral. It was what had drawn him to her from the start.

Then he noticed her hands tremble in her lap.

Griff sank back in his seat and waited for his temper to calm. Bloody hell. Why had he yelled at her?

"I'm sorry. I don't usually react so violently."

She didn't look away from him but drilled him with a glare that brimmed with serious intensity. "I won't have a marriage where we raise our voices in anger," she said firmly. "It achieves no good purpose."

He raked his fingers through his hair. "I agree. Please, accept my apology."

The expression on her face told him her reaction to his raised voice was based on something more personal. "Did your parents often argue?"

She turned her face away from him to look out the window. "Their relationship was unique. I do not intend to mirror their example."

"Our marriage will not be like your parents', Anne. Neither of us will be antagonistic toward the other."

"You think my parents were antagonistic to each other?"

"Yes. Freddie led me to believe they fought a great deal."

"Only my mother fought, sir. She never ceased trying to make her life better. She never ceased trying to change what everyone knew would never change. You see, she made one fatal mistake even before she married my father."

He lifted his brows, waiting for her to continue. "And her mistake was?"

"She fell hopelessly in love with him and would have done anything if only he would have returned that love."

"Was your father in love with someone else?"

"Not someone. Something. His next drink. My father loved his next bottle of whiskey too much to even know how he destroyed everything he touched."

Griff didn't move. He couldn't. He felt the color drain from his face and sank back as if a heavy weight had dropped onto his chest.

The air in the close confines of the carriage stilled as if both of them had ceased breathing.

*I need to know which one of us you choose.*

Bloody hell. This was the risk she was taking.

"Your father was a drunkard?"

She lowered her gaze to her hands twisting in her lap. "I don't remember him ever being sober."

"I didn't know."

"Not many did. For the most part, he kept to himself in the country and did his drinking where no one could see him. We rarely went to London, where anyone would realize his problem."

"How did he die? I remember he had an accident of some sort."

"His pride and joy were his stables. He loved to ride. The more inebriated he was, the faster he rode and the more chances he took. When I was sixteen, he took out a new horse he'd just purchased. The horse was not as tame as the others, nor was it used to Father. He was drunk and had no business riding. He tried to jump a row of hedges and missed. He broke his neck in the fall. Mother died of loneliness less than a year later. She'd lived her whole life thinking her love could make him stop drinking. After he was gone, she could not live with her failure. She loved him too much to go on without him."

"And you will not make that same mistake?"

He heard the soft gasp that caught the air in her throat. She appeared untouchable. He waited, but she didn't answer him.

Her silence was more telling than a thousand words.

"Are you afraid I might be like your father?"

She opened her mouth to speak, then closed it again as if she couldn't find the courage to tell him she did. Couldn't find the courage to tell him she was terrified that someday a bottle of liquor would be more important to him than she. Instead, she said the last words he ever expected to come from her mouth.

"We will go day by day. One day at a time."

The air drained from his lungs. "What did you say?"

"I said, we'll go day by day, one day at a time, and we'll be fine."

His mind raced back to the time right after he'd brought her to London. To when he lay in a secluded room at Adam's town house and thought he would die before the liquor in his body left him. To the time when he thought Julia had come to him, held his hand, placed a cool cloth on his forehead, and whispered encouragement in his ear. To when the words *just stay with me and I'll help you, day by day, one day at a time* had been all that kept him going.

But Julia hadn't spoken those words. They'd been spoken by Anne. She'd been the one at his bedside, not Julia. Anne knew how strong a hold liquor had on him. She knew he was a drunkard just like her father, struggling to stay away from that next drink, wondering when he could no longer push it away, when the blessed relief of a drink would be more important than his wife or his family. No wonder she didn't want to marry him. No wonder she had demanded that he choose between her and the glass of whiskey he'd cradled in his hand.

"May I ask you a question, sir?"

He slowly turned his head to look at her.

"The day you came to see me at the cottage to tell me I had to go to London to find a husband, I made the mistake of assuming you had come to offer marriage yourself. You told me then you would rather face a firing squad than marry. Is the idea of marriage still so reprehensible?"

"That is a moot point, wife. Just as your reasons for not wanting to marry me are no longer of importance. Any reason we might have had before for avoiding matrimony was taken out of our hands when Lord Portsmouth walked through that door and found us together."

He turned to keep watch out the window. "We have both made the devil's bargain."

Before he could see her reaction to his statement, a loud pop stopped him from saying whatever else he intended to say. The carriage jerked hard to the right.

Before he had time to reach for the pistol in his jacket pocket, the carriage lurched forward. The jolt tossed him across the seat. The sound of horses' screaming clashed with the driver's loud yells. The carriage tipped precariously, then rolled end over end.

Griff clutched Anne tightly as the carriage turned over. They were tossed about like little marbles shaken in a cup. His only thought was to protect her from being hurt.

There was a loud crack of splintering wood, then the carriage careened headlong down a sharp ravine and through the thick underbrush off the side of the road. The frightened look on Anne's face and her bloodcurdling scream were the last things Griff remembered before they came to a jarring halt.

\* \* \*

Anne couldn't move. Every muscle in her body refused to obey her orders to move. She had a stitch in her side where she'd slammed against the edge of the seat, and her head pounded as if she'd knocked it against something hard. Otherwise, she thought she was unhurt.

Griff lay sprawled on top of her. He'd taken the brunt of the bruises in his effort to protect her.

She pushed against him to ease him off of her, but she couldn't move him. She needed to see if he was hurt.

"Griff?" She pressed her hands between their bodies until she touched his face. Her fingers felt something warm and wet. "Griff!" she yelled, pushing harder to ease him from on top of her.

His weight shifted and he moaned.

"Griff, let me up so I can see how badly you're hurt."

He pushed himself off her then shook his head as if trying to clear it.

She knew the exact moment he remembered what happened.

He clasped his hands on either side of her face. "Are you all right?"

"I'm fine. But I think you may need some assistance."

"No, it isn't serious." He touched her arms and straightened her legs, then tipped her face to check for any cuts or bruises. "Are you sure you're unhurt?"

"Yes." She looked up. The bottom of the carriage was where the top should be. They had tipped over. "Is it possible for us to get out?"

He pushed on a door until it opened. "Here, let me crawl over you and I'll help you out."

Anne moved her skirts and made room for him to step over her, then sat up when he was out of the carriage. She turned around in a very unladylike manner, then climbed out of the carriage with little trouble.

"Are you sure you're uninjured?" he asked again, running his hands up and down her arms.

"Yes, but you have a gash above your eye. Here, let me see it."

He stood still barely long enough for her to take the handkerchief from his pocket and wipe the blood away. She was relieved to see the gash was not very deep and had already stopped bleeding. Before she finished, their driver ran up with the two horses in tow.

"Mr. Blackmoor"—the driver dropped the reins and let the horses munch on the thick grass—"are you and the mistress all right?"

"Yes, Franklin. Thank you."

"I can't understand what could have happened. One minute everything was fine, then there was this loud pop and the horses took off. It's a good thing I had just slowed down for that crossing there." He pointed to a small path that intersected with theirs. "Or it would have been a lot worse. You could have gone into the stream and drowned."

Griff walked over to where the front of the carriage hung in the air. Franklin followed him, still scratching his head.

"Well, don't that look odd," Franklin said, reaching up to touch the splintered bar of wood that was the tongue of the carriage. "You just got this carriage not too long ago, and look how that piece looks rotted through. Like it wasn't a good piece of wood to start with. Or like someone mighta sawed it part of the way through."

The breath caught in Anne's throat. She turned her gaze to Griff's. The hard look on his face blazed with smoldering fury.

"Did someone tamper with the carriage, Griff?"

His face was pale, the dangerous look in his eyes sent shivers down her spine. He didn't answer but fisted his hands at his side.

"We need to get you home. Are you capable of riding a horse if I hold you?"

She nodded in answer.

"Franklin, bring the horses. We'll ride them home, and you can come back for the carriage later. Don't touch anything until I have a chance to look at it."

The groom nodded in understanding, then brought the horses over. Griff helped her mount, then got up behind her.

They rode in silence the rest of the way. With each turn in the road, Anne felt him distance himself from her. Even though his arms still held her close and his broad chest shielded her from harm, his silence told her he blamed himself for the accident. The manner in which he kept her at arm's length told her he was afraid his nearness was what had caused her harm.

As soon as they reached Covington Manor, he lifted her in his arms and carried her to the house.

"I'm not hurt, Griff. I am quite capable of walking by myself."

He ignored her protests and carried her through the front door and up the stairs. He issued orders with every step upward. He instructed the maid, Martha, to follow. For a warm bath to be sent up. For a tea tray to be prepared. For Anne to be waited on and her every need seen to.

The minute he was assured the staff had done his bidding, he turned his back and left without a word.

If the carriage ride were a sign of things to come, it was an ominous beginning to their marriage and her life at Covington Manor.

# Chapter 22

❧

*A*nne was glad he didn't make her wait long after she'd bathed and dressed before he came to her. She sat in the window seat overlooking the garden below when he knocked. She bid him enter.

"Are you better?" he asked when he came into the room.

She couldn't keep her eyes from taking in every inch of him. He'd shed the strict black tailcoat he'd worn to their wedding and now wore a casual burgundy jacket that brought out the vivid blue of his eyes and his dark features. The snow-white linen shirt and cravat he wore beneath the jacket only accentuated his bronzed complexion. Her hands ached to reach out and touch him.

"I'm fine. I wasn't hurt. Just tossed around a bit." She stood. "Was the carriage tampered with?"

He avoided looking at her. "I'm not sure."

"Yes, you are."

His gaze darted to hers, the tight clench of his mouth an indication of his harshly controlled emotions. "Yes, it was. But I've increased the guards. You'll be safe as long as you don't go any farther than the gardens."

"I don't blame you for what happened to the carriage."

"Well, you should," he fired back. "You should wish we had never met. We had never married. That we had never kissed that first time."

"Because that is what you wish?" She was unable to ignore the rigid expression on his face.

She heard him breathe a heavy sigh. When he spoke again, his voice was much softer, his words much calmer. He had distanced himself from her again.

"Does your room meet with your approval? Is there anything else you need?"

"I have everything I need. The room is lovely. Thank you." She let her gaze focus on their bedroom. It was beautifully decorated in rose and burgundy and cream, and accented in shades of blue. A huge four-poster bed took up most of one side of the room, and a dressing table, mirror, and two chaise longues sat off to the other side. A large, open window covered a major portion of the wall facing the garden, and beneath it was a long, embroidery-cushioned window seat.

"I'm glad you like it," he answered. "There is a sitting room through here"—he led her beyond a door on the opposite side of the room—"with a sofa and chairs, and a small fireplace. And a writing desk and window seat over here. My bedroom is through that door." He pointed to the far side of the room.

A small pain stabbed through her. He didn't intend to share the same room with her.

"Is it normal for husbands and wives to keep separate bedrooms?" she asked.

He dropped his hand from around her and took a step away. "I think it would be best in our case."

She lifted her gaze. "Why?"

He looked uncomfortable. "Perhaps when we know each other better..."

"I see," she said, although she did not see at all. "When do you anticipate that will be?"

"In time."

He turned away from her, indicating that the topic was closed.

"Do you feel well enough to go below and meet your staff, then perhaps eat a bite for supper?"

"Of course. I am anxious to meet them, and to be quite honest," she said, trying to hide the hurt she felt, "I'm famished."

He offered her his arm.

She placed her hand on his, then walked with him down the hallway and to the long, spiraled staircase. A tall, distinguished-looking gentleman stood below and bowed elegantly.

"This is Carter," he said, introducing their butler. "And Martha, your lady's maid. And Mrs. Buttonsly, our cook. And Hodges..." He walked at her side as they made their way down the long row of servants.

She met the warm smiles on their faces and tried to remember them all. But the fact she was most aware of was the way he held himself away from her. She didn't understand it. His indifference caused a riot of confusing emotions to race through her body.

"On behalf of the staff, my lady," Carter said, nodding to emphasize the sincerity of his words, "we would like to welcome you to Covington Manor. We trust you have recovered from the incident this afternoon, and wish to tell you how pleased we are to have you here."

"Thank you," she said. "Thank you all." Bright smiles greeted her when she spoke.

"If there is anything you need, you have only to ask, my lady."

"Thank you," she answered.

"Dinner is ready whenever you are, sir," the butler announced.

"Very good, Carter. My wife tells me she's famished."

They ate the light supper Mrs. Buttonsly had prepared for them in strained silence, and when they finished, Griff stood.

"It's been an exhausting day, Anne. I'm sure you're ready to retire."

Without waiting for her to say otherwise, he held out his hand to escort her to her room. When they reached her bedroom door, he leaned down and pressed his lips lightly against her forehead. "Good night." He bowed slightly. "Sleep well."

"Are you retiring as well?" she asked, hoping he could not hear the nervousness in her voice.

"There are several details I promised Adam I would see to when we arrived. I need to take care of some of them immediately."

She tried to hide her disappointment. Even if there were details his brother had asked that he see to, she doubted Lord Covington expected his brother to see to them on his wedding night. "Very well. Good night, Griff."

He held open the door, then closed it after she entered her room.

Anne fought the heavy lump that sank to the pit of her stomach as she walked across the room to where Martha waited for her. A gown and robe lay across the bed and, thankfully, Martha chattered constantly about the working of the house and which stable hand was interested in which kitchen lass.

Anne tried not to think about the words her husband had said before he left her. Surely he did not mean he would not come to her tonight? On their wedding night?

Martha helped her remove her gown and get ready for bed. When she finally met with Martha's approval, Anne sat on the stool before the mirror while she brushed her hair.

"Everyone was glad you weren't injured today, my lady."

"Thank you, Martha."

"And even more glad the master has married again and brought you here." She continued to brush Anne's hair in long, smooth strokes.

"Have you been here long, Martha?"

"Good gracious, yes, my lady. I was born on Covington property. My father was a gamekeeper, and Mother was the countess's maid. I practically grew up in the manor."

"Were you Mr. Blackmoor's first wife's maid, too?"

Martha stopped in the middle of picking up Anne's slippers from the floor. "Yes, my lady. My mother decided when the dowager countess died that she was too old to be a lady's maid. For a few years there wasn't a need for me to step into her shoes, seeing as how Mr. Blackmoor wasn't married. Then he brought home his new wife, and I came upstairs to take my mother's place."

"Her name was Julia, wasn't it?"

"Yes."

"What was she like?"

Martha looked uncomfortable, but Anne had too many questions to be deterred. She had to know what it had been like between Griff and his first wife.

"She was very beautiful, with long golden hair, the color of ripened wheat, and laughing eyes as blue as a clear summer sky. She had a soft voice and a smile that never failed to brighten Mr. Blackmoor's day. The master was devastated when he lost her. We were all afraid he would never recover after the tragedy."

"There was a son, too, wasn't there?"

Martha smiled and clutched her hands to her breasts. "Ah, yes. Little Andrew. What a precious bundle of energy. Every time his nurse set him on his feet, he would take off at a run. He never walked anywhere." Martha put Anne's shoes in the upright clothes chest. "Someday, it will be your little ones we will chase through the manor. We are all awaiting that day."

Martha gathered the clothes Anne had taken off. "Will there be anything else, my lady?"

"No," Anne whispered.

"I'd best be going then so you can rest awhile before…" Martha smiled. "I imagine the master will be here before long."

Martha reached for the door, but Anne had one more question she needed to ask. "Martha?"

"Yes, my lady."

"Was this their room?"

Martha clutched the clothes in her arms closer to her chest. "No, my lady. The master and his wife had their suite of rooms on the other side of the manor. In the west wing."

Anne was startled at the relief she felt. "Good night, Martha."

"Good night, my lady."

When she was alone, Anne looked at the big, four-poster bed. A shiver of apprehension raced through her body, warming her from the top of her head to the tips of her toes.

This may not be how she thought her life would be, but it was too late to change anything now. Even if Griffin Blackmoor was not the husband she'd envisioned, at least there would be children. Children she would love and who would love her in return.

She would not be so foolish as her mother. She would not spend her life waiting for her husband to love her when even the blind could see he could not. She would give her love and attention to the children he would give her and let them be her life.

Anne walked across the room and stared down at the bed. Perhaps he would plant the seed of her first child inside her tonight. Perhaps he would give her a babe to love soon, before she came to care for him more than she did at this moment. Perhaps if she had a child, she would not want him so.

Anne sat on the edge of the bed to wait.

\* \* \*

The hours passed in agonizing slowness as she waited for Griff to come to her. She'd moved to the window seat long ago to watch the full moon shine high in the sky.

At first she'd been nervous, anticipating his arrival. But as the hours passed, her nervousness dissipated, and disappointment settled over her like a heavy weight.

She'd waited nearly all night, praying he would come. But he hadn't.

Her husband hadn't been able to force himself to come to her.

Anne tucked her legs close to her chest and smoothed the gown of filmy, white gauze over soft peach satin that Patience had given her for her wedding night. The knot deep inside her stomach tightened. She'd lived with the fear her whole life that if she married, her husband might be like her father. That the man she married might want his next drink more than he wanted her. She suddenly realized she had more to fear than a bottle of whiskey.

*The master was devastated when he lost her.*

She closed her eyes and took several deep breaths. Griff had told her from the start he did not want to marry. Now she knew the reason why. His reason had wheat-colored hair and laughing blue eyes the color of a clear summer sky. It was Julia's name he'd called out when he was sick. Julia's face that haunted his dreams. Julia's love he still cherished.

How could Anne expect him to care for her when he still loved a wife who had died four years ago?

She closed her eyes to the rising sun and willed the tears not to fall.

# Chapter 23

❧

The promise of dawn brightened the early morning sky, and Griff stretched out over his stallion's neck to let his thoroughbred thunder across the open meadows of Covington Estate. His horse's hooves dug up huge clods of wet, grassy mud that flew through the air and splattered against his back and legs. Mammoth drops of sweat formed on his forehead and poured down his face. He flung the salty wetness from his eyes with the back of his hand while he pushed his mount even harder.

He raced as if the hounds of hell were on his heels. They were. They had tormented him since he'd walked away from his bride on her wedding night.

His chest heaved as violently as his horse's, both their breathing labored and heavy. He knew he should slow down, but he couldn't chance it. Slowing down meant giving his mind an opportunity to chastise him for what he'd done. It meant giving his conscience time to revolt against his unconscionable act.

He dug his heels into his stallion's sides and let the early morning air whip his hair as he continued to race over the open spaces even faster. Damn it, but he wanted a drink.

He wanted his wife.

A loud, anguished cry escaped into the hazy, early morning sunshine, and he realized it had come from deep inside him.

He pulled back on the reins to slow his horse. When the stallion stopped, Griff jumped to the ground and doubled over in exhaustion. He braced his hands on his knees and gasped for air as if his lungs might burst.

She was a threat to everything he'd protected himself from since he'd lost Julia. And she was everything his heart cried out to have again.

Every time he was in the same room with her he wanted to take her in his arms and hold her. Every time he looked into her face he wanted to press his lips against hers and feel her mouth open beneath his. Every time he stood near her he remembered how she felt in his arms, how his flesh burned when he held her. How eagerly she wrapped her arms around his neck and clung to him.

He ached until the pain was unbearable. Thinking about how desperately he wanted to look at every glorious inch of her gnawed a hole deep in his gut. He wanted to touch her, stretch his naked body atop hers, and feel her beneath him. He wanted to bury himself deep within her and truly make her his wife.

He stood, then raked his fingers through his wind-whipped hair. Dear God, how had it come to this? When had he allowed himself to forget the painful lesson he'd been taught? Giving Anne his heart amounted to a death sentence. Attempts had already been made. She'd nearly been run down by a carriage. The carriage "accident" on their way here wasn't an accident. What more proof did he need that he was incapable of protecting her?

Griff wiped the sweat that poured from his face. He couldn't be a loving husband to her until he was sure she was out of danger. He couldn't risk getting her with child until he knew he could keep both her and the child safe. And he couldn't do either until he knew the identity of the man intent on revenge.

Griff dropped his head back on his shoulders and breathed a heavy sigh that stretched his lungs and burned his chest. He walked back to where his horse stood grazing on lush meadow grass and looked around. If someone was out there, he'd find him. He wasn't going to let Anne die like Freddie had.

Great rivers of sweat ran down the horse's neck and his flanks. Griff had worked him hard. He patted the horse lovingly, then put his foot in the stirrup and swung up. He settled himself in the saddle and stopped. A slight movement to his right caught his attention.

Griff slowly turned his mount. He kept his gaze on the grove of trees where he'd seen the disturbance, and urged his horse forward.

Someone was there. He felt him watching.

Griff reached for the pistol he kept in his jacket pocket and brought it out. He wasn't sure what good it would do—perhaps none if the sniper shot at him without stepping into the open—but at least he would have it. He wouldn't die without a fight.

He nudged his horse forward and slowly made his way toward the copse of trees. If his enemy was there, he would find him. He would put an end to this right now, before another attempt was made on Anne's life.

His heart pounded in his chest like hammer against anvil. The blood thundered in his head, causing tiny white spots to dance in front of his eyes. He thought of Anne, of never seeing her again. He foolishly wanted one memory to hold on to—one night of having her in his arms, of loving her, of burying himself deep inside her before his enemy's bullet killed him. He wished he had loved her just once before it was too late to ever have her.

He neared the trees and saw a slight movement again in front of him.

The killer was still there.

A light sheen of perspiration gathered on Griff's forehead as he rode toward the targeted spot.

Nothing happened. No shot rang out. No figure barreled through the trees. No piercing pain from a bullet seared his flesh.

Griff slid to the ground and held his pistol at his side. This is the spot where he'd seen movement. The spot where the person watching him had waited.

Griff walked among the trees, then crouched down to look for any sign someone had been there. He rubbed his hand over the thick grass behind one of the trees. A footprint. It was nothing that could help him identify who'd stood there, but it was proof that he hadn't imagined being watched.

Griff followed the prints until they disappeared. Whoever it was knew what he was doing. Griff's mind flashed to Jack Hawkins. If the killer was Jack, why hadn't he fired? He'd had a clear shot, but he'd let Griff go. That meant he was still waiting, watching.

Griff searched the area but found nothing more. At last he mounted, then dug his heels into his stallion's flanks and rode him at an easy pace. What game was the bastard playing? Why hadn't Hawkins shown himself?

Griff's blood ran cold. Maybe Hawkins didn't want him. Maybe he wanted Anne. Just like Griff had taken his brother from him, maybe Jack Hawkins intended to take Anne's life in return.

Griff pushed his mount harder. He had to keep her safe. He'd double the men who watched the grounds and post guards all around the house. Nothing would happen to her. He'd make damn sure.

When he reached the manor, he jumped to the ground. He handed his groom the reins, then raced up the walk. Carter was waiting at the front door. "Send Franklin to me right away. Then have water sent up for a bath."

"At once, sir."

Griff put his foot on the first step, then stopped.

Anne stood at the top of the long, spiral staircase. She wore a blue-and-white checked morning dress, the skirt so full it made her waist appear even more minimal than he remembered from when he held her. She wore her hair swept loosely up to the top of her head, tiny stray tendrils framing her face and resting against her long, graceful neck. Her lips were full and rosy, and he remembered the feel of them beneath his.

His body responded with an ache he wished the long, hard ride would have eased but hadn't. Her skin was pure and flawless, and his fingers ached to touch her silky smoothness. Then he looked into her eyes.

Regret slammed him in the gut. Her eyes were dull and lifeless. Dark circles rimmed her ebony eyes. She looked tired, as if she hadn't slept the night before. As if she'd lain awake waiting for him, wondering why her husband had not come to her.

She stood at the top and did not move.

He climbed the stairs until he was even with her. "Good morning." He leaned over to kiss her gently on the cheek.

She stiffened. "Good morning, sir." Her voice was soft, placid, resigned. "You must have risen early."

"Yes. I went for a ride."

"Did you find what you were searching for?"

He clenched his jaw. "Yes." Their gazes locked. He saw the understanding in her eyes. "Have you eaten yet?" he asked, knowing she probably had not.

"No."

"I'll bathe, then be down to join you."

"That isn't necessary."

He tried to smile. "It's silly for us to eat separately."

"But not for us to spend our wedding night separated?"

He took a harsh breath and waited until he had rein on his temper. "I'll be down shortly," he said through clenched teeth.

She shrugged her shoulders, indicating she didn't care one way or another. "As you wish."

He recognized her efforts to distance herself from him. Even though he realized that would keep her safest, he was loath to have it happen. "At your convenience, Martha can show you the house. Make a list of anything you need or want changed, and I'll see that it gets done. The house has gone without a mistress for over four years. I'm sure there is much that needs attention."

"Am I confined then to the house?"

The chill in her voice sent a shiver down his spine. "No. You are free to go outside. But I will go with you. After we've eaten, I'll show you the gardens. They are quite spacious. I'm sure you will not find them confining."

She breathed a sigh that nearly screamed her frustration. The harsh clip of her words confirmed it. "Thank you, sir. I look forward to your company."

The look on her face said there were a hundred things she looked forward to before his company—including a trip to the gallows. He didn't blame her for feeling this way. He'd been a disappointment so far. But he'd had no choice—not until either he or the killer was dead. Until then he could neither take her heart, nor offer her his own. He could offer her nothing more than his promise to keep her safe, and pray he didn't fail her as he'd failed Julia.

"I won't be long." He stepped aside so she could pass him.

With a stiff nod, she made her way down the stairs. She didn't look back.

The knot in his stomach tightened as he watched her. He knew his absence from her bed had hurt her last night.

He watched until she was out of sight, then turned. As he was about to walk away, the front door opened, and Franklin entered the foyer.

"You wanted to see me, sir?"

"Yes, Franklin. Double the guards to watch the grounds. Post another dozen men in the garden and close to the house."

"Yes, sir. Right away."

"And Franklin," Griff added when the agent turned to leave. "Tell the men to keep their eyes open."

"Yes, sir."

Franklin left and Griff walked to his room. He had to get this over with soon. He couldn't take a chance with her. He couldn't risk her getting hurt.

# Chapter 24

❧

When they had finished their meal, Griff offered her his arm to give her a quick tour of some of the rooms in the house before they visited the gardens. She lifted her hand as soon as she could. It was hard enough being this near him. Touching him was an unbearable torture. They walked in silence, just as they'd eaten.

He escorted her to a wide set of stairs that led to a separate wing of Covington Manor. They climbed the five steps, then through a spacious entryway that opened to a magnificent ballroom large enough to entertain more than a hundred guests. Anne stood in awe at the top of the stairs. The room was elegantly ornate and furnished in the most stylish décor.

She wondered how often he and Julia had entertained here, how often their home had been filled with gay laughter and soft music. She pushed the thought away and tried to concentrate on anything other than the wife Griff wished hadn't died.

She walked down the five steps, then across the ballroom floor. On the far side of the room, four wide double doors stood open as if in invitation for her to walk through. Once outside, she got her first glimpse of the mammoth gardens he'd mentioned.

She stood on the wide stone terrace and took in the scene before her. It was breathtaking. Everywhere she looked flowers and bushes flourished in riotous color while trees and shrubbery stood out in healthy perfection.

"It's beautiful," she whispered.

"Do you like it?"

"How could one not like it?"

She walked to the edge of the terrace and leaned against the cement railing. She suddenly felt like a child let loose in a fairyland. She wanted to run this way and that so she could see everything that was there.

"Was this your wife's creation?" she asked, the question out of her mouth before she could stop herself.

"Julia?" He laughed. "Heavens no. She wasn't fond of anything without a roof on it. She used to stand before the window to look out and say that was as close to the outdoors as she wanted to get. The gardens were my mother's. She was the one who envisioned it all and badgered the gardeners until they planted every tree and bush and flower she wanted."

"And you have kept it up?"

"Yes."

There were three paths that wound through the trees and bushes. Anne rushed down the three center steps that led off the terrace. She walked past beds of azaleas, rhododendrons, and roses and lilies of every color imaginable, past stone benches scattered along the path and tucked beneath trees.

When they reached the fork where the path split, she stopped to take in the magnificent sight that surrounded her. She sat for a second on a bench beneath a huge, spreading beechnut tree and looked at the daisies at her feet.

"Are you fond of the outdoors?" Griff asked.

"Yes. We had a lovely garden at Brentwood Manor, but it was nothing as beautiful as this. Freddie used to tease me that one of the reasons he could not take me to London was because it would take me too long to get the dirt from beneath my fingernails."

Griff leaned down and snapped off three daisies and held them out to her. When she reached for them, their fingers touched. He turned his palm in to her palm and held her hand. He did not let go.

A thousand pinpricks raced through her body along with a heat so intense she thought she might suffocate. She would not let him do this. It would only hurt worse when his disposition changed again from warm to cold. She took the flowers and pulled away.

"Come here, Anne." Griff held out his hand.

She hesitated, then took his hand. Together they walked down the path to her right.

Griff stopped and Anne took in the sight before her. Her breath caught.

A huge fountain bubbled in the center of a large circle of neatly trimmed grass. A number of stone statues stood as sentinels around the water's edge. Anne's mouth dropped when she saw them.

"Father is responsible for the statues."

Griff put his arm around her waist and led her down one path, then crossed over to another. More statues lined the path.

"Mother fell in love with the statues when she and Father visited abroad. She wanted to bring one or two of them back but was too embarrassed to have "naked people" where visitors and guests might see them, so she refused to let Father purchase them. Father bought them without her knowing and had them shipped over. He placed them in various spots throughout the garden.

"Quite often Mother would have them moved so they were more hidden, but Father always had them moved back. He finally told her that moving them was going to cause the gardeners to injure their backs, so she finally stopped having them moved. He told her if anyone objected to them, she was to tell them the statues were his and he refused to get rid of them. Do they embarrass you?"

"Not at all. They're beautiful."

She thought she noticed a smile on his face but couldn't be sure. When he turned to speak to her, the serious set to his features was back.

"Let me show you one more part of the garden."

Anne placed her hand atop his arm and walked with him down another path, this one to the left. The paths twisted and turned, going off in every direction imaginable. They were walking through a maze. Every foot was lined with bushes that were taller than Griff by at least half a head. The mystical effect of this secluded area of the garden was remarkable.

"This is remarkable," she exclaimed. She rushed ahead of him to see which direction their path would take next.

"Adam and I used to spend hours in here hiding from each other when we were young. Turn to your left." He let her go a few feet before he was at her side. "Look ahead."

"Oh," she said on a whisper. "It's beautiful." Ahead of them was a large wooden gazebo.

Anne walked to it, then climbed the steps that led to the covered interior of the summerhouse. She slowly walked the circumference, studying the landscape from every angle.

"Once you make it this far," he said from behind her, "it's easy to get back. Just follow this path. When you have to turn, always take the path to your right. In time you will reach the house."

"What happens if I take the paths to the left?"

There was a slight hesitation before he answered. "It will take you to the chapel and the cemetery where all the Blackmoor ancestors are buried."

Something drew her there. Anne went down the three steps and took the first turn to the left. Then the next. She walked until she saw the small, brown stone building ahead of her. She knew without asking that this was the chapel. She stood outside the door until he opened it, then went inside.

The chapel was small, not nearly as big as she anticipated it would be. But it was beautiful inside. The moment she passed through the doors, she felt as if a strange force welcomed her—as if God's voice whispered in her ear to assure her she had nothing to fear.

She reverently walked toward the altar but stopped midway down the aisle. The sun streamed through the stained-glass windows on both sides of the chapel. A glow of muted shades encompassed them. Her breath caught and all she could manage was a small, solemn sigh.

She turned and her gaze took in the surreal expression on Griff's face.

"This is where we should have married," he said. "It's where Blackmoors have said their vows for generations."

"Did you and Julia say your vows here?"

"Yes."

Anne stepped closer to the front of the chapel. "It is a special place. I feel as if the angels are here with us. As if they are hovering close to guard and protect us." She turned her head to look at him. "Is that how it is for you?"

"Yes. I never came here much until after I lost Julia and Andrew. Then, every time I walked through the doors, I experienced a peace I needed badly. I come here often, and it's always the same."

He touched her elbow and they walked the rest of the way down the short aisle. When they reached the front, he turned her in his arms and clasped her hands in his. "Do you know what I would have liked to have said to you the day we married?"

She shook her head. There was a serious expression on his face.

"I would have told you that I realize you would not have willingly chosen me for your husband. Now I understand why. I understand your fears. But I promise I will not be like your father. I will never choose a drink over doing what is best for you. Look how long I've gone already."

"And you don't want to have another drink?" she asked.

The air caught in his throat. "Only a dozen times a day or more." His gaze remained locked with hers. "But I have not let myself give in to the temptation. And I will not."

She tried to smile, though she wasn't sure she was successful.

"I wish things could be different," he whispered, brushing the backs of his fingers down her cheek.

"So do I. Only not in the same sense as you want them to be different."

"How is that?"

"I would wish for the strength to be content with only the blessings of each day."

"Perhaps that's because you've never received the world's blessings and had to give them back."

Anne wanted to cry out that she knew she wasn't Julia—that she could never be Julia. No matter how much he wished it.

"If there's anything you want," he said, his tone containing a softness she was not used to, "you have only to ask. If it's within my power, I'll give it to you." He took a deep breath. "That is all I have to offer."

The warmth Anne saw in his eyes the moment before vanished. In its place was the hard, unyielding resolve she'd lived with since she'd spoken her vows.

"Is it enough?" he asked.

She looked at him and blinked twice to stop the wetness that blurred her vision. "I do not want for much, sir. Only—" She stopped.

"Only what?"

*Only to be your wife.*

*Only to be loved.*

How could she tell him? She could not say the words. It was like wishing for the moon.

"Nothing, sir. I only want what you are willing to give. I will give you what I can, along with my hand to hold when you lose your way, as I promised."

He touched his fingers to her cheek, then his gaze moved to her mouth. A moan of anguish came from deep inside him and he lowered his head and pressed his lips to hers.

His kiss was soft and reverent, filled with only a sampling of the emotions they both struggled to keep at bay whenever they were near each other. He kissed her again.

She wrapped her arms around his neck and held him. Yes, this is what she wanted there to be between them. This is what she needed to know was still there.

When their kiss ended, she remained close to him.

Griff brushed his fingers down her cheek as if he needed a reminder of what had transpired between them. Then he stepped away from her. His separation indicated that Julia still possessed a large part of his heart. He couldn't allow himself to care for Anne like he'd cared for Julia. The love he still felt for his dead wife would not let him.

He looked at her as if he'd read her mind, then walked toward a side door that led from the chapel.

Bright sunlight blinded her when he opened the door, then the chapel darkened again when he closed the door behind him.

She stood at the front of the chapel with her hands fisted at her sides. A quiet anger built within her. She was his wife now, the woman he should want at his side. How could he kiss her with such passion one minute and run away from her the next? It was as if a part of him refused to give himself over to her—as if a likeness of his dead wife flashed before him, and he regretted that he'd besmirched her memory.

Anne followed him out the door and to the place where he stood. He anchored his hands against the wrought-iron fence as if he needed its support to help him carry the heavy load placed on his shoulders. The fence surrounded a small, private graveyard. She knew in an instant who was buried here.

She looked down. Her gaze rested on two fairly new stones that marked two well-tended graves.

"They're not really here, you know." His voice was filled with pain. "Their bodies were never recovered."

She wanted to reach out to him, to hold his hand and comfort him, but she could not.

"I could lie and tell you I never loved her. That we had married young and afterward discovered we were not suited to each other, but that wouldn't be true."

Anne thought she would be ill. Her stomach clenched and rolled. It took every ounce of her self-control to keep from running away from him and taking a carriage back to London.

"I loved her very much, and she loved me. Together we had a son who was the joy of our lives. When I lost them, I thought I would die." He lowered his head between his outstretched arms. "It's my fault they are dead."

He took a deep breath that expanded his shoulders and chest. "Julia was terrified of sailing. I had some business to attend to in France and wanted her to go with me. She didn't want to go, but I forced her. I promised her nothing would happen to her and Andrew. That I would take care of them. Then the storm came up.

"The wind tossed our ship around like a toy boat. We crashed into some rocks off the coast of France and began taking on water. The captain ordered all the passengers to board the longboats.

"Julia's fear was irrational. She didn't want to leave the cabin, but I made her. I took her and Andrew atop to wait to board one of the boats, then went below to help the other passengers. When I returned, Julia was gone. She'd taken Andrew back to our cabin."

Griff swiped his hand down his face. "I shouldn't have left them. I knew she was too frightened to wait there without me."

"So you blame yourself because they died?" For the first time she understood the guilt he carried with him.

"Who else is there to blame?"

"No one, as long as you have a need to blame someone."

He shot her a confused look.

"We often assign blame when something tragic happens that we can't understand. I tried to blame you when Freddie was shot."

"But I was responsible—"

"No. You were there, nothing more. Perhaps the bullet that killed him was intended for you. Perhaps it wasn't. Maybe we will never know. But what good would have been served if you had died, too? Would Rebecca and I have been better off if you had died?"

The muscles across his shoulders bunched and she heard his shaky sigh.

"That's what makes death so unbearable to some," she continued. "Sometimes there is just no one to blame. I think you'd like to blame God, but you aren't brave enough, so you blame yourself."

Anne turned away from his angry expression and looked down. The wrought-iron fence was lined with wildflowers of every color. She reached down and picked two bunches, then entered the gate and laid flowers on each grave.

"There is no one there," Griff repeated, his voice hoarse and riddled with emotion.

"To me they are there. This is their final resting place. You are the one who cannot let them go. You're the one who can't accept their deaths and go on with your life."

"I can't forget them," he whispered, the agony and hurt inside him plain to hear.

"I would never ask you to forget them. I only ask that you make room in your life for me, too."

Anne ran her fingers across Griff's child's headstone, and walked back out through the gate. She did not wait for him but headed down the path that would take her back to the manor. She refused to live the rest of her life in the shadow of a woman she had never met, a woman she could never replace.

She swiped the back of her hand across the tears that threatened to spill from her eyes. She refused to give in to the hurt she felt.

Her options were so few. He'd told her she only had to ask, and if it was within his power, he would give it to her. He would live to regret his words. She would not let him go until she had exactly what she wanted.

If he could never love her, she would have the next best thing.

*　*　*

Griff tossed and turned as sleep eluded him again. He knew tonight would be another sleepless night. He'd hurt her again today. For as much as he'd tried to make her first day tolerable, it had turned out to be a day riddled with painful truths and unpleasant memories. Now she knew. Knew about Julia. Knew he hadn't protected Julia after he'd promised. Now Anne knew his promise to protect her was just as hollow.

He lay on his back and crossed his arms beneath his head. He shouldn't have kissed her.

It was almost more than he could do not to go to her. It nearly took more willpower than he possessed not to walk through that door and into her room and take her. Bloody hell, but he wanted her. Wanted her with a desperation he did not think he would ever feel again. Most of all, he wanted her to know that she didn't have to compete with Julia. Julia was his past. Anne was his future.

He wanted to make a life with her, have a family with her. Watch the children they created grow. He wanted to laugh with her and talk with her and hold her through the night. He wanted to share his every thought with her and have her share her thoughts with him. And then...

Griff remembered the sabotaged carriage and the movement in the trees. He could not risk it. The attempts on his life proved it could all be taken away from him in the blink of an eye.

He broke out in a cold sweat. He couldn't stand to lose her, too. He couldn't survive if he had to give up another child.

Griff threw back the covers and jumped from his bed. The moment his feet hit the floor, his bedroom door opened. He turned to face her.

Anne stood in the doorway, holding a flickering candle in her hand. Her face looked pale in the candlelight. "Anne? What's wrong?"

She stepped into the room and closed the door behind her.

"Anne? What is it? Are you all right?"

She looked at him with a determination he'd never seen before. She opened her mouth to speak, but the sight of his naked body obviously startled her. Her gaze moved over him.

Griff muttered an oath and reached for his robe to cover himself. He pulled it closed in the front, but not before he caught her gaze riveted just below his waist. For a moment he thought she was going to run from the room, but she held her ground and took her first step closer.

He tied the belt that held his robe secure and stepped close to her. When he was close enough, he took the flickering candle from her trembling hand and set it on the table beside the bed. "What's wrong? Has something happened?"

She swallowed hard. "Did you mean it when you said if there was anything I wanted, and if it was within your power, I only had to ask and you would give it to me?"

His heart fell to the pit of his stomach. A feeling of dread consumed him. "Yes."

"Then I have something I want. Something you have within your power to give me."

He turned and walked to the window. A cold chill washed over him. He was going to lose her. He'd been afraid that when she found out about Julia she would leave him. What woman wanted to stay with a husband who couldn't protect his family? What woman wanted to stay with a man someone was trying to kill? What woman wanted to stay with a man she was not certain could survive another day without a drink? Why the hell would she want to risk spending her life with him? He wasn't worth it.

After a long while, he turned back to her. "Very well. What would you like from me?"

She swallowed again. At least telling him she intended to leave him was not easy for her.

"What is it, Anne? What would you like me to give you? An annulment?"

Her eyes opened wide as if she couldn't believe he had read her thoughts.

"Is that what *you* want?" she asked on a hoarse whisper. "Do you want our marriage to be annulled?"

"No, but I would understand if you did. I have not been much of a husband to you."

"You have not been *any* kind of a husband to me."

Her words stunned him. "No, I suppose I haven't. You would certainly be within your rights to ask for an annulment."

"I do not wish to be separated from you."

He felt the air leave his lungs. "If not an annulment, what do you want?"

The relief he felt was so great, he vowed she could ask for the moon and he would give it to her. He would give her anything if she would not leave him.

He looked into her eyes and saw the determination. "What is it, Anne? What do you want?"

"A child. I want to have a child."

Griff caught himself on the edge of his bedside table. She'd just asked for more than the moon.

# Chapter 25

❧

His mouth dropped. "You can't be serious."

Anne saw his horrified look but didn't give him time to voice his refusal. She couldn't back down. Her future rested on this moment. "I know you didn't want to marry me. That you weren't ready to take another wife, but it's too late to undo what has been done." A cold chill washed over her. "Unless *you* want an annulment." She looked into his eyes, praying she would see his true feelings. "It is not too late. Our marriage hasn't been consummated."

"No, I don't want an annulment."

Anne breathed a sigh of relief when Griff didn't hesitate. "Neither do I. I married you knowing how things would be between us. I married you knowing that I could never replace what you'd lost when your wife and child were taken from you. But I do not intend to allow you to dictate what I must give up because of your reservations."

She took a step closer to him.

"I will not spend my life alone. If I—"

She stopped. She did not have the courage to tell him if she could not have a husband who cared for her, she would at least have children she could love. "You promised you would give me whatever I asked, as long as it was in your power," she finished.

"You don't know what you are asking of me."

"I'm not asking anything of you. I'm demanding that you be a husband to me, at least until I am carrying a child."

"It's not just *a* child. It will be *my* child."

"It will be *mine!*" she yelled. The frustration and anxiety she felt stripped her of her patience. "You do not have to love it, as you do not have to love me. You only have to provide for me and the child I will bear so that we do not go homeless or hungry."

"Bloody hell, woman! Do you think I could watch you grow large with my child and not marvel because I gave it life? That I could ignore the fact that the babe growing inside you is flesh of my flesh and that it carries my blood in its veins?" Griff slapped his hand against his thigh and walked away from her. "Do you think it's possible for us to couple like two animals, then walk away from each other as if what we shared meant nothing?"

"It is a risk I am willing to take."

"Well, I'm not!" His deep voice caused her to flinch.

The air cracked in mocking silence as his words echoed in her ears. The door to his secret fears opened, and for the first time she saw what he truly feared. "Is that what you are afraid of? That if you lie with me you might come to care for me?"

"I already care for you. That's why I married you, because I care for you."

"No. You married me because you felt obligated to me and because Portsmouth left you no choice."

"Perhaps you don't remember the kisses we shared, wife, but I do. There was nothing uncaring or unemotional about them. I all but had you naked in my arms when the earl walked in on us."

"That doesn't prove anything except there is a certain attraction between us."

"There is more than an attraction. Every time I hold you I forget why I should not."

His words stunned her. "Why shouldn't you hold me?"

"Because neither of us can take such a risk. I don't want anything to happen to you. There has been an attempt on my life twice, and both times someone else paid the price. First Freddie. Then you. That same person was my shadow wherever I went in London, and now he has followed us to Covington Manor. This morning when I went for my ride, he was in the bushes waiting for me."

"You saw him?"

"No. But he was there." Griff paced the room. His hands fisted in tight knots at his side. "Don't you see, Anne? I can't risk that something might happen to you. Just give me until I find who it is that wants to kill me."

She squared her shoulders. "I have lived my whole life afraid to take risks. When Father was alive, we couldn't go to London for fear Society would discover his sickness. Then I was afraid to risk taking a husband because I might end up living the same life as my mother. I don't want to be afraid any longer, Griff. I don't want to be alone."

He closed his eyes. "You don't know what you are asking."

"I do," she said softly. "I am asking you to give up one small piece of your life. I am asking you to find a tiny place in your heart for a wife and child. You don't have to promise we'll have your whole heart, just a corner where we can find contentment."

She paused to take a breath. "I am asking you to give me however many hours or days or years God grants us together."

He shook his head as if struggling with all the fears he'd harbored since he'd lost his wife and son in the storm. She knew his agony as if it were her own.

"Would it be so terrible to love me, Griff?"

He shook his head, then reached out his arms and clasped his hands around her shoulders. He pulled her close to him. "No. It would not be so terrible to love you. It would be impossible to lose you."

"You won't lose me, Griff. I promise."

He placed his finger beneath her chin and tilted her head, then brought his mouth down over hers. His lips were warm and firm pressed against hers. He pulled away from her, then kissed her again, his touch gentle at first, then harsh and demanding, with a certain desperation she tried to meet and satisfy.

She knew what he expected, what he wanted. He opened his mouth and she opened hers, anticipating, expecting the thrust of his tongue. The swirling inside her yearned with a savage desperation. She pressed herself closer and wrapped her arms around his neck. She urged him to kiss her like he had before. But he held back.

When she could not wait any longer, she raked her fingers through his hair and brought his head closer to her. She needed to touch him, feel him, and she explored further.

His tongue darted forward, touching, then mating with hers in a frenzy she could not control. She withdrew, leaving him to savagely breach the warmth of her mouth. He kissed her long and hard, then pulled his mouth from hers.

"Do you have any idea what you do to me?" he whispered, trailing kisses over her cheek and down her neck.

"Yes," she whispered back. She spanned her hands across his back and shoulders to keep him close. "But I am not near the expert as you."

His hands cupped her cheeks, holding her steady while his face lingered only inches from hers. "You are expert enough, wife."

He brought his mouth down over hers again, kissing her with ravenous hunger and a fierceness that left her gasping. She had no choice but to hold on to his shoulders and arms and let him be her strength.

He kissed her with frenzied urgency, then with a consummate completion. With each assault, a hunger raged inside her that was nearly uncontrollable. She wanted more than his kisses. She wanted to feel his hands on her naked flesh.

She wanted to be his wife.

As if she'd spoken her thoughts aloud, he pulled her close. He kissed her again then looked down at her with eyes black and mysterious with passion.

"Are you sure? Do you have any doubts at all, Anne?"

"No. The time for doubts was before I let you kiss me that first time. Heaven help me, I think I will die if you stop now."

His fingers worked the ribbons at her neck. He loosened the lacing down the front and pushed the material from her shoulders.

Filmy white gauze and soft peach satin slid over her hips and landed in a puddle at her feet. When she was naked, he picked her up in his arms and placed her on the bed.

She watched as he loosened the tie at his waist and shrugged out of his robe. He stood naked before her, so virile and handsome she wanted to cry.

"You are beautiful," she whispered.

He chuckled as he brought himself down over her. "I think those are words that I am supposed to say, my lady."

"I don't need to hear that I am beautiful."

She lifted her hand and stroked her fingers down his face. Oh, but he was handsome. More handsome than she ever imagined her husband would be.

He nestled his face in the crook of her neck, nuzzling her skin and kissing her to distraction. "Then what do you need to hear, Anne?"

"Only that you want me. For this. For tonight. For as long as we have together."

"I will always want you, Anne," he whispered. Then he made her his wife.

\* \* \*

Griff slept peacefully. She could tell by the slow, relaxed breaths he took. He'd dropped one arm and one leg over her, and lay in quiet contentment.

She wrapped her arms around him, marveling at the rightness of his weight atop her and how complete she felt. Marveling at how perfect loving him was.

Knowing what they'd shared was worth the risk.

She closed her eyes and slept in his arms. She would not worry that Julia or Andrew held the largest part of his heart, just as she would not worry that he would want a drink more than he wanted a life with her.

She would live her life with him one day at a time. And she would be happy.

# Chapter 26

✤

Anne looked up from the letter she was compos-
ing to Becca and sighed. How could she put into
words how her life had changed since she had become
Griff's wife? How could she explain that marrying Griff
wasn't the tragedy she'd feared at the time?

She thought of the man she'd married and realized
she didn't regret becoming his wife. She'd come to care
for him and rely on him. She'd come to look to him to fill
the part of herself she'd never known was missing—a part
that made her feel whole.

Although he was still a mystery to her, she knew that
given the chance, she wouldn't do anything differently. She
wouldn't wish to be married to anyone else if it meant she
would have to live a future without Griff. She would take
one day at a time and trust that her life would be complete.

He had changed little in the past two weeks. He still
kept her at arm's length more often than not, refusing to
open up to her or show her that he might care for her.
She understood now that he was terrified that something
might happen to her.

He went out every day to search for the enemy he was
certain was waiting to do her harm. He'd increased the
number of men guarding her to the point that she'd given

up trying to call them all by name. She was never alone. There was always someone with her, watching over her.

Every night he came to her, whether out of need, or because of her demand, she wasn't sure. She preferred not to know for certain. She'd come to care for him entirely too much to realize his reason might only be one of obligation.

She blushed when she remembered the hours she had spent in his arms. Every night for the two weeks they'd been together, he'd shown her how passionate it could be between a husband and wife. How marvelous it was to receive what he gave her.

Some nights he made slow, languorous love, touching and caressing her until she was wild with passion. Other nights, his lovemaking contained a desperation to hold her, to consume her. On those occasions it was as if he feared this might be the last night they had together.

Even though they shared no words of love, words weren't necessary. Losing someone he'd loved as completely as he'd loved Julia was an obstacle between them. But the obstacle wasn't insurmountable.

Anne knew he wanted her. Perhaps in time he would even come to love her. Especially once there was a child.

She placed her hand on her stomach and breathed deeply. Perhaps he'd already placed a babe inside her. She would not know for at least another week.

She couldn't stop the smile that covered her face. Perhaps when there was a child…

Carter's voice brought her back to the present.

"My lady," he announced from the doorway. "You have a visitor. The Marquess of Brentwood is here to see you."

Anne hesitated but couldn't invent a plausible reason to refuse him. "Show him in, Carter."

"Yes, my lady."

The marquess entered the room and Anne struggled to appear hospitable. "Good day, Lord Brentwood." She rose and stepped around the desk.

The marquess walked toward her with a purpose, as though he was eager to see her. "My dear Anne," he said, reaching out his hands to take hers. "You look radiant. As if marriage truly agrees with you."

"It does," she answered.

Brentwood lifted her hands to his lips.

The second she was able, she pulled her hands out of his grasp. "I didn't realize you'd returned to the country," she said.

"London can occupy only so much of my time before I yearn to be back to the quiet solitude of the country. And, as you are aware, Brentwood Manor is a perfect place to find such contentment."

"Yes. It is beautiful."

Anne sat on the settee in the middle of the room and held out her hand to indicate one of the overstuffed chairs that faced her. Brentwood sat. When Carter brought tea, she poured, then handed him a cup.

"Is your husband away?" he asked, taking one of the small sandwiches she offered.

"Yes, but I expect him back any moment. He went out to visit one of the tenants." The lie came easily to her. Griff had left early that morning to continue his search. He was obsessed with finding the person responsible for the attempts on her life.

She prayed someone would go for Griff so she wouldn't have to be alone with the man who held Freddie's title. She couldn't explain it, but he made her uneasy.

"I'm glad to see you looking so happy," he said. "I was not the only one surprised by your hasty wedding. Half of London is still in shock."

"There is no reason for them to be," she said.

"On the contrary. No one was even aware that you and Blackmoor were enamored of each other. Especially your suitors. If we had known, we would have each pressed our suits with much more fervor. We didn't realize we had such formidable competition."

She didn't say anything but lifted her cup to her lips and took a sip of tea.

"I have to admit," he said, "that I'm glad you returned to the country. It's wonderful to have neighbors again. After you settle in, I will have to have a dinner party to celebrate your marriage. Just a small, intimate dinner, as many of our neighbors are still in town."

"That would be nice," she managed, without displaying her true feelings. "Perhaps in a month or two."

Brentwood arched his brows. "Of course." He set his cup and saucer down on the small table beside his chair and steadied his gaze on her. "There is one other matter that brought me here today." He leaned back in a relaxed pose, as if he were about to discuss some insignificant detail.

Anne raised her brows. "Yes?"

"It concerns the strip of land your brother left you in his will."

Her mind tried to grasp what he was talking about. She'd almost forgotten about the small piece of land Freddie had bequeathed to her.

"As you are probably aware, the land is worthless. It is nothing but craggy rocks that cannot be negotiated by man nor beast. It is riddled with dangerous caverns and caves that flood with each tide. The land has no conceivable value to anyone."

"But you are interested in purchasing it?"

"Yes."

"Why?"

"Because it belongs to Brentwood. It was originally a part of the estate before your brother had it separated. Even though it is uninhabitable, I want it back to make it part of the original Brentwood Estate."

"I see."

"I would, of course, offer you a fair price. Say, ten thousand pounds."

Anne couldn't believe she'd heard him right. "Ten thousand pounds, my lord?"

"Yes."

"But I thought you said the land was worthless."

"It is, to everyone but me. It's worth that much so that Brentwood is not partitioned off."

Anne sat back against the sofa and remembered the letter Freddie left her concerning the land.

*I regret that I have not yet acquired enough wealth to adequately support you, Annie, but at the moment this parcel of land is all I have to leave you to preserve the Brentwood name. Know that there is no one else I would have possess it but you, and promise that you will never sell it.*

"I'm afraid I cannot consider selling the land, my lord."

A frown covered his face. "But why? What possible use can you have for it?"

She stiffened her spine. "I have no use for it. But it is all I have from Freddie. I have no desire to part with it, no matter how much you offer me for it."

"But that is foolish. It is nothing but a dangerous piece of land, littered with rocks and boulders, and caves that flood with each swell of the ocean. Surely you don't intend to let sentimentality lead you to make such a foolish decision?"

"I'm afraid I do, sir."

"Then I will offer more. Twelve thousand pounds."

"No, sir. It is not the money."

Large, angry veins stood out on his neck. "You are being ridiculous! The land is worthless."

"It is not to me," she said.

Brentwood got to his feet and raised his voice. "I will not take no for an answer. I will not give up until—"

"Enough!"

Griff charged into the room and made his way to her side. "You will not speak to my wife in that manner, Brentwood." Griff rested his hand on her shoulder. "What is this all about?"

Anne looked at the livid expression on Griff's face. "Lord Brentwood has come to extend an offer to buy the land Freddie left me when he died. It is evidently a worthless strip of coastline and of no value to either of us, except it is all I have from Freddie."

"And you do not wish to sell it?"

"No, sir," she said, hating the tears that swelled in her eyes.

"Very well," he whispered, lifting her chin with his finger as if telling her to be brave a little longer.

He turned to Brentwood. If the look on Griff's face did not send trepidation racing through the marquess, then he was not capable of feeling fear.

"My wife does not wish to sell the land, Brentwood."

"But—"

"Enough! She does not wish to part with it. She thanks you for your kind offer, but she is not interested. I do not wish to have the matter brought up again. Is that understood?"

"It is," Brentwood hissed through clenched teeth. "If you will excuse me, I think I have overstayed my welcome."

Carter appeared to show the marquess out. Not until they heard the door close behind him did either of them speak.

"What exactly did Brentwood tell you about the land Freddie left you in his will?" Griff asked, sitting down beside her on the sofa and taking her hands in his.

"Nothing, other than he wanted to buy it."

"Do you have a copy of the will?"

"Yes."

"I'd like to see it, Anne."

Anne got the will and the note Freddie had written her from a small wooden box in her bedroom where she kept the few personal mementos she had, and brought them down.

"This is what the solicitor gave me, and this is the note Freddie left. Perhaps you will know what it means."

Griff took both papers from her. He read the will first.

Anne sat quietly beside him and watched his face while he read. The frown on his forehead deepened. When he finished, he opened Freddie's letter and read it.

"What does it mean?" she asked when he said nothing.

Griff shook his head. "I'm not sure. I can't imagine why Freddie went to such pains to purchase it. He had to petition the courts to get it, and submit a mountain of paperwork as well as pay a staggering amount in legal fees for something that is seemingly worthless."

"Did he ever speak to you about it?"

"No. Never."

Griff read the papers again. The look on his face indicated he didn't understand them any more the second time he read them.

"How much did Brentwood offer you for it?"

"Twelve thousand pounds."

His eyes widened, then he looked back down at the papers in his hands.

"Griff?"

He looked up from the will.

"I want to see the land Freddie left me."

"It's too dangerous to go there, Anne. We would have to travel in the open, and I don't want to take the risk."

"We can go in a closed carriage. We will not be in danger if no one can see us."

"I said no."

"Then I will give you tonight to change your mind and agree to take me, or allow me to go on my own. Either way, tomorrow morning I intend to see what Freddie left me that is so important to the new Marquess of Brentwood that he would offer twelve thousand pounds to have it."

She spun on her heels and left him before he had a chance to argue with her. She knew their discussion was not over, but before she was finished he would find out how stubborn she could be, and that when she made up her mind to do something, nothing could stop her.

Besides, she had all night to convince him.

Her blood ran hot just thinking of the delightful things she could do to change his mind.

# Chapter 27

❧

Anne pressed back against the carriage seat and held her breath as the young lad Timothy snapped the reins and drove the horses away from Covington Manor. With every clop of the horses' hooves, she waited for one of her guard's booming voices to call her carriage to a stop.

It had been much harder than she'd anticipated to get away from their watchful eyes. There must be a dozen or more men surrounding the house keeping watch. She'd had to sneak past every one of them.

There'd be hell to pay when Griff realized she'd left the grounds without him. But she didn't care. She'd cross that bridge when she came to it.

She'd tried every bit of persuasion imaginable last night to get him to agree to take her to see the strip of land Freddie had left her, but he'd been adamant in his refusal. He forbade her to even consider it. That was when she had devised her plan. She'd only have to make sure Timothy did not pay for her stubbornness.

She'd perfected her scheme all day, making sure she hadn't overlooked one detail. She had the description of the land so Timothy could find it, and a pistol she'd taken from Griff's desk drawer—just in case she had trouble.

She had a lantern to explore the caves she knew were on the land, and some matches.

When she was certain she had everything she needed, she made arrangements for Timothy to take the carriage down the lane and wait for her on the other side of the garden wall. Once Griff was gone for the day, she made her escape.

Anne wasn't delusional enough to think she could accomplish her goal without Griff finding out what she'd done. Even if she returned before he did, she had no doubt one of the men would inform him that she'd left.

She rubbed her hands up and down her arms to ease the nervousness. She would worry about Griff later. He would no doubt be furious with her, and in a way, she didn't blame him. She'd promised him she wouldn't leave the house unless he was with her. But…

She touched her hand to the pistol, then looked out the window at the countryside. He would have to understand this was something she had to do.

When she returned, he would yell at her and double the guards to make certain she couldn't get out again. But by then it would be too late. She would have seen what Freddie had left her. She would know what was so important about the so-called worthless strip of land that Brentwood had offered her twelve thousand pounds for it.

"We're here, my lady," Timothy called, slowing the horses.

When the carriage stopped, Anne waited until Timothy opened the door, then stepped out. "Are you sure this is it?" she asked, looking around.

"Yes, my lady. According to the papers you gave me, the place you came to see starts over here where the land juts in, and goes to that big boulder down there." Timothy pointed to a huge rock that seemed far away.

"Are we on Brentwood land right now?"

"Yes. As far as that boulder. That is where Covington Estate starts."

Anne walked closer to the edge. A steep drop-off overlooked the ocean. From here she could see straight down to where the waves slapped against the sandy shore.

It was midafternoon and the tide was low. Every large rock and boulder was exposed, plus the openings to dozens of caves.

There was nothing there. Only a long stretch of desolate sand that no one should care about.

Why would Freddie go to such lengths to bequeath her this part of the estate? Brentwood was right. It looked worthless.

Anne walked closer to the edge, searching for a way to get down.

"Be careful, my lady. It's terribly steep right here, and the ground is rough. It's easy to lose your balance and slip."

"I would like to go down, Timothy."

"Are you sure, my lady? I don't think it's safe for you to attempt the climb down."

"I'm sure your master would agree with you, but since he is not here at the moment, I'll go down."

"Very well, my lady," he said shaking his head. "But I don't think it's wise."

"Don't worry. I'll be careful." Anne looked around. "Where would be the best place to get to the bottom?"

Timothy released a worried sigh. "Over here, then," he said. He offered her his arm and led her a few feet to the left. "I think the climb down will be easiest from here, where the slope is not so steep."

"Look, here's a path. Someone must come here, then."

"It looks that way, my lady. Do you want I should go down with you?"

"Yes, Timothy. I might need your help. I'd like to see what's down there. I brought a lantern with me."

Timothy picked up the lantern and gave her his hand as they made their way down the rocky hillside.

Rocks and boulders slowed their progress, and Anne had to watch every step she took. The small, pointed stones cut through her soft kid slippers, and she soon regretted she hadn't worn a heavier pair of shoes.

"I envy you your boots, Timothy," she muttered, wincing in pain when she stepped on another small stone. "Next time I will be more prepared."

"I have a feeling when the master finds out that you came here without him, there won't be no next time, ma'am."

Timothy's words caused a tremor to race through her. He was probably right. She just hoped she survived Griff's temper when he found out.

"Let's walk around a bit, Timothy," she said when they reached the bottom. "I want to get a look at everything."

"There don't seem to be anything of value here, ma'am. It looks kinda worthless."

"That's what I think, too," she said, looking up and down the desolate coast. "But we'll look anyway."

"Very well, mistress. But we can't be too long. The tide will come in after a bit, and we don't want to be caught down here when it does. See that line there." He pointed to where it looked as if someone had drawn a chalk line across the cliff. "That's the waterline. When the tide comes in, that's how far the water rushes up. There'll be no way for us to climb up fast enough if we stay here too long."

"Don't worry, Timothy. We'll be gone long before the tide comes in."

Timothy lit the lantern and stepped in front of her to lead the way. She followed close as he took her into the first cave to explore. The inside was dark and damp, and she doubted if it was big enough for Griff to stand upright without hitting his head on the rocky top. They walked forward a few feet, then stopped when they came to a dead end.

"Ain't nothin' here, my lady. We'd best try another one," Timothy said, turning around.

They went to a second cave, then a third. They carefully made their way down the coastline, entering a dozen more caves just like the first. Finally, they walked through an opening she knew was more than large enough for Griff to stand in with room to spare.

Timothy held the lantern high and gave a whistle. This cave was huge compared to the others. The tunnel seemed at least twenty feet across, and when she stopped to take a breath, the air seemed lighter, not as stale and musty as the air in the other caves.

She turned in a complete circle, then stopped and looked down at the floor. She bent down and stared in confusion at the mass of footprints in the sandy floor.

"Look, Timothy. Look at all these footprints."

Timothy hunkered down to study the sandy floor, then stood back up. "It looks like this cave has had a lot of visitors and they were here real recent, or the tide would have erased their boot marks."

"Lift the lantern," she said, and Timothy held the light high. "Let's see where this cave leads."

"Perhaps it would be best if we left, my lady. If someone is using this cave, it's hard telling when they might come back."

Anne knew Timothy was right, but she also knew how difficult it would be to come back. "Just a few more minutes. I want to see where this cave goes."

She walked farther into the cave, with Timothy holding the light high to show the way.

"Is the ground slanting upward?" she asked, lifting her skirts in her hands and struggling to keep up with Timothy. It seemed to her as if they were climbing up a very steep hill.

"Yes, my lady. Do you want to turn back?"

"No. I'm fine," she lied. She was getting tired. The farther they went, the harder it was for her to breathe. Even though the cave seemed to be getting larger, the walls seemed to close in around her. She didn't like it here. What on earth had possessed Freddie to give her this land?

They walked a little farther, and suddenly the cave opened up. The ground flattened, and they stepped into a large room. Timothy lifted the lantern and turned a circle so they could see every foot of the huge cavern. It was empty now, but even Anne could see from the scrape marks and footprints on the floor, it had been a hive of activity not long ago.

"What do you make of it, my lady?" Timothy asked, still studying the marks.

"I think it's time to leave before whoever was here earlier comes back."

"Yes, ma'am. This place makes me shiver. Besides, it won't be long before the tide comes in. I wouldn't want to be caught down here when it does."

Anne let Timothy lead the way. The minute they walked through the opening of the large room, she looked down. The ground was already wet, and more water inched its way across the floor until it was nearly to the bottom of the incline.

"Run, my lady!" Timothy hollered. "The tide is coming in."

Anne and Timothy ran down the steep incline and into the swirling water. It was already over her slippers and rising steadily.

A fear unlike anything she'd ever felt raced through her. The minute she stepped into the water, her skirts soaked up the liquid, turning her gown into a heavy weight that made it almost impossible to move. She knew she would never make it to safety on her own, and if Timothy stayed to help her, she would risk his life, too.

"Timothy, run ahead and get help. Find your master and tell him where I am."

"Are you sure?" Timothy said, sloshing through the water.

"Yes. Hurry!"

Anne saw him race ahead of her to the mouth of the cave, and a wave of panic washed over her. She tried to keep her heavy skirts out of the water and move forward, but she could only creep ahead by inches.

She wished she'd listened to Griff when he'd told her not to come here. She knew he was going to be furious, but right now, his temper was the least of her worries. Even if he ranted at her for being so foolish, it was better than never hearing him yell at her again.

# Chapter 28

❦

"Would you like me to send some men back out, sir?" Franklin asked when they returned to the manor house. "I think we were close this time. We almost had him."

Griff dismounted and handed his reins to the stable boy, who came running to get his horse. "No. We won't find him again today. But we were close."

"Yes, sir," Franklin said. "Maybe tomorrow."

"Maybe," Griff answered, although he knew they wouldn't catch Jack Hawkins tomorrow or the day after— not until Hawkins wanted them to find him.

Griff strode up the walk, trying to keep his frustration under control, then took the steps to the house two at a time. "Where's my wife?" Griff asked Carter as he handed the butler his coat.

"She's either in the library or her room or the garden, sir."

Griff gave Carter a hooded look, then waited for him to explain what he meant.

"She told me she would be in the library, but she told Martha she would be in the garden. And she told William she was going to her room. She wasn't in the library when I went to check on her, and William has not left his post on the terrace. He assures me she hasn't gone outside."

"Then that leaves her room. I'll go up to get her."

Griff mounted the stairs at a fast pace. He wanted to see her, to try to smooth over the harsh words they'd shared last night. They'd nearly passed the point of just arguing when he'd refused to take her to see the land Freddie had left her. He knew how important seeing the parcel was to her, but he couldn't let her go. It was too dangerous. Even if she wasn't convinced someone was out there, he knew someone was.

Someday, when Jack Hawkins was no longer a threat, he would take her to see the land. Until then, he could not risk letting her go out.

The door to her room was open and the room was dark. The first niggling of unease washed over him. He walked into an empty room and called her name. No one answered. From there, he went to the room that had become theirs together. And the sitting room in between. She wasn't there, either.

"Carter!" he hollered, racing down the stairs. "Have the servants check the house and the gardens. Tell my wife I want to see her right away."

Blood pounded in his head as he made his way to search the garden. Surely she wouldn't have…But he knew she would and was afraid she had. She was determined to see the land Freddie had left her. And she'd told him in no uncertain terms she intended to go whether he took her or not. His blood ran cold.

"Sir!" Franklin said, rushing through the patio doors. "One of the carriages is gone. And the lad Timothy."

His heart pounded in his chest. He raced through the house and out the door, fighting the same fear he'd battled several times before. The same fear he'd fought when Freddie had died in his arms. The same fear that had consumed him during the storm that had claimed Andrew and Julia. He'd made the same fatal mistake with Anne that he had with Julia. He shouldn't have left Julia alone, nor should he have left Anne alone.

A groomsman had a horse waiting for him, and he jumped into the saddle. He knew where she was.

He rode across the meadows with Franklin and a small army of men following him. He took every path he thought might save him a minute or more.

He had to reach her as quickly as he could. He refused to think she might be injured or hurt. He refused to think Hawkins might have found her, and she was lying somewhere dead. He focused instead on the harsh scolding he would give her when he reached her. On the pleasure he would take locking her in the house and placing a guard at every door and window so she couldn't pull such a dangerous stunt again. Mostly, though, he focused on the relief he would feel when he found her safe and sound, and he could hold her in his arms. He pushed his horse harder.

"Please, God. Please. Let her be all right."

Franklin and the other men followed behind him, but he didn't slow to let them catch up. The relief he felt when he saw the carriage ahead was unbelievable. He wanted to shout with joy.

"Anne! Annie, where are you?"

"Sir!"

Griff looked but didn't see the owner of the voice.

"Sir! Here. Over here!"

Griff brought his horse to a stop at the edge of the cliff and jumped down just as the lad Timothy climbed over the top.

"Where is she?" Griff bellowed, clasping the lad by his shoulders. "Where is your mistress?"

Tears streamed down the boy's face.

"Where is she?" he hollered again.

"Down there, sir. Still in the cave."

Griff looked at the water rushing into the caves. "No!"

He raced down the steep slope, falling part of the way, sliding the rest. When he reached the bottom, the water was already past his ankles.

"Anne!" he hollered, wading through the frothy brine. "Where are you?" He raced on farther, hollering her name into every opening. Which bloody cave was she in? There had to be a hundred of them down here. Where the hell was she?

"Anne! Damn it, Anne! Answer me!"

He raced on farther. The water swirled around his calves, slowing him even more.

"Anne! Where are you?"

"Griff! Help me!"

Griff barely heard her voice over the rushing water but knew she was close. He raced ahead to the spot where he thought her cry for help had come from. "Where are you, Anne?"

"Here. I'm here."

Griff made his way to the cave he thought she'd called him from and stopped. It was pitch-black inside the opening, and he couldn't see a thing. "Anne!"

"I'm here, Griff. Straight ahead of you."

Griff listened. He could hear her sloshing through the water. He walked forward with his arms outstretched. Finally, he saw her faint outline in the darkness as she struggled to make her way toward him. When she was close enough for him to reach her, he wrapped his arms around her waist and clasped her to him.

"Oh, Griff." She clung to him as he pulled her with him toward the opening.

By now the water swirled around his knees. He knew even if they made it out of the cave, they would play hell trying to get up the steep slope. The material of her skirts had soaked up enough water to make her gown weigh a ton. He was surprised she'd even made it this far.

"Keep moving, Anne. Don't stop!"

"I'm tired, Griff."

"I know. But keep moving."

Griff knew she was struggling to keep up with him, her cumbersome skirts slowing her down. She lagged behind with every step and he tightened his grip around her waist and pulled her along. Her knees buckled once or twice, and she nearly fell, but he held her up as they made their way out of the cave and into the sunshine.

If they were lucky, they might make it to the spot where they could climb the slope. But the water was higher now, almost above their knees. They took a few more steps and she stumbled again, nearly going down.

"Wrap your arm around my neck and hold on."

He picked her up in his arms and carried her. She held on tight as he made his way along the coast.

His chest burned as he sloshed through the rushing water. When they reached the path, he set her on her feet but still held on to her hand.

"Keep moving, Anne, and don't let go of me. I'll lead and you follow. But hold on to my hand!"

Water rushed around him and he felt a fear he'd prayed never to feel again. He knew how the rushing waves could suck you under. How the water could steal the air from your lungs. How it could kill. Destroy. Take away the people you loved. She would not be safe until they were out of the water.

Griff grabbed Anne's hand and pulled her along with him. He didn't give her a chance to stop.

Their progress was slow. The water lapped at their heels with each step up the steep slope. But finally they made it to dry ground. Each step was still a struggle, but now they could move away from the angry waves at a faster pace.

His chest burned. His legs were numb and trembled beneath him. She had to be twice as tired. Blood pounded inside his head from fear and exhaustion. He clasped his arm around her to drag her the final few steps, not taking the chance she might slip or fall behind. When he was almost to the top, Franklin reached out his hand and helped him the last few feet. Griff kept his grasp tight on her and pulled her up with him.

When they reached the top, Griff brought her up against him. He wrapped his arms around her and crushed her to him. He never wanted to let her go.

His body trembled and his chest heaved, but he knew exertion was only partially responsible for his lack of air. He sank to his knees on the grassy knoll and looked down on the rushing waters below.

He feared he might be sick. Rushing to reach Anne was like when he'd lost Julia. Water was everywhere, rushing around their feet, pulling them under. Just like on the ship. The fear was the same, a mind-numbing, chilling fear.

He swiped his hand across his face and took another deep breath. *He could have lost her.*

His stomach revolted again, the pressure in his chest growing increasingly more painful. He held her tighter. He wouldn't let her go. He wouldn't chance losing her.

"Griff," she said, pushing against him. "I can't breathe."

He lessened his grasp and touched his fingers to her cheek. He needed to leave, to be far away from this place. "Franklin, have the men prepare to go. Let's get out of here."

Franklin issued the order and the men who were with them went to their horses.

Griff clasped his hand around hers and pulled her to her feet. Even though the sun shone bright from above, she shivered. Her clothes were soaked and cumbersome, the weight of her skirts now impossible to manage. She stumbled as he led her to the carriage. When Griff looked down at her, her face was pale and drawn.

*He'd almost lost her.*

She stumbled a second time, and he lifted her in his arms to carry her to the carriage. His muscles bunched when she wrapped her arms around his neck and held on to him. A heavy fist pelted him in his gut.

*He could have lost her.*

She was shivering now, both from fear and from the cold. He walked to the carriage where the lad Timothy stood. "There should be blankets in the back. Get them."

Timothy ran around the carriage and brought back two blankets. Griff stepped inside with Anne, then wrapped both blankets around her. When he had her cocooned in the blankets, he sat with her in his arms.

She was exhausted. Her lips were blue, her cheeks lacked the slightest hint of pink, and deep, dark circles rimmed her eyes. But at least she was alive.

The relief he felt nearly overwhelmed him. He released his pent-up emotions the only way he knew—in anger. "What the hell did you think you were doing? You could have drowned!" his voice bellowed in raspy gasps. "Of all the bloody fool things to do!" He gulped hard to take in air. He couldn't breathe. "I could have lost you."

He pointed a trembling finger at her. "You will never, ever come here again. Do you hear me? Never!"

"I hear you," she answered, then shivered again.

He cradled her in his arms as the carriage carried them home. Her eyes were closed and she lay her head against his chest.

"I thought the sea was going to take you," he whispered. "I thought I was going to lose you, too."

She answered him not with words, but by nestling closer to him and wrapping her arms around him.

"You're safe now, Anne. I won't let anything hurt you."

"I know you won't, Griff." She breathed a deep sigh. "I know you won't."

His chest still burned from the fear that ran rampant through him. He could never let anything happen to her. He wouldn't survive if it did.

He closed his eyes and rested his chin on the top of her head. He ignored the hot tears that streamed down his face.

He'd done exactly what he'd sworn he would never do—risked his heart.

# Chapter 29

e loved her.

Bloody hell and damnation. He'd done exactly what he'd sworn never to do. He'd risked it all. And yesterday he'd found out how quickly she could have been taken away from him.

Griff paced the floor in his study like a desperate animal. He'd been as surly as a bear with a hurt paw. But it was because he was so damned afraid. Why on earth had she done something so stupid and irresponsible as to sneak away from the house when she knew someone was out there? When she knew someone wanted to hurt her to get at him? Didn't she know he couldn't survive if he lost her? He'd never been so terrified in his life. And because he was so afraid, he'd taken it out on her.

He'd yelled and bellowed and threatened her within an inch of her life. Then he'd ignored her. He'd avoided her and tried to make her life a living hell because she'd terrified him so. To her credit, she weathered his tirades with as much bravery as he'd ever seen. He even thought he caught her smiling at him during one of his lectures. How could she be so calm? Didn't she know how valiantly he was fighting to keep his feelings hidden?

Didn't she know he couldn't survive if he lost her, too?

He hadn't been kind but had stormed about like a dark thundercloud. The more he had lectured, the more she tried to placate him, to involve him in some kind of conversation—idle prattle about Freddie's antics when they were young, questions about the running of the estate, or a multitude of inquiries concerning his youth. He didn't want her to be so perfect and understanding. And yet the more he fought to distance himself, the more he wanted her.

He told himself he'd gone to her last night because giving her a child was the only request she'd made of him. But that was a lie. The reason was he couldn't stay away from her. He wanted her too desperately and needed to hold her close to him. And she welcomed him with open arms, satisfying his most base needs as well as something else he couldn't explain.

Their lovemaking was all-consuming and frantic, each of them taking and giving with complete abandon. And this morning, when he left her, he knew it would be only a few hours before he'd want her again.

He fisted his hands tight. Damn, he wanted her now—wanted her like he'd never thought he'd want another woman after Julia.

He walked the length of the room, his nerves so on edge he couldn't stand it. Nights were the worst. Darkness brought to life all the terrors he wanted to forget—the rushing water swirling at their feet, the panicked look on her face, the fear that almost took his breath when he thought she might drown. He paced the length of the room again. Damn! He had lived his worst nightmare. He needed a drink.

He stopped short and almost laughed. No. He needed his wife.

He braced his hands on either side of the curtained window and stared out into the darkness as if he might find the answers he searched for. He'd put her in the middle of one tragedy after another. He needed to figure out why Freddie had gone to such lengths to bequeath that seemingly worthless piece of land to Anne. What was so special that Freddie thought owning it would preserve their good name?

He needed to find Jack Hawkins and have this done.

He was scared—scared something would happen to her if he let her out of his sight. Or that something would happen to him, and he wouldn't be able to protect her from a threat he wasn't sure he understood.

He picked up the letter he'd received from London that afternoon and reread it. It was from Fitzhugh, informing him that Jack Hawkins had left London the same time he and Anne had. He'd given the excuse that he needed to settle some family matters.

That had been weeks ago. Griff knew now it was Jack Hawkins who'd been following him and who was out there, watching, waiting.

He looked around the room, praying a bottle would magically appear. All he wanted was one drink. Just one to settle his nerves and figure out answers to all his questions. Like why Hawkins hadn't killed him already. Griff had given him plenty of opportunity. Why was he playing games with him?

He heard the clock strike midnight. He'd stayed away from her longer than usual, but tonight she'd seemed terribly quiet. Perhaps it would be best if he didn't go to her at all. Perhaps she wouldn't want him tonight.

He extinguished the lantern on his desk and walked across the room as if some unseen force controlled his movements. He couldn't stay away from her. He just wanted to see her and hold her. Perhaps she would already be asleep. That didn't matter. He would lie down beside her and hold her, because there was no place he'd rather be than at her side.

Griff made his way up the stairs and readied himself for bed. He washed, then slipped his arms through the sleeves in his robe and walked through the sitting room that separated Anne's room from his. He quietly opened the door, in case she was sleeping.

He stepped inside and stopped short. The bed was empty, the covers pulled back as Martha would have left them, but the bed had not been slept in. Anne was not there.

Griff stepped closer, then saw her standing in the shadows, her head bowed, her arms wrapped around her middle.

"Anne?"

"Did you finish what you had to do?"

"Yes." He took a step toward her but stopped when he saw her shoulders tense. "Aren't you tired?"

"I couldn't sleep."

"I see. Is something wrong?"

"No," she whispered, shaking her head. She took in a deep breath that trembled and when she spoke, her voice cracked. "Perhaps it would be best if you slept in your own bed tonight, Griff?"

"Are you feeling all right?"

"Fine. I'd just like to be alone."

"And if I refuse?"

She stopped as if unable to find the strength to argue with him.

Griff worried even more when he saw her tighten her arms around her middle. He closed the gap that separated them.

He placed his hands on her shoulders to turn her around, but the minute he touched her, she stepped out of his grasp. "Anne? What's wrong?"

Wetness pooled in her eyes and threatened to spill down her cheeks. He didn't want to see her like this, couldn't stand to think he was the cause of her unhappiness. The guilt he felt because he knew he'd been such an ass pelted him in the gut, sickening him. It wasn't her fault he was too much of a coward to face his own fears.

He pulled her to him and wrapped his arms around her. Her cheek rested against his chest.

"We can't make love tonight." Her voice was hoarse.

"We don't have to make love every night. We can wait until tomorrow night."

"We can't then, either. I have my monthly." She hesitated. "I'm not carrying a child."

Griff closed his eyes. He knew how desperate she'd been to conceive. He rubbed his hands over her back and arms. "It's all right."

"It's not all right."

A single tear trickled down her cheek. There was nothing he could do to take away her hurt. "There's time, Anne. There will be a child eventually."

She wrapped her arms around him tighter and buried her face in his chest. He loved the feel of her there.

Griff held her until the soft tears no longer fell, then tenderly kissed her forehead. "Come on," he whispered in her ear. "Let me take you to bed."

"But we can't—"

"I know. But that doesn't mean we can't lie together. That I cannot hold you in my arms. That we cannot wake up together so you are the first sight I see when I open my eyes. But we will wake up in my bed. My bed is better. Your bed is too short for me to sleep comfortably."

She followed him to his room and lay down in the center of his bed. He lay down beside her and pulled her close. This was the way he always wanted them to be.

"I was so certain we had made a babe," she said, breathing a shaky sigh.

She shivered in his arms and he held her tight. This was the only way he knew to take away some of her disappointment. "We will. In time there will be a babe."

"When I was young, I overheard Cook tell our upstairs maid that it only took once. We've done it so often, I was sure…"

Griff smiled and kissed the top of her head. "It sometimes only takes once. But mostly, couples have to try more often before a babe is made."

"But I was so sure. I didn't want you to go through such torture for so long."

He tried not to laugh but couldn't help it. "Don't worry about me enduring such torture. Worry more about how I will survive not touching you for the next few days." He brushed a stray lock of hair that fell to her cheek. How had he thought he could keep from loving her? He knew now how impossible that would have been. "Are you in pain?"

She shook her head.

He kissed her gently on the forehead. "Good. Now go to sleep."

She breathed a contented sigh. He thought she'd smiled and wondered what she was thinking, then suddenly realized something he should have known long before now.

That it would be more possible to live without air to breathe than without her love.

\* \* \*

Griff dropped to the ground and handed his reins to one of his stable hands before making his way to the house. He'd left Anne early, kissing her when she awoke, then telling her to go back to sleep. He'd gone out to see if he could find Jack Hawkins but had come up empty-handed, as always. This morning, at least, his shadow did not stay quite so hidden. Once Griff thought he'd even seen Jack's outline.

"Is your mistress up?" he asked Carter, shrugging out of his coat.

"Yes. She's waiting breakfast for you."

Griff walked to the chair where she sat and kissed her on the lips. His body reacted to the way she returned his kiss.

"How was your ride?" she asked when he'd filled a plate and sat down at the head of the table.

"Fine. It's a beautiful morning."

"Did you find him?"

Griff's fork stopped midway to his mouth. "What makes you think I was looking for someone?"

"Because you look for him every time you go out. He's why I cannot step foot out of the house."

Griff finished the eggs on his plate and spread warm jam on a piece of toast. He decided it would be futile to try to keep anything from her. "No. I didn't find him, although today I spotted him. He's becoming more careless."

"Or he is tired of playing his cat-and-mouse game with you."

"Perhaps." He pushed his empty plate away and lifted a cup of tea to his lips. "This will be over soon."

"And then what? Will I be a widow?"

"No," he answered, though not as confidently as he wanted. "I will know what this is all about."

"I received a note from Lord Brentwood. He's going to call on us again today. I think he intends to make another offer for the land."

He leaned back in his chair. "Are you considering selling now?"

"No."

"Good."

She smiled. "Would you have let me if I really wanted to?"

"The land is yours. Freddie left it to you."

"But as my husband, you now control everything I have."

"The land is yours. You can do whatever you want with it."

"Then I will keep it. There is something that is not right about the land. Something we don't know yet. Why would Freddie go to such lengths to have something so desolate? And why is Brentwood so desperate to possess it? Why has he offered to pay such an extravagant amount for something he claims as worthless? I think there is a secret there that we have to uncover. Something that could even be illegal. There were tracks all over inside some of the caves."

Griff frowned. "What do you mean, tracks?"

"Footprints and tracks, as if someone had slid something heavy around inside them."

Griff stamped down another stab of worry. "Stay away from there, Anne. The caves are dangerous. We've already discovered that."

"No more dangerous, I think, than Brentwood. Perhaps they are connected somehow."

"Don't meet with him unless I am here, Anne. I don't trust the man."

"Neither do I. For some reason, he—"

"Excuse me, sir," Carter interrupted from the doorway. "But Hodges says he needs to speak to you concerning a matter of importance."

"Tell him I'll be right there," Griff answered, and got up to leave. "I'll be back before Brentwood comes." He kissed her lightly on the lips.

"Good," she said. "I don't like being alone with him."

Griff gave her a last smile, then walked out the door. He was going to have to settle the matter with the land once and for all today. Brentwood was undoubtedly someone who refused to give up until he had what he wanted.

Griff walked across the yard, already forming in his mind what he would say when they met with Brentwood later.

Griff pulled his mind back to the problem at hand. "Is something wrong, Hodges?"

"Yes, sir." The groomsman twisted his hat in his hands. "I found something you need to look at."

Hodges walked to the carriage house. Griff followed.

Hodges had taken care of every Covington horse, carriage, and wagon for as long as Griff could remember. The post had been his father's before him, and he had already been an expert when he stepped into the position.

Hodges stopped before the carriage. "I discovered this when I inspected the carriages like I have every day since the accident. It must have happened during the night. There was nothing wrong with this carriage yesterday." He pointed to the vehicle's underside.

Griff knelt down to look. Someone had nearly sawed through the main frame that supported the carriage. There was another cut in the crossbar that held the horses in place. From the way the two pieces had been sawed, they would not have snapped immediately but would have held together until enough speed pulled against the wood and weakened it. Even if the carriage was traveling no faster than the regular rate of speed, there would be no way for any driver, no matter how cautious, to control the vehicle. It was guaranteed to overturn.

Griff felt his temper snap. "Saddle me a fresh horse, Hodges." Griff checked to make sure the pistol in his jacket pocket was loaded. "Send word to Lady Anne that I had to leave for a while but will return as quickly as possible."

The minute Hodges brought his mount from the stables, Griff swung into the saddle.

"Do you need someone to go with you, sir?" Hodges asked.

"No. I need to handle this on my own." Griff turned the black stallion away from the stable, then stopped. "If something happens to me, send someone to London to get Lord Covington. He will know what to do."

Before Hodges could answer, Griff slapped the reins against the horse's flanks and rode toward the grove of trees where he'd last seen Hawkins. He had no doubt he would find him there. This time, only one of them would ride away.

# Chapter 30

❋

*G*riff slowed his mount when he neared the grove. To the untrained eye, Jack's movements had been so minute that no one who wasn't looking for him would have realized he was there. But Griff knew, just as he knew Hawkins had watched him every day since he and Anne had come to Covington Manor.

Just as he'd watched him in London.

Griff reined in his horse and stopped in the open meadow. He was out of firing range. If Hawkins wanted him dead, he would have to come closer to kill him.

"Hawkins! I know you're there. We've played this game of yours long enough. Come out and face me. Let's get it settled once and for all."

Griff waited. The blood pounded against his ears as he watched for some movement in front of him. His horse pranced nervously beneath him as if he understood the danger. Griff gripped the reins tighter to hold his stallion steady.

The seconds ticked by with agonizing slowness. Griff reached for the pistol in his pocket, then stopped when Hawkins stepped out from the grove of trees.

"How long have you known I was here?" Hawkins asked, taking a few steps closer, but not enough for either of them to get off an accurate shot.

Griff dismounted and stepped around his horse. "You followed us from London."

Jack Hawkins laughed. "I guess I'm not as good as I thought."

"You're good," Griff said. "You should be. We both learned from the best."

Hawkins took a few steps closer, then planted his feet wide apart and loosened the buttons on his jacket. Griff saw the pistol Hawkins had in the belt at his waist.

"I didn't get a chance to express my congratulations on your marriage." Hawkins's hands hung loose at his side, his pose calm and relaxed. "You have a lovely bride."

"I won't let you hurt her. I'll kill you first." Griff watched him make a slow circle to his left, moving so the sun was behind his back and shone in Griff's eyes.

"Is that what you think? That I want to hurt her?" He took a few steps closer and closed the gap between them. "Because of what happened to my brother?"

Griff didn't answer him.

"What if I told you I had nothing to do with what's happened to you so far?"

Griff paused. "I'd want to know why you've been following me. What was so important that you followed me here?"

"I need to prove to you that I can be trusted. I need to clear my name."

Griff looked at the man he'd spent nearly two years fighting beside, trusting to watch his back and protect him. There'd been a bond that had connected them. "You think you need to clear your name?"

"Yes. The name my brother disgraced. I have a responsibility to my family." Jack lifted his shoulders a little higher. "I am a cousin to the Earl of Stratmont."

"You are a cousin to Stratmont?"

"Yes. My father was the late earl's youngest brother."

Griff understood Jack Hawkins's concern. If his brother's activities were made public, the scandal would no doubt ruin Stratmont's reputation.

"Thankfully, my brother didn't use our family surname, Hawkins, but chose a fictitious name. He lived and died as Nigel Stoneworth. That's the name you knew him by, Griff. He was one of the spies we executed at the end of the war." Hawkins turned to face him straight on. "I can't let you think I am like him."

Griff didn't say anything. He waited to see what Jack Hawkins would do.

"When Fitzhugh discovered that Nigel was my brother, I knew that you knew, too."

"Why didn't you tell us when it happened?"

A smile lifted the corners of his mouth but didn't come close to reaching his eyes. "What would your reaction have been? What reaction would I have gotten from Fitzhugh and every man in intelligence?"

"They'd have sympathized with you and felt a deeper admiration for you—"

"Perhaps to my face," Hawkins interrupted, his voice stronger and more forceful than before. "But behind my back they would have wondered what kind of man could stand by and watch his brother be arrested and tried for treason without lifting a finger to help."

Hawkins paced a few angry steps, then stopped. "Then the doubts would have started. They would have watched every move I made. They would have watched for any sign that I was a traitor, too. Rumor and speculation would have followed me wherever I went.

"I'm not like you, Blackmoor. I didn't want to put my military career behind me. I don't have an estate waiting for me at home. I intend to make intelligence work my career. But how long do you think even Fitzhugh could have defended me once the questions started? How long before it would have been impossible for him to trust me with anything more important than escorting the general's wife to and from an occasional social affair?"

Griff released a deep sigh. "So you said nothing. You suffered in silence when your brother faced a firing squad and was executed."

"My brother made his own choices. I tried to stop him before he got in too deep, but I failed. Afterward, I did what I had to do to protect my family's reputation."

"Why have you been following me?"

Hawkins smiled. "I wasn't the only one following you at first. We all were—Johnston, Turner, and myself. We were all trying to save you from yourself. Between the liquor and the brawling, you were bloody well bent on killing yourself." Hawkins stopped. His features turned more serious. "I'm glad to see you've left the bottle alone. We were worried about you."

Griff felt his face flush. "But you were the only one to follow me when I left London."

"I wasn't following *you*."

"Then who?"

"Your wife."

Griff's heart skipped a beat. "Now you want me to believe you followed me here to protect my wife?"

"You can believe what you want. I know you think an assassin wants you dead, but you were never the intended target. Your wife was."

Griff considered what Jack Hawkins told him. "It seems odd that every time something happened to either of us, you weren't far away."

"But not close enough to catch the culprit."

"What are you saying?" Griff's heartbeats quickened.

"I'm saying that the carriage that ran Lady Anne down meant to do exactly that. Just as I will wager every pound of my pension that the bullet that killed your friend Brentwood hit its mark, too."

The earth shifted beneath him. He didn't want to believe Hawkins. Freddie didn't have an enemy in the world. Surely no one had wanted him dead. Or Anne. Why in heaven's name would they want to hurt either of them? There was no reason.

Hawkins shook his head. "You need proof, don't you? I should have known. Follow me."

Hawkins walked toward the grove of trees. Griff had no choice but to follow him to a secluded place where only a little sunshine filtered through the thick leaves. Hawkins stopped, then pointed to a medium-size wooden chest on the ground. He walked to the chest and flicked open the lid.

Griff stared down at the chest, then picked up one of the small oval cakes wrapped in poppy leaves and cotton cloth. "Where did you get this?" he asked, his voice nearly choking on the lump he couldn't swallow past.

"From the caves. The new Marquess of Brentwood is smuggling in opium and using the caves to hide his contraband until he sells it."

"That's why the bastard is so desperate to have that pile of rocks."

"There's only one cave on the whole coastline large enough and deep enough in which to store and hide the opium. Your wife was in it the other day when she nearly got trapped by the tide."

Griff's gaze darted to Hawkins's.

"You gave me quite a scare," Hawkins said. The grave expression on his face confirmed his confession. "I didn't realize she'd gone there until you went after her. I went back this morning and looked around."

"And you found this?"

Hawkins nodded.

"The floor slants upward as you go toward a large open area near the back of the cave. The water never reaches that part, but it prevents anyone from entering the cave once the tide comes in. It's the perfect hiding place. Brentwood's men unload the opium into the cave, then guard it until the water rises. Once the tide comes in, it's impossible for anyone to enter or exit the cave. When the tide goes back out, Brentwood removes his contraband, and the water erases any sign they've been there."

"The bastard."

Hawkins closed the lid to the chest and sat down on it. "My guess is that Brentwood's been using the caves for quite some time, and your friend discovered it. That was why he was killed."

"But Brentwood didn't get the land. Freddie willed it to Anne."

"Brentwood didn't know that until the will was read. I talked to your wife's solicitor before leaving London, and he told me Brentwood was shocked to learn that Freddie had petitioned to have that strip of land removed from the rest of the entailed estate."

Griff's temper rose. "That's why he went after Anne. He sought to marry her first. As his wife, anything she owned would belong to him. When she refused, he tried to kill her, knowing as long as she wasn't married, her possessions would go next to Rebecca, who would undoubtedly sell him the land with little resistance."

"But before he could accomplish either, she married you," Hawkins added.

"That was why he attempted to kill us both."

"He had to," Hawkins added. "Just killing her would do him no good. Upon her death, the land would go to you. He knew he had no chance of getting it then."

Griff looked down at Jack Hawkins. He sat on the lid of the chest. For the first time he noticed his pale complexion and the uncharacteristic way his shoulders slumped. Then he noticed the dark spot on the sleeve of his jacket. "What happened?"

Hawkins tapped the chest with his good hand. "It's a scratch. Let's just say I didn't escape with the proof of Brentwood's crimes without a reminder."

"Brentwood was there?"

"Not in person, although I'm sure by now he knows someone has discovered his hiding place. This shipment came in at dawn, and one of the men he had guarding it saw me as I was trying to leave. I'm afraid I had to kill him."

Griff felt the first unsettling wave of fear take hold of him. "I have to get home. I have to get to Anne. Brentwood sent word earlier he was coming. It's hard to tell what he'll do if he knows he's been found out."

Jack Hawkins rose from the chest and concealed the opium beneath some bushes. "I'll go with you."

"Are you sure you're all right?" Griff hollered over his shoulder as he raced to where he'd left his horse.

"I sustained worse than this saving your sorry hide in the barroom brawls you weren't sober enough to remember."

But Griff barely heard him. His thoughts were on Anne and his need to get to her before Brentwood did.

# Chapter 31

❦

*A*nne heard Brentwood's voice from the foyer and fought the dread that consumed her. She clenched her hands in her lap and worried her bottom lip, hoping whatever Griff had to do wouldn't take long.

"Good afternoon, Lady Anne," he said, his words clipped as he marched past Carter and into the room.

She took a deep breath and braced herself to fend him off. She focused on the severe expression on his face and the anger in his gaze. He seemed different today, dangerous. The desperate expression on his face gave her warning.

She reluctantly held out her hand as was expected. The familiar way in which he held her fingers made her flesh crawl. She wanted to pull her arm back, but he held her fingers in his grasp and wouldn't let go.

"Are we alone?"

"For the moment. My husband will be here soon. Would you care to sit while we wait?" She pointed to the chair farthest from where she sat.

"No, I think not," he answered. "I don't think I will be here long enough to get comfortable."

She breathed a sigh of relief. Good, he didn't intend to stay.

"In fact, I think neither of us will be here long enough to make ourselves comfortable."

She lifted her gaze and stared at him. The bone-chilling glare in his eyes sent a shiver of fear through her. "I can't imagine where you think I am going, Lord Brentwood."

"It's quite simple, my lady. I have decided you should come with me."

"Surely you're joking." She couldn't believe his audacity.

"Not in the least. I think having your husband hunt for me where I am in control is preferable to waiting here for him to arrive." Perspiration glazed his forehead.

Anne was suddenly more than a little afraid.

Brentwood looked around the room and shook his head. "Being here is like walking into the proverbial lion's den. You can almost feel him here, can't you?" A malevolent sneer lifted the corners of his lips. "He has that kind of power. Have you noticed?" He laughed. "Of course you have."

He turned his attention back to her and offered her his hand. "If you would be so kind," he said. He motioned toward the door. He expected her to leave with him.

"Get out. I have no intention of going anywhere with you. I want you out of my house. Now."

The marquess opened his jacket and pulled out a pistol. He pointed it at her. "I would be glad to leave, my lady. But you are coming with me."

Anne jumped from the settee and darted to the left. Before she could get out of his reach, he grabbed her arm and swung her around.

"Please, don't cause me trouble, cousin. For your own good."

Anne struggled to get out of his grasp, but he had too tight a hold on her. Every attempt was useless, and as a last effort, she reached out and grabbed a vase sitting on a small table at the end of the sofa and brought it down against him.

He ducked his head to the side, but the vase hit his shoulder and broke. A broken piece skimmed his face and a narrow stream of dark blood oozed from the cut on his cheek.

"Damn you!" He slashed his hand in front of him and slapped her across the face.

Anne clutched her hand to her burning cheek and staggered backward. This couldn't be happening. "It's the land, isn't it? You're using it for something illegal."

He laughed, the sound even more frightening than the look on his face. "You might say that. And I don't intend to lose control of it. I'll take care of you first, then your husband. He's been a problem since he first arrived."

He clamped his fingers on her shoulder to push her. Before he got a tight hold, she twisted hard and felt his grip loosen.

He bellowed a vile curse and reached for her. She wasn't free long enough to get away, and the next time he reached for her, he wrapped his fingers around her arm like a vise.

His hold bit into her flesh, and she cried out in pain. He pulled her up against him and pinned her arm behind her back so she couldn't move. Before she could gather her breath, he poked the pistol against her ribs.

"Now, Lady Anne. You are going with me. I would hate to have to kill you here. Finding you shot in your own drawing room would cause too many unnecessary questions.

But I will if you force me. I have nothing to lose anymore. By now your husband knows all my little secrets."

"What secrets?"

"Quiet!" He brought his hand down across her mouth hard enough for her to taste blood. "Move!"

He pushed her forward.

She tried once more to escape him. She stomped down hard on his foot and yelled as loud as she could. "Carter! Help me!"

The butler came around the corner at record speed, but before she could issue a warning, Brentwood raised his arm and fired the pistol in his hand. Carter staggered backward, clutching the round red spot that darkened his shoulder.

Anne watched in stunned horror as Carter sank to his knees, then crumpled in a heap on the floor.

The doors burst open, and Franklin and several of the guards Griff had hired to protect her rushed into the room. Brentwood grabbed her from behind and pressed the pistol to the side of her neck.

"Come one step closer and I'll blow her pretty head off."

Franklin lifted his hand and the guards stopped.

"Now, drop your weapons."

The guards looked to Franklin for instructions. There was little hesitation before Franklin ordered the men to drop their weapons.

"Wise choice," Brentwood said as he pulled her toward the door. "Now, stay where you are and don't follow, or she dies."

They walked past Carter lying on the floor, and Anne prayed that he was still alive, but she didn't have a chance to see how badly he was hurt. Brentwood held the pistol to the side of her neck and pulled her along with him.

"Move," he hissed when she held back. "Cause any trouble and I'll kill them all."

Anne choked back her fear. She had no choice but to go with him. She walked past the shocked expressions on the servants brave enough to hide behind half-open doors.

"Help Carter," she managed to say as Brentwood pushed her across the foyer.

He led her out the door, past more stunned servants racing to the house. Past the guards and Hodges, who'd come with a weapon, an old rifle probably only used to kill predators who were a threat to the animals.

"Drop it," Brentwood said, shoving his pistol against Anne's head, "or I'll kill her right here."

The men hesitated as if debating what to do, then dropped their rifles to the ground.

"Now, someone bring my horse and help your mistress mount."

Hodges brought Brentwood's horse, then helped Anne to the saddle. The tortured look on his face was almost more that Anne could stand.

"Do not fear, my lady," Hodges whispered before he left her side. "The master won't let anything happen to you."

"I know," she answered, struggling to give Hodges a reassuring smile.

"Quiet!" Brentwood bellowed. He swung his arm through the air and knocked Hodges to the ground. Before Hodges could rise to his feet, Brentwood leaped atop the horse. He dug his heels into the horse's side and the stallion took off at a run. Anne was forced to hang on to the saddle in order to avoid leaning back into Brentwood's body. She couldn't stand to have him touch her.

"You won't get away with this," she said as they raced down the lane. "The minute Griff returns, he'll come after you."

Anne was sure she heard Brentwood laugh. "I'm counting on it, my lady. Oh, yes. I'm counting on it."

The air caught in her throat. He intended to kill them both.

There was no opportunity to talk to him and no need. She already knew the answer to the only question she wanted to ask. She recognized where they were going. Brentwood was taking her to the caves.

Her stomach rolled until she thought she would be ill. It was midafternoon already, and it would not be long before the tide came in. If he left her in the caves now…

Anne looked around her, praying she would see Griff coming to help her. But all she saw were the cliffs. All she heard were the ocean waves as they slammed against the rocks.

All she felt was a fear unlike anything she'd ever felt before.

# Chapter 32

❋

*G*riff brought his horse to a halt before he reached the manor house. Franklin, Hodges, and a group of men rode toward them.

"Do you know them?" Jack Hawkins asked.

"They're from the manor, the guards I hired to protect Anne. Something must be wrong."

Griff urged his mount ahead. "What's wrong, Franklin? Where's your mistress?"

"He's got her, sir. Lord Brentwood. He came to the manor with a gun and shot Carter when he tried to stop him. The mistress put up a brave fight, but she wasn't no match for the marquess."

Griff couldn't believe the anger that surged through his body. "Which way did they go?"

Franklin pointed toward the caves.

Griff swore. "Georgie. Ben. Give us your mounts. We need fresh horses."

"They can't be too far ahead of you," Franklin said while Griff mounted a fresh horse. "Just the time it took us to saddle our horses."

Griff turned his mount around, then stopped. "Did he hurt her, Hodges?"

The groomsman hesitated and Griff had his answer.

"The mistress is all right, though," Hodges said. "She's a brave lady, and I told her before she rode away that you would be right behind her."

"Let's go," Griff said. His body was numb with fear. He couldn't let anything happen to her.

"Send someone back for a length of rope," Jack said to Hodges before he followed after Griff. "At least fifty feet or more."

Griff pushed his mount forward. Neither he nor Jack said anything until they reached the flat area just before the drop-off that led down to the caves.

"Do you see anything?" Jack asked.

"No. They're probably down below. They know I'll come after her. Brentwood is no doubt waiting for me."

"But he's not expecting me. You go down from here, and I'll circle around. They won't expect anyone to come from that direction."

"That's because it's nearly impassable. Are you sure…?"

"Don't worry about me. You just keep the bastard occupied until I can get to you. Don't try being a bloody hero until I'm there to watch your back."

Griff dropped to the ground and handed Franklin his horse's reins. "Keep the rest of the men up here. If any of Brentwood's men make a run for it, do what you have to, but don't let them get away."

"You can count on us, sir."

Jack took the rope from the rider who'd just come and looped it over his shoulder.

Griff started for the edge, then stopped. "How many of them are there, Hawkins?"

"I took care of one earlier today, so there's only five left, but with Brentwood, they're up to six."

"We've faced worse odds."

Jack smiled. "Just get her to the back of the cave, Griff. Don't try to take her out. There won't be enough time."

Griff grasped the hand Jack held out to him, then walked toward the path. He made his way down, wondering how she'd gotten to the bottom without falling.

Griff finally reached the bottom. He took only a few steps before Brentwood's voice stopped him.

"That's far enough, Blackmoor. I've been waiting for you."

Griff turned toward Brentwood's voice. "Where is she? What have you done with my wife?"

"She's right here." He pointed toward the cave. "Inside."

Griff saw the pistol in Brentwood's hand and the cocky tilt to his head. He wanted to wipe the sneering grin off his face. If he would just step closer...

"I can't tell you how relieved I am she didn't accept my marriage proposal," Brentwood said, pacing before him. "This Lady Anne is not at all the meek little mouse I thought she was. She was a great deal of trouble on the way, but don't worry, I put her in her place as I know you would have wanted me to."

Griff seethed with anger. "So help me, if you hurt her, I'll—"

Brentwood swung out his arm. "I don't think you are in any position to issue threats, Blackmoor." Five men stepped out from behind the rocks. Each one had a rifle aimed at him.

Griff ignored the men and the guns, and walked toward the mouth of the cave. Brentwood's voice stopped him. "First lay down your weapons."

Griff pulled the pistol out of his jacket pocket and dropped it to the ground. Brentwood smiled but indicated with his hand that he knew there were more. Griff pulled out a second weapon he'd tucked into the waistband of his breeches, and dropped it, too.

"That's better," Brentwood said, then moved to the side to make room for Griff to pass. "I'm sure she's quite anxious to see you."

Instinct warned Griff to go slowly, but he couldn't. He needed to see her with his own eyes. He needed to make sure she was all right. He strode past Brentwood and almost ran into the cave.

"That's far enough!" Brentwood bellowed as Griff got near enough to almost touch her.

Griff stopped but didn't take his eyes from her. His breathing came in ragged gasps while he fought to keep from racing to her, from loosening her from the pole Brentwood had her tied to.

The only light in the cave came from torches in the holders anchored on the wall. At first Griff didn't notice the dark bruises on her cheeks. When he realized what they were, he experienced a fury greater than he'd ever felt before. Her dress was torn at the sleeve, exposing her scraped and bloody shoulder. He fisted his hands at his side, swearing that no matter what, Brentwood would die."Griff?" she whispered, her voice weak, the luster in her eyes faded. "You shouldn't have come."

"It's all right," he whispered, reaching out to cup his hand against her face. She winced when he touched her. "Everything will be all right."

Brentwood laughed behind him. "What an optimistic sentiment." He circled the pole where Anne was tied.

Griff stepped closer to her and felt the thick ropes and the knots that bound her. Each knot had been tied separately. It would take hours to cut through the ropes and free her.

"Aren't you going to ask why I've gone to all this trouble?" Brentwood cocked his head to the side.

"I already know. You're using this cave as a hideaway for the opium you smuggle into the country."

"Very astute of you, Blackmoor. I knew you must have been the culprit who came earlier and left one of my men dead. When we did a count of our goods, we came up one chest short. That's when I knew I had no choice. I had to eliminate you and your wife now. Today."

"Even if you kill us, you won't get the land. My brother, Lord Covington, will never sell it to you."

"Yes, he will. I realize my mistake when I came to you. I offered too much money for something seemingly so worthless. It aroused your suspicions immediately. I won't make that mistake again."

"Did Freddie discover what you were doing?" Griff asked. "Is that why you killed him?"

Griff heard Anne's shocked gasp. Brentwood laughed. "Unfortunately, yes. I really wasn't all that interested in the title, nor did I care overly much for possessing Brentwood Manor, although it is rather nice. I just wanted to use this little section of isolated coast where I could unload and store my goods, then distribute them without anyone the wiser."

"But Freddie discovered what you were doing."

"Yes. I think perhaps he even knew his life was in danger. Why else would he go to such lengths to have this piece of Brentwood Estate removed so it was no longer entailed? To spite me. He made sure even if I possessed the rest of his inheritance, I would never possess the portion I truly wanted."

"You won't get away with this, Brentwood."

"I already have. I'm a very wealthy man, thanks to my little venture here."

"That was before your smuggling was discovered."

"By you? You think you can stop me, Blackmoor? Look around you. There are five rifles pointed at you, and"— Brentwood stopped and pointed to the opening of the cave—"and the tide is coming in."

Griff saw the water seeping into the mouth of the cave. He moved closer to Brentwood, praying he could get close enough to grab him. "You're going to shoot us?"

"Oh, no. That would cause too many questions. But I'm going to make sure neither of you make it out alive. It will be such an unfortunate accident, the two newlyweds trapped, unable to escape before the tide came in. The story will cause tears to fall and soften even the hardest hearts in Society."

Griff held back. He needed to give Jack more time to get down the cliff, but he couldn't wait too long. Water was now seeping farther into the cave.

"You two," Brentwood said to two of his men. "Get the boat ready."

The two men closest to the entrance left.

The odds were better now. He prayed Jack was out there and could eliminate the men who had left. He'd only have four to watch. If he could get his hands on Brentwood and hold him captive until the water rose, he had no doubt his men would abandon him to save their own skins. If only he could get close enough to him.

"I still don't understand one thing," Griff said, taking a step closer. "How do you think you will be able to convince anyone that our drowning was accidental when they find our bodies bound to poles?"

Brentwood's brows shot upward. "You are not tied, are you, Blackmoor? Are you that anxious to make your escape that much more difficult?"

Griff stopped where he was. The water now reached the tips of his boots. "You bastard! What are you up to?"

"Nothing, Blackmoor."

Brentwood turned to the three men still standing guard. "Harley, see what's taking the others so long. We can't wait much longer. We have to get out of here." Another man standing close to the entrance left the cave.

Brentwood turned his attention back to Griff. "Where was I?" He took another step closer to Griff.

Just a little closer, and Griff could grab him.

"Oh, yes. I just couldn't live with myself if I did not give you a fighting chance to survive. So, even though I have made it impossible for poor Lady Anne to escape, I have decided to leave you free. Then, when the water rushes into the cave, filling this part of it to the ceiling, you can stay with your true love and perish together, or"—Brentwood laughed as he waded through water that now swirled around his boots—"you can leave her to her death and save yourself. And live with what you did for the rest of your life. Even if you did survive and told what you know, who would believe a man who'd abandoned his wife to save himself?"

Brentwood laughed, the sound sending chills down Griff's spine. "I wish I could stay around and see how this little drama unfolds. I believe you may be the only man in all of England who has the habit of surviving his wives while they drown."

Griff knew he should give Jack more time before making his move, but Brentwood's words affected him more than he could stand. With a roar, he leaped through the air. He grabbed Brentwood around the throat and wrestled him to the ground.

One of the men standing guard got off a shot before Griff tackled Brentwood into the swirling water. Griff felt a burning sting to his upper arm, but he wasn't hurt enough to impede his movements.

"Get him!" he heard Brentwood holler, but when the two remaining men made a move to come closer, Jack rushed into the cave and tackled them both.

Griff hit Brentwood hard in the gut. The bastard doubled over in pain but recovered and came to his feet with a knife in his hand.

Griff wanted to get this over quickly. The water already swirled around their ankles, which made going after him difficult. Griff had to hurry. The longer Brentwood held him off, the less time he had to free Anne.

He rushed forward, focusing his attention on the knife in Brentwood's hand. He lunged, then pulled Brentwood's hand to the side and twisted up. Brentwood staggered backward, then went beneath the water. He came up sputtering.

Neither of them could move now. The water was nearly to their knees, and made even the smallest steps extremely difficult.

Brentwood lunged forward and locked his arms around Griff's shoulder. He brought his hand down to stab Griff in the back, but Griff twisted to the left. When Brentwood reached for him, Griff grabbed his arm and thrust the knife upward. He buried it deep in Brentwood's chest.

Brentwood's eyes opened in disbelieving horror as the water turned red with his blood.

Griff kept his hand on the knife until he was sure Brentwood was dead, then pulled the knife from his body and released him. He didn't take time to watch their nemesis float facedown away from them. He needed to get to Anne. The water was already past his knees.

"You're safe now, Anne." Griff wanted to hold her in his arms, but he didn't have time. He had to get her loose before the water rose so high they couldn't work with the ropes.

"I've tried, but I can't get loose."

"I know. We'll free you. Just hold still."

"If you don't—"

Blood pounded inside his head. "We will."

Griff checked the ropes. Blood dripped from Anne's wrists where she'd struggled to free herself from the ropes that bound her to the pole.

"How are we going to handle this?" Jack hollered, wading over to Griff's side. No fewer than ten separate ropes held Anne, from her chest to her ankles. "I'm afraid the pole is too strong and big around for us to break."

"We're going to have to cut the ropes. It's the only way."

"Even with both our knives, there's no way we can cut through this many ropes in time. They're too thick."

"Hold still, Anne. Don't move." Griff took his knife and slit her gown at the waist, then pulled on her petticoats until they drooped downward. "Do you have your gun? Is your powder dry, Jack?"

"Yes." Jack pulled it from his jacket and held it.

"I want you to shoot as many of the ropes as you can from the back. Fire against the pole. The bullets won't go through. I'm going to try to cut all these layers of skirt. Once all this excess material is gone, the ropes should be loose enough to fall to Anne's feet and she can step out of them."

"There's not enough time, Griff," Anne said as the water rose to her hips. "Get out before it's too late."

Griff ignored her and kept working while Jack stepped back and fired the first shot. The bullet sliced the lowest rope just below the water line and it fell to the water.

Six ropes held her tight above the waist, and six below. Jack fired six shots, one after another, freeing Anne from the waist up. Now she was tied only by her hands and by the six ropes that bound her from her hips to her feet. Griff worked frantically to stuff her layers of clothing beneath to give them some slack. Already, though, he had to work underwater, coming up only long enough to take a breath before going back under.

"Can you shoot the rope loose from her wrists?" Griff gasped when he came up and saw that Anne was free on top.

"If you hold her steady and keep her wrists as far apart as possible."

Without hesitating, Griff stood in front of Anne and wrapped his arms around her. He grabbed hold of each hand and pulled her wrists apart. Griff didn't doubt Jack could put a bullet between her hands without harming her. He was that good.

Griff pressed himself against her and looked into her eyes. What he saw made him more afraid than he'd ever been. What if he lost her? What if they couldn't free her in time? What if she drowned, too? Just like…

"I love you, Anne," he whispered, bringing his lips down on hers. "I love you," he repeated as the gunshot blew through the rushing water. The rope fell in two and her arms were free.

Tears rolled down her cheeks. "I love you, too, Griff."

Griff released her and dove beneath the water to push her skirts beneath the ropes.

He was frantic to get her loose. Even with Jack's help, they couldn't free her fast enough. The water was already up to her chest and rushing into the cave faster than before. His chest burned and his lungs screamed for air, but he forced himself to stay underwater as long as possible. Four ropes still held her.

No matter how fast he worked, he was afraid she would not be free in time. He was afraid he could not save her before the water rose above her head. Afraid there was no way he could keep from losing her.

Griff rose to the top and took a deep breath, then dove back down. The pain was unbearable. His head spun in dizzying circles. He was so tired and weak he couldn't stay below as long as he had before. His heart pounded so hard he thought it might explode.

Jack's knife sawed through the second rope. They had only two more ropes to cut and she would be free. He was frantic. His hands trembled while he worked. If only the water would stop rising, but it didn't. If anything, it seemed to rush in faster.

He and Jack needed another breath and they both pushed to the surface. The water was up to Anne's shoulders and she lifted her chin to be able to breathe.

"We're almost done, Anne," he cried out, but she didn't answer him, only looked at him as if to memorize his features, as if knowing this could be the last time she might see him.

"I won't lose you," he promised, then dove back to the bottom.

Jack worked on the lowest rope until it snapped apart, then swam away to get the long length of rope he'd brought with him. When he came back, he tied it around Griff's waist and swam to the large open room, where it was dry. Griff was glad. He wasn't sure he had the strength to carry Anne that far on his own.

Griff cut at the rope and the material that bound her, thinking he would not need another breath to free her, but the knife wasn't as sharp now and wouldn't cut through the wet rope. He couldn't make it. He needed another breath.

He pushed to the top to gulp a huge breath, and before he dove back down, he looked at Anne. The water covered most of her face now, with her nose lifted high so she could breathe.

He dove back down and sawed at the rope with frantic urgency. He couldn't lose her, couldn't live without her.

He'd die before he'd let her drown. But it was taking so bloody long to get the last rope off.

Finally, it fell loose and he pushed upward, reaching for her to pull her to safety. But he was too late.

Water covered her head.

Griff freed her, then pulled her above water, but she didn't struggle for air. Instead, she floated facedown in the water.

"No!"

He heard the hoarse echo of his voice as fear took over every part of his body. He reached for her, turning her to keep her face above the water, but she didn't take a breath. "Anne! Oh, God, Anne. No!"

Her face was pale, almost blue, and she lay in his arms like a limp rag doll while Jack pulled them toward dry ground.

Terror raged through him until he couldn't breathe, until he couldn't think. He couldn't lose her.

"Dear God. Please don't take her away from me," he prayed over and over. "I love her too much."

# Chapter 33

✤

Griff felt solid ground beneath his feet and tried to stand but his legs were too weak to support him. He went under with Anne in his arms. He struggled to his feet and Jack pulled on the rope to help him walk the slope upward until he was on dry ground.

"She's not breathing, Jack! Help me!"

Jack rolled a barrel out from the corner and Griff laid her facedown over it. He pressed on her back, gently at first, then harder when it didn't do any good.

"It's not working," Griff yelled, placing Anne on her side and pounding her back. Her face was blue, her lips a deathly gray, and she was so limp she nearly folded when he laid her down.

"Anne! Anne, breathe, damn it!" He shook her by the shoulders, then held her to him, rocking her back and forth. "What should I do? I can't make her breathe!"

Jack's face was pale, a helpless look of panic in his eyes. "I saw a man a couple years ago save his little boy when the lad fell into a river and nearly drowned."

"What did he do?"

"He held the little boy's nose and covered his mouth with his own and breathed for him."

Griff didn't hesitate. With one hand he held Anne's nose and with the other he pushed her chin downward until her mouth gaped open. He covered her mouth with his own and breathed a deep breath in, then pulled it out, then breathed it in, and pulled it out.

"Breathe, Anne! Breathe!" he ordered, pushing his hand on her stomach as if he could make it move for him.

"Do it again!" Jack yelled, pushing on Anne's stomach like Griff had done.

Griff pushed a deep breath into Anne, then pulled a deep breath out. On the second deep breath, water spewed from her mouth and she coughed and gagged. She spit out what seemed like half the ocean. Griff held her in his arms while she retched more water. It took forever, but finally she gasped for air, then breathed on her own.

"Oh, Anne." He held her to him while tears ran down his face. He waited until she moved on her own, then wrapped her in one of the rough blankets Jack found covering some of the wooden chests lined against the wall. "Are you all right?"

She nodded, then tipped her face to look at him. She pressed her cheek back against his chest and leaned against him. "Are you all right?" she whispered, her voice weak and hoarse.

He laughed. How could he be anything else now that he had her back with him?

\* \* \*

Griff held Anne in his arms while she slept. He refused to let her out of his sight. He couldn't chance that she'd stop breathing. He couldn't chance that he might lose her.

She slept for several hours. Finally she shifted in his arms and struggled to open her eyes.

"Are you waking?" he asked, brushing a strand of hair from her face.

"I'm trying, but it's difficult."

"I don't doubt it. You took quite a beating."

"Is Brentwood dead?"

Griff nodded. "We're safe now. He can't harm us any longer."

"Who was that man with you? Was he the one you were trying to find?"

"Yes." Griff lifted his gaze to where Jack sat. "Come here, Jack. I'd like to introduce you to my wife."

Jack walked to them, then knelt down beside Anne. "Jack, this is my wife, Lady Anne. Anne, this is the man who saved your life. Jack Hawkins."

"How do you do, Lady Anne. I'm very glad to make your acquaintance."

"And I'm very glad to be alive to make yours." She reached through the slit in the blanket to shake his hand. "I will forever be indebted to you."

"I'm glad I could be of service. You gave us quite a scare."

She smiled, but her effort was weak. "I didn't mean to."

She shivered and Griff pulled the blanket around her more tightly. "Are you cold?" he asked, unable to keep the concern out of his voice.

"Just a little."

Jack stood. "I'll tear apart more chests and put more wood on the fire. It would be a shame to save you from drowning only to have you freeze to death."

Jack built up the fire, and before long the cave was warmer.

"Is that better?" Griff asked, holding her closer.

"Yes, much," she answered. "Especially being in your arms."

"I don't ever intend to let you out of my arms again."

"That sounds very nice," she said, laying her head back against his chest and closing her eyes. "I'm tired, Griff."

"You sleep now, Anne." He picked her up in his arms and lay with her on the blankets Jack had spread out for them. "You're safe now."

She snuggled closer and closed her eyes.

"She's asleep already, Jack," Griff whispered, watching Anne slumber in his arms.

"I don't doubt it. She's been through hell. She'll no doubt want to sleep until she can forget it."

"No doubt." Griff couldn't keep his eyes off her, couldn't keep his hands from brushing the hair from her face, from tracing her ears and narrow throat. He couldn't keep the unbelievable joy from nearly bursting his heart. He loved her. He knew it without a doubt.

"Jack?"

Jack looked up from the fire. "Yes."

"Thank you. I'll never be able to repay you for what you did. Never."

"You already have. You trusted me even after you knew what my brother did."

"You weren't responsible for your brother's actions. You had no control over the choices he made."

Jack Hawkins sat back on his haunches and fanned the burgeoning fire. He was a large man, as tall as Griff, with shoulders equally as wide. Griff always knew if he ever needed someone to watch his back or be his right hand, Jack was the one he wanted beside him. He knew that now more than ever.

"Do you know what it's like," Jack said, adding wooden slats from the crates to the fire, "to watch your brother die and know there's nothing you can do to stop it from happening? Or to be so ashamed that you can't admit to the world that the traitor about to die is family? Or to live with yourself afterward because somehow what he did must have been your fault?"

"You weren't responsible for his actions. He was a grown man. Old enough to make his own choices."

"He was my younger brother. Do you know what his last words were to me?"

Griff waited.

"He told me he couldn't compete with me any longer, that I cast too large a shadow. What did I do, Griff? What is wrong with me that my own brother hated me so much that every choice he made was to defy the principles I upheld? Every choice he made was to destroy me?"

"There was nothing you could have done, Jack. He forged his own path."

"And I am forced to live with his death."

"Don't let your doubts destroy you. I learned that lesson the hard way. For years, I tried to blame myself for my wife and child's deaths. I thought they died because of something I did, but that wasn't true.

"Then, I thought I was responsible for Freddie's death, and for Anne nearly being run over. Do you know what Anne told me once? She said we humans often feel the need to assign blame when something tragic happens, and sometimes there is no one to blame." Griff smiled. "She said she thought I would like to blame God, but that I was not brave enough, so I blamed myself instead."

"Perhaps she's right."

"I have no doubt she is." Griff smiled down at Anne, then turned to his friend. "Get some rest, Jack. If you're half as tired as I am, you're probably dead on your feet."

"You're a lucky man, Griff," Jack said, looking at Anne's sleeping form.

"I know I am. And I'll never forget it." Griff pulled her closer into his arms.

* * *

*Anne was fighting the rising water and losing the battle. She was suffocating. Water rose to her chin, then covered her mouth and her nose. She took in huge gulps until she couldn't see. Couldn't breathe. She was going to die.*

*She tried to scream but couldn't. The water covering her face only muffled her sound. Ropes held her tight, and she struggled harder but could not get free.*

"Anne," a voice whispered in her ear, and two strong arms wrapped around her and held her. She was safe. When she finally woke up enough to realize she'd been dreaming, every muscle in her body ached. At first she wasn't sure where she was. The minute she remembered, her heart skipped a beat and she jolted in fear.

"Everything's all right, Anne," Griff whispered again, touching her, holding her. Kissing her.

"I couldn't breathe. The water was too high."

"It's all right. You're safe now."

"I was so scared, Griff."

"I know."

"How did you know to come here for me?"

"Hawkins figured it out. He found out Brentwood was using this cave to hide his opium shipments."

"Did Brentwood really kill Freddie, Griff?"

"Yes, then he tried to kill you when you refused to marry him. If I hadn't been so blind, I would have figured it out long before now. But I was so convinced I was the one the killer was after. I didn't think anyone could want Freddie dead. Or you. If it hadn't been for Hawkins…"

Anne looked over to where Jack Hawkins slept in the corner on the other side of the cave. His ebony hair shone in the firelight, and the flickering flames cast shadows over his face.

"He saved my life," she whispered in case Jack was awake. "How can I ever repay him?"

Griff lowered his head to whisper in her ear. "Perhaps someday he'll need our help, and we'll go to him."

Before he lifted his head, Anne turned until her face was next to his. She raised her hand and cupped his cheek, then traced her fingers over his jaw. "Please, kiss me," she whispered, and he smiled.

"I'd be glad to, my love."

He lowered his head and covered her mouth. His kiss was warm and gentle. His lips touched her lips, tasted her, drank from her, worshipped her.

Anne wrapped her arms around his neck and held him to her while he deepened his kisses. His mouth opened above hers.

"I love you," he said. He lifted his head and cupped her cheek in the palm of one hand. "I love you more than I thought it was possible to ever love another person again. I know the risk you took in marrying me. You were afraid I would end up like your father. That I'd want a drink more than I wanted you or the children we will have. But that won't happen, Anne. Nothing will ever be more important to me than you are."

"Oh, Griff." Anne wrapped her arm around his neck and brought his lips down to hers again. She kissed him hard, with enough desperation to show him how much she wanted him.

"I love you," she said when they broke apart, each of them gasping for air. "And I will love you until the day I die, and beyond. Loving you was a risk worth taking."

"And I intend to prove that to you every day of our lives," he whispered, then kissed her again. "I'll make sure you never regret the risk you took."

# About the Author

Laura Landon taught high school for ten years before leaving the classroom to open her very own ice-cream shop. As much as she loved serving up sundaes and malts from behind the counter, she closed up shop after penning her first novel. Now she spends nearly every waking minute writing, guiding her heroes and heroines to happily ever after. The author of more than a dozen historical novels, her books are enjoyed by readers around the world. She lives with her family in the rural Midwest, where she devotes what free time she has to volunteering in her community.